# BLINK OF AN EYE

# BLINK OF AN EYE

# IRIS JOHANSEN

# ROY JOHANSEN

GRAND CENTRAL
PUBLISHING

NEW YORK   BOSTON

Grand Central Publishing

Hachette Book Group

1290 Avenue of the Americas, New York, NY 10104

grandcentralpublishing.com

twitter.com/grandcentralpub

First Edition: February 2021

Grand Central Publishing is a division of Hachette Book Group, Inc. The Grand Central Publishing name and logo is a trademark of Hachette Book Group, Inc.

The publisher is not responsible for websites (or their content) that are not owned by the publisher.

The Hachette Speakers Bureau provides a wide range of authors for speaking events. To find out more, go to www.hachettespeakersbureau.com or call (866) 376-6591.

Library of Congress Cataloging-in-Publication Data has been applied for.

ISBNs: 9781538762882 (hardcover), 978-1-5387-1907-7 (large print), 978-1-5387-6287-5 (ebook)

Printed in the United States of America

LSC-C

Printing 1, 2020

# BLINK OF AN EYE

# CHAPTER

# 1

WOODWARD ACADEMY FOR THE PHYSICALLY
DISABLED
OCEANSIDE, CALIFORNIA

S he's here *again?*" Dr. Allison Walker's tone was low and
almost menacing as she whirled on Kendra Michaels. "We
discussed this, Kendra. I believe I made myself clear. What
didn't you understand?"

"Nothing," Kendra said quickly. She found herself feeling
the same sense of panic and intimidation she'd had when
she'd been scolded by the school's head administrator during
the time she'd attended here as a child. Which was totally
ridiculous. Yes, Allison was impressive, but between Kendra's
work in music therapy and her investigations with the FBI,
she had significant credentials of her own. So why was she
backing away instead of defending herself? "It was kind of a
surprise visit. We weren't expecting Delilah Winter to show
up here today."

"*I* certainly wasn't expecting her," Allison said coldly. "And
I wasn't expecting to have to tell the guards at the front gates

to clear away all the fans and paparazzi who followed her onto the property. There were even more than there were last time. I understand they had to whisk away Congressman Dalborne, who'd just arrived here for a visit, to keep him from being trampled. Do you realize how important he is? Everyone knows he's getting his ducks in a row to run for president."

"You're exaggerating. Congressman Dalborne was actually a good sport about it all," Kendra said defensively. "And Delilah Winter took him with her when the guards were getting her through the gates. He was laughing about it."

"Which is more than I'm doing," Allison said. "This is a school, not a rock concert. Those students are here to learn how to handle their disabilities, not worship at the feet of some pop star. There's been enough disturbance here at Woodward Academy in the last months. I agreed to go along with your plans to improve our image, but not at the expense of the students. You promised me that wouldn't happen."

"And it's not," Kendra said. "Be fair, Allison. I've kept my word. A few months ago, this school we both love was going to be forced to shut down. You'd lost the funding to keep it open because no donors were willing to be associated with it. Not only had there been three murders on the property, but a drug lord kingpin and his men were killed here. We had to get another donor as well as convincing the parents of those special kids to bring them back. Something had to be done quickly."

"So you decided we had to develop a relationship with the media that would cause everyone to forget what happened here and make them think we were St. Jude or Shriners." She added sourly, "We don't need to copy any other schools or hospitals. We work hard and we're one of the best schools in the world for helping the disabled."

"But we had to make the public remember that and forget the ugliness they'd seen recently on TV," Kendra said urgently. "We're making progress, Allison. I was able to arrange one interview with *60 Minutes* and two with CNN. Four positive feature articles have been written about celebrities visiting the campus and raving about the classes and students here." Allison's expression wasn't changing, so Kendra rushed on: "And I managed to get that billionaire from Silicon Valley as a prime donor for the academy. That might not have happened if he hadn't seen those CNN shots of the kids in the classroom."

Allison nodded grudgingly. "If he doesn't back out when he sees how Delilah Winter is turning this campus into her personal playground. Favorable publicity is one thing, notoriety is something entirely different. She's been here *five* times, Kendra. She's a disruption. Those paparazzi rob the school of any dignity it might have. Your friend Jessie Mercado arranged for her first visits here to the school. Can't she tell her to go on tour or something?"

"That might be difficult when Delilah is a superstar and she and Jessie are just good friends," Kendra said dryly. "We're only having a small communication problem with her. Jessie didn't even know she was here until I called her and asked her to drive down from L.A. and talk to her. She should be here by now." Time to escape. She'd done all she could to soothe Allison. She turned and started across the campus.

3

"I'll go down to Big Rock where Delilah is performing and meet her."

"Big Rock?" Allison asked. "Now it's an outdoor concert?"

"It's not really a concert." Big Rock was an enormous flat rock on the grassy expanse of the gentle hills that overlooked the ocean. Kendra and generations of other students had sat there on the rock, carved their initials, and told their secrets to each other. "No one could call Big Rock a stage. She liked what I told her about how the kids felt about it. She just sits on the rock, sings a little, and talks to the kids. By having it outdoors, it gives the kids more room to spread out." She was hurrying away. "It's going to be fine, Allison. We'll take care of it."

"Then take care of keeping her away from here," she called after her. "I don't know why she would even want to come."

"Because she likes it here, Allison," Kendra said quietly as she headed across the huge campus toward the hill that led to Big Rock. "She likes the kids. And there's no way we're going to hurt her feelings."

She could hear the sound of Delilah's guitar in the distance, but she wasn't singing. Laughter. She must have said something funny to the kids while she was strumming. Delilah was so good with the kids. Why not? She wasn't much more than a kid herself, barely twenty. She'd hit it big with her first platinum record when she was fifteen and kept on climbing.

Yet Kendra had always been aware of something youthful and wistful about her from the first moment Jessie had introduced them. Jessie had told her she'd had a few big headaches from the time she'd taken over Delilah's personal protection, but it had only been because the girl was young and scared. She'd never turned into a spoiled brat—which could well have happened considering her sudden fame. Kendra knew Jessie had become really fond of her before she'd turned her over to another protection service, and it was obvious Delilah adored her. Kendra had wondered whether she'd first come to the school because it would give more opportunity to be with Jessie. If that had been the reason, it wasn't now. She'd told Allison the truth: She'd seen both the gentleness and the affection whenever Delilah interacted with the students.

"Coward," Jessie jeered from behind Kendra. "Here I am to the rescue. Maybe you should have called your friends Griffin and Metcalf with the FBI to keep Dee under control. Or how about Lynch? As a black ops specialist, he should have been able to handle her."

"Shut up." Kendra turned to watch Jessie Mercado walk toward her. Those huge brown eyes and pixie features echoed the mischief in Jessie's voice, but Kendra had already had enough. "I took the flak Allison was handing me, but I had no intention of yanking Delilah out of here by myself."

"She told you to call her Dee." Jessie fell into step with her. "Do you want to hurt her feelings? She thinks you're her friend."

"And I'm trying to maintain a professional relationship." Which was difficult when Dee was so damn wistful and appealing. "And I am her friend, I just don't want to have to be the bad guy. She did us a favor the first couple times she came here for interviews with the kids."

"And you don't want to tell her to get lost now that all that celebrity bullshit is getting in the way. Well, Dee has to live with it twenty-four seven." Jessie added bluntly, "You're too soft. By all means, call in the FBI."

"I'm calling in Jessie Mercado. Why didn't you know she was going to show up here today?"

"We don't live in each other's pockets. She didn't mention it. When I phoned her, she told me she didn't know herself until her car picked her up this morning. It was an impulse. She didn't even notify her security detail." Jessie's lips tightened. "She was halfway to Oceanside before those agents thought to check on why she was late for rehearsal. I'd have fired them if I'd still been heading her security."

"It was her fault."

She shook her head. "They had a job to do. Cooperation with a client is nice, but you can never count on it. Though I'll read her the riot act for being stupid. I taught her better than that." She glanced soberly at Kendra. "But she really wasn't being stupid. She's very smart and canny about what's going on around her. Sometimes she just has to let go and forget about being Delilah the Superstar. It keeps her sane and all the phoniness at bay. These visits here with the kids have been good for her. She's only a kid, too, you know." She made a face. "Not that her mother or all those sycophants around her have ever let her act like one. She's been a meal ticket since her first Disney Channel show when they found out she could sing."

"That's terrible," Kendra said. "I'm glad she had you for a friend during that time right after her record went platinum."

"Maybe I wasn't her friend." Her lips twisted. "She wanted me to stay with her longer, offered me a fortune to do it. But much as I like her, I could only stand that bullshit pop-star life for so long. Then I set her up with another security head, Colin Parks, and moved on."

"You were her friend," Kendra said quietly. "You *are* her friend. I've seen you with her."

They had come over the hill and suddenly could see the huge crowd of students below surrounding the enormous flat rock where Delilah Winter was sitting, holding her guitar, with one torn-jean-clad leg tucked beneath her. Dewy complexion, tousled red hair, gray-green eyes, and that eager smile as she gazed out at her audience and tried to reach them. She was full of life that lit her entire face with warmth.

Jessie's lips softened as she looked down at her.

"You're right, maybe I was her friend." She started down the hill. "Though how that will turn out after today, we'll have to see."

———

Dee saw them the minute they got close to the Big Rock. She smiled as she waved enthusiastically at them, then turned to the people in the audience. "Hey guys, two of my old friends have just dropped in. Jessie Mercado is an awesome private investigator who's usually busy saving not only Hollywood but the entire planet, and Kendra Michaels was once a student here just like you. You all know her story. Blind girl has miracle operation, regains sight, and becomes an FBI superstar." She gave a mock yawn. "That script has been written a hundred times before, but I guess it's a classic. But I thought *my* audience deserved more so I got Kendra to agree to come up here and show you what the shouting was really all about." Her face was suddenly alive with mischief. "So give her a hand to encourage her to tell us how a kid who had been blind all her life could make those FBI wizards sit up and take notice."

"What?" Jessie murmured in shock over the wild shouts and applause of Dee's audience. Her gaze flew to Kendra's face. "You didn't do that, did you?"

"Of course I didn't," Kendra hissed. She couldn't believe it, either. "I'm going to *kill* Dee. Whatever possessed her?"

"She's always had a puckish sense of humor. And Dee's so used to show business, she probably thought it was no big deal to put you on the spot in front of hundreds of people." She suddenly chuckled. "Good Lord, your face!" Her smile was almost as mischievous as Dee's as she started to applaud. "Maybe look on it as a challenge?"

"Not funny. Talk about tough audiences."

"Then you're on your own."

"Why am I not surprised?" she said grimly. "It's been that kind of day." She started to make her way through the crowd toward Big Rock where Dee was sitting.

If anything, the young girl's smile was even more impish than before as she met Kendra's eyes. She made a sweeping gesture of welcome and handed her the microphone. "Have a great show, Kendra."

Kendra gazed blankly down at the mike. What the hell was she supposed to do now?

Well, not freeze or stutter like an idiot.

*Look on it as a challenge*, Jessie had said.

She smiled and fell silent a moment, thinking.

Then she lifted her eyes to the audience and started to speak. "It wasn't long ago that this school was in trouble. Serious trouble. It looked like it was going to close forever. But thanks to Delilah Winter, Congressman Dalborne, and a lot of other people, that's changed. We have hope now."

The crowd cheered.

"Do your stuff, Kendra!" It was a girl's voice from the front row. "Do what Delilah said!"

Kendra glanced down to see a fragile-looking child with a broad grin on her face: Ariel Jones, a little blind girl she'd met during her previous case. "Do it!" Ariel was clapping her hands enthusiastically. "Come on! Show us!"

"What a troublemaker you are, Ariel." Kendra shook her head. "You guys don't really want me to do a bunch of lame parlor tricks, do you?"

More cheers, more applause. Okay, she'd give them what they wanted. As much as Kendra usually hated performing like a trained monkey, today was different. Of course these kids loved to see what was possible with the hand they'd been dealt.

She turned toward the politician. "Congressman Dalborne, thanks for coming out today."

"My pleasure." He stepped toward Kendra and waved to the crowd.

Kendra looked him up and down. "I always like politicians who patronize local businesses. You ate at the Breakfast Club

Diner down on North Coast Highway this morning. I hope you enjoyed it."

He frowned, puzzled. "You saw me there?"

"No. I haven't been to the BCD in years."

"Then how...?"

"You read the newspaper while you ate. Not on your phone or a computer, but a paper you probably got from a machine. And it wasn't the *San Diego Union*. You went local again. The *Coast News*, probably."

Dalborne turned to a bespectacled young aide standing a few yards away. "Curtis, did you tell her...?"

The aide shook his head no.

Kendra paced in front of the congressman's group for a moment. "You wore braces as a child, didn't you, sir? You were young. Younger than most kids when they wear braces."

Dalborne flashed his perfect smile. "Right again. Though I'd really rather forget those days."

"You managed to recover. From that childhood trauma *and* the cold you had last week. There's been a bug going around. I caught it myself."

Dalborne nodded. "It's a nasty one, isn't it?"

"Absolutely." Kendra stared at his feet. "You grew up wearing flip-flops, and I'd say you probably still wear them quite a bit when you're off the clock. I don't know where you call home, but this seems to indicate you live on or near the beach somewhere."

Dalborne blinked, staring at her in disbelief. "You're right about the shoes. And I live in a beach house in Del Mar."

"Nice neighborhood."

"Very." His brows rose quizzically. "So are you going to tell us how you knew all this?"

"By doing something most of the kids here do better than anyone else. I just pay attention."

"How did you know where I ate breakfast?"

She shrugged. "I smelled your breath. The Breakfast Club Diner serves up a mean plate of huevos rancheros, with a homemade sauce to die for." She wrinkled her nose. "And that sauce hasn't changed in twenty years, and it's on your breath right now."

The kids loved that.

After the laughter subsided, Kendra continued. "They're also famous for their orange marmalade muffins. It's a very distinctive color."

Dalborne squinted at her. "I didn't have a muffin."

"No, but your assistant did."

The assistant quickly looked down at his shirt and tie.

"Not on your clothes," she said to the assistant. "There's a distinctive orange splotch under your right thumbnail." She turned back to Dalborne. "Your breath and his orange thumb can only mean you guys ate at the Breakfast Club Diner."

"The newspaper?"

"Your right fingers have newspaper ink on them, meaning you're left-handed, by the way."

"How do you figure that?"

"Only one hand is stained, meaning you were probably eating with the other hand. If you were holding the newspaper with your right hand, you were holding your fork with your left. Your dominant hand."

"How did you know which paper?"

"The *San Diego Union* doesn't come off on the hands nearly as much as the Coast Group of neighborhood papers. It's a pretty safe assumption you were reading the *Coast*."

"The fact that I wore braces?"

"Aside from that perfect smile of yours?"

"Thank you." He smiled again. "Aside from that."

"You have a habit of breathing in through your teeth. A lot of kids who wore braces do that. And it's a habit some people carry with them throughout their lives, even if they aren't aware of it."

"Trust me, I'm aware of it. Every time I watch replays of myself at debates. It's that obvious?"

"Not to most people. But I bet a lot of these kids could hear it."

"Interesting," he said as he heard sounds of agreement from the audience. "I think I just found my next debate prep team. What else can they hear?"

"A very slight rattle in your chest, a postnasal drip that's probably a residual effect from your cold. I'm sensitive to it, because I also had it. And they might also hear the sound of your very elegant loafers snapping up against your heel. It's the same sound someone makes when they wear flip-flops. That says to me you're probably used to wearing flip-flops more than any other type of shoe."

Dalborne shook his head. "Incredible. Now I know why the FBI likes you so much."

"What they like about me is that I just pay attention and can help them do what they do a little better." Kendra whirled toward Dee. "And paying attention is how I know Delilah Winter didn't show up at the recording studio night before last and left the crew and musicians waiting for her the entire session. Right, Dee?"

Dee's eyes widened and her jaw went slack. After a shocked moment, she finally responded. "Yeah, I was on the beach working on writing a new song. Time got away from me. I was in another world." She added quickly to the audience, "But trust me, I felt really guilty, and I paid overtime to each and every one of the crew. That was very unprofessional of me. So you guys do as I say and not as I do. Okay?" Then her face suddenly lit with a rueful smile. "And be sure and watch your back when you're doing something bad around Kendra Michaels!"

The kids were clapping and laughing wildly at this sudden sign of naughtiness and vulnerability in the superstar they adored. As well as at the idea that she had been bested by one of their own.

A perfect time to end the performance, Kendra thought. She stepped forward and waved her hand at the audience. Then she bowed low as the applause washed over her. The next moment she jumped down off the rock and tried to escape through the crowd.

But she found Dee in front of her, hurling herself into her arms. "You were terrific! Just what I wanted. Just what they needed. I'm window dressing, but you're the real thing." She pushed back and grinned up at Kendra. "Wanna go on the road with me?"

"No, I don't." But she had to smile back at Dee. "And

that was a dirty trick catching me off guard. What if I'd blown it?"

"You didn't. I have an instinct about things like that. I knew you were a natural. And how could I resist doing it when I've wanted to know how you do all that stuff myself? I knew I wasn't going to have much more time to find out, so I laid my trap." She made a face. "But how in hell did you know about that session I missed the other night?"

Kendra smiled. "Jessie told me. She said your manager called her when they were searching for you."

"That's cheating."

"A little. But you deserved it for putting me on the spot." She paused. "Is anything wrong? You worried a lot of people that night. It's not like you."

Dee shrugged. "Yeah, like I told you, time got away. I was really into creating something great with that new song." She nibbled at her lower lip. "And maybe I wasn't into anything else that night. With music you can't do it if you can't feel it, you know?"

"Sure." It was only half true. She could understand the artistic problems, but balancing them with the fame and emotional traumas could only be solved by Dee herself. It troubled Kendra that there didn't seem to be anything she could do to help her. She said lightly, "But you must have been feeling it today. You gave those kids a fantastic show."

"You helped. It was great fun, wasn't it?" She gave Kendra another hug and stepped back. She said quietly, "Don't worry, I'll do a couple more songs and then I'll say goodbye to these guys. I'll be off your hands in an hour and on my way back to L.A. with Jessie. I'll even promise that we'll lead all those paparazzi creeps out front away from here. Jessie is terrific at stuff like that."

"I know she is," Kendra said hesitantly, her gaze searching Dee's expression. The last thing she'd wanted to do was to hurt her. "It's not that we don't like you and appreciate everything you've done for us. You're a very special person, Dee."

"But so are these kids," she said softly. "And they belong here. I know I don't. It was just nice being able to watch them, be with them for a little while. They're so strong, much stronger than me."

"No, they aren't. Jessie keeps telling me what a tough cookie you can be."

"That's different." She gave Kendra another quick hug. "Now stop looking at me like that. Everything's okay. I understand." Her hand tightened on the mic, and she jumped back on top of Big Rock. She shouted, "Hey, I'm jealous. Kendra was just a guest artist. Let me show you what I can do. You heard her tattle how bad I was about writing that song when I should have been at work? Well, it might have been a bad thing to do, but the song turned out pretty darn good. Who wants to hear the new song I just wrote?"

The audience erupted with a clamor of shouts and applause.

"Come on, you're now ancient history." Jessie was suddenly beside Kendra and leading her out of the crowd. "Though you did a damn good job. Dee was impressed with you."

Kendra gazed over her shoulder at Dee Winter, glowing, intense, giving everything, who had started to sing again. "Then she wasn't the only one. I was very impressed by her..."

———◆———

"I was right, you know," Allison Walker said as she came to stand beside Kendra at the front gates of the school. She watched Jessie drive Dee Winter past the crowd of paparazzi at the curb in her black Range Rover SUV. "She was disruptive. Look how those paparazzi are jumping into their cars to follow her."

"Yes, she was disruptive," Kendra agreed. "But those paparazzi are doing exactly what she wants them to do right now. Jessie is leading them away from here like a Pied Piper." She added quietly, "And the kids had a wonderful, memorable experience."

"I understand you had something to do with that," Allison said dryly.

"A little. But that was Dee Winter, too." She smiled. "And I can't deny you were right. How could I?"

"You can't." She was silent a moment. "I . . . like her."

"I know you do. She was just a problem you felt you had to solve."

"She stopped by my office and thanked me for being so kind to her. She actually . . . hugged me. I was a little uncomfortable."

"I'm sure she wasn't. And I'm sure she meant everything she said to you."

"I believe she did." She was silent a moment. "Perhaps we'll invite her again . . . in a year or so." She shrugged. "At any rate, she's on her way to where she belongs now. Thank heavens your friend Jessie brought a car and not her motorcycle this time. I wouldn't want to be responsible for an accident happening to a guest at our academy."

"I don't think our 'guest' would mind. Dee would find riding on the back of Jessie's motorcycle a blast. She's probably done it many times before." Kendra sighed as Jessie's SUV disappeared around a corner, followed by a parade of screeching paparazzi vehicles. She wished she was with them. She was suddenly feeling very much alone after the excitement that had gone before.

She turned away and headed for her Toyota in the parking lot. "Now I've got to go back to my condo and have dinner with my friend Olivia. I had to cancel on her twice this week, and Olivia doesn't tolerate that kind of discourtesy. She let me know it wasn't to happen again. It seems as if I'm up here all the time these days."

"I know you are," Allison said. "And I'm grateful. Don't think I'm not. You've practically saved the academy. It's just that things are different now. It's hard for me to get used to it."

"Me too. And you've worked just as hard as I have, Allison. We've done it together." She got into the Toyota. "I'll see you tomorrow."

"Have a good dinner." She paused. "I haven't seen that extraordinary Lamborghini that belongs to Lynch up here for the last week." She hesitated again. "Is there some problem?"

Allison was trying to be tactful, Kendra realized. Unusual for her these days. Bluntness ruled her life except when dealing with business associates or parents of students. But evidently, she didn't want to come straight out and ask her if the man she assumed to be Kendra's lover had left her and gone on the lam.

"No problem other than the usual one with Adam Lynch. The Justice Department wanted him to save the world and he was sent somewhere in Tibet to do it. I haven't heard from him since he left last week." She backed out of the parking space. "But I'm sure he's missing the Lamborghini."

---

HIGHWAY 5

OCEANSIDE, CALIFORNIA

"They're gaining on us." Dee's voice was tense with excitement as she looked at the rearview mirror. "I think it's that red Subaru who's in the lead." She tilted her head. "Though that Chrysler is pretty close."

"You sound like you're calling a horse race." Jessie cast her an amused glance. "And enjoying every minute of it."

"I always have fun with you." Dee's gaze was fixed on the vehicles careening around the curb behind them. "That green jeep took that turn on two wheels. He definitely has potential."

"Potential to kill himself, maybe. Or someone else on the road."

"Can you lose 'em before that happens?"

Jessie pulled the wheel hard right and spun onto Oceanside Boulevard. "We'll see. By the way, are you going to tell me where you left your security detail this morning?"

"Not sure. They're probably still at Thunder Road recording studios, wondering where in the hell I went."

"You slipped out on them?"

"Maybe." She looked away from Jessie. "They would have tried to stop me. The recording company pays them."

"And you wonder why I quit as your security director."

Dee grinned as she leaned back in her seat. "I wouldn't have tried to slip out on you. Admit it, you've never had a more fun job."

"I had more fun dodging gunfire in Afghanistan."

"You miss me."

"How can I miss you when you're always hanging out at my office?"

"Not when I'm on tour. Are you sure you don't want to come back?"

"Positive. Buckle your seat belt. It's about to get hairy."

Dee's smile deepened as she pulled the belt across her chest. "Now that's what I like to hear."

Jessie punched the accelerator and sped toward the I-5 entrance ramp. As the paparazzi's vehicles fell in line behind them, Jessie slowed to a crawl.

"What are you doing?" Dee asked.

"Waiting for that eighteen-wheeler to catch up to us."

"Why?"

Jessie was still looking in her side-view mirror. "Gotta time it just right…"

The cargo truck pulled alongside them and most of the other photographers' cars. Just as the lane turned right onto the I-5 northbound entrance ramp, Jessie gunned the engine, jumped the median, and swerved left in front of the truck. She sped down Oceanside Boulevard and checked the rearview. The paparazzi caravan, still blocked from the left by the eighteen-wheeler, could only continue onto the freeway.

"Well done, my friend." Dee initiated a fist bump that Jessie didn't return.

"There's still a couple stragglers back there." Jessie's hands tightened on the wheel as she sped up and turned right onto South Coast Highway. "And the others will get off at the next exit and try to intercept us."

Dee's eyes were glittering with excitement. "Then let's change cars."

"How do you propose we do that?"

"We find someone to loan us theirs."

"That's your plan?"

"Yes. We'll find someone, and I'll strike the *Summer on the Beach* album pose." Dee flipped back her hair, cocked her head to the side, and smiled in a perfect re-creation of her multi-platinum debut album cover. "I'll offer 'em ten back-stage passes, and if that doesn't work, I'll volunteer to show up at their daughter's next birthday party."

"That actually works?"

"Yes." She was beaming. "For almost everything."

"I'm *really* glad I don't work for you anymore."

Dee was ignoring her. "Slow down, I think I see a house-wife getting into a Suburban."

"I have my own plan, Dee. And it doesn't involve a meet-and-greet at a kid's birthday party."

She frowned. "I'm *not* naming a song after someone."

"Also not on the table. Hang on." Jessie spun hard left

into a restaurant parking lot and raced down a narrow driveway to the building's rear side, where a deck overlooked the narrow beach.

Dee looked around. "So we're just gonna hide back here? I like my plan better."

"No. We are switching vehicles, but not in the way you think." Jessie put the SUV in park and killed the ignition. "Let's go."

"Go where? Is someone meeting us? Did you send for an Uber?"

Jessie climbed out and slammed the door closed.

Dee scrambled out and joined her on the blacktop parking lot. "Come on, what's the plan?"

Jessie motioned ahead, where a black fourteen-foot bowrider boat was partially beached on the sand.

Dee's eyes lit up. "The *Moon Shadow*! What's it doing here?"

"Saving your sorry ass from the paparazzi."

"You brought it down here for me?"

"I came prepared." She sighed. "You know, it's almost as hard being your friend as it was being your employee." They approached the sleek craft, which Jessie occasionally used for surveillance and tracking along the coast. "Let's push this back and get out of here."

Within five minutes, they were on the boat and speeding north on the waters past Camp Pendleton.

"We got away from them!" Dee collapsed back in her seat, her face wreathed in smiles. "For a minute, I thought they had us. What a way to go, Jessie!"

"I'm glad you approve," Jessie said dryly. "Given how close

we came to going off that cliff near the school. And those cars following us came even closer."

"I knew you'd find a way to lose them." She reached out and squeezed Jessie's arm. "You're one of the best stunt drivers in Hollywood. You're totally awesome behind the wheel. Remember, you let me watch you on the set a couple times when you were working as the head of my security."

"That was a mistake," Jessie said grimly. "I only did it because we were just getting to know each other, and I wanted you to have faith in my driving in case the situation called for it."

"And this situation called for it," she said with satisfaction. "So it wasn't a mistake."

"Except that I'm no longer heading your security team. And today you blew off the people who have that job. Not good, Dee."

"You're going to yell at me." Her smile faded. "I thought you would. I deserve it. I'm a professional, and I knew I didn't have any right to breach my security contract with my recording company. But I thought maybe it wouldn't hurt to do it one more time before I became Delilah again." She added coaxingly, "Give me a break. I'll apologize to everyone. I've already told Kendra I'm sorry I put her on the spot by showing up at the school." She made a face. "I really thought I could sneak past the paparazzi at the front gate."

"They had it staked out because they knew you'd been there four times before." Jessie frowned. "And you don't have to apologize to me. You're not that crazy sixteen-year-old kid I watched over any longer, Dee. You shouldn't have to apologize to anyone. You're grown up and you should have your own standards and abide by them." She paused. "And usually I believe you do. I think this time you went off the rails a bit. Is everything okay with you?"

"Sure, fine." She smiled brilliantly. "Why not? My last record went platinum."

"Is everything okay with you?" Jessie repeated.

Dee glanced out the window. "I've missed you. You're the only one I can really talk to, Jessie. I know you're always busy. Hell, you were even on that job in Afghanistan for a while this year." She went on quickly, "I'm not complaining. You're right, I'm grown up and you don't work for me any longer. But if I sent you tickets, would you come to my concert tomorrow night? I'm playing the Hollywood Bowl."

Oh, shit.

Jessie hadn't realized how long it had been since she'd made more than passing contact with Dee. She was right, Jessie had been swamped for the last months, and Dee's career had also appeared to be operating on hyperdrive. Other than setting up Dee's appearances at Woodward Academy, she'd barely seen her. But Jessie should have remembered how vulnerable and lonely Dee could be even surrounded by hordes of fans. "I wouldn't miss it," she said lightly. "But I thought it was already sold out."

Dee grinned. "Lucky for you I know someone at the box office."

"Yeah, lucky for me." She grinned back at her before she paused to ask, "Is your mother going to be able to make it this time?"

"Gina?" Dee shook her head. "Be for real. She's in France

with husband number five. She said she'd try to see me when I go on tour."

"Hey, then maybe you'll be able to have dinner with me after the concert? I'll understand if you can't. But I'd be willing to fight my way back through all your friends and fans if I had a chance."

"You have a chance," she said quietly. "Thanks, Jessie."

"For what? It's just a meal." She tilted her head. "And talking about meals, would you mind if I didn't take you right back to that mansion you call home? I'm starved. Maybe we could stop at Pink's and get a hot dog?"

"Maybe we could." Dee's gray-green eyes were suddenly twinkling. "Since you're the only one in my circle who will let me load mine with onions for fear of media reprisal."

"I'll brave it. We've gone through worse together." She pulled back on the throttle. "And I have a hunch there are even better times ahead…"

---

KENDRA'S CONDO

"Stop checking up on me. I told you I was coming to dinner," Kendra said when she received Olivia's call as she got out of her car in the parking garage. "I'll be in the elevator in seconds. But I thought I'd go up to my place and shower first. I was outside on the grounds of the school for a while today and I'm a little mussed."

"Bad idea," Olivia said flatly. "Get off at my condo instead.

Harley has been missing you, and that means you'll end up more than 'mussed' when he gets through with his first attack. And you'll probably smell like chopped liver. I don't think those new breath mints are working."

Kendra groaned. "I thought you told me that dog training was making a big difference."

"Oh, it has, but with a unique dog like Harley, you have to consider that his superb intelligence would let him know that he's being ignored, and he'd feel as if he had to do something about it." She paused. "He might even think you have to be punished."

Kendra didn't like the sound of that. There were times these days when she regretted persuading Olivia to take a Seeing Eye dog into her home. Her friend had sworn she didn't need a service dog since she considered herself, though blind, to be totally independent. She'd even built a successful web destination called *Outasite* that earned her seven figures. Yet she'd fallen in love with Harley. Perhaps they'd become entirely too close in both nature and spirit, Kendra thought gloomily. "You wouldn't have been coaching him?"

"I never coach Harley in bad behavior. But you'll have to take responsibility for your own misbehavior. Neither of us approved of you canceling dinner for the second time in a week. I'll see you in a few minutes." She ended the call.

Kendra sighed as she pressed the button for Olivia's fourth-floor condo. Might as well accept whatever Olivia and Harley had in store for her. Olivia had been her best friend since they'd both been students at the academy as children. When Kendra had gained her sight, it hadn't changed anything about the relationship but the fact they'd both gotten stronger and more determined to be their own people.

She heard Harley's hideous bark as she hurried down the hall so the neighbors wouldn't complain. Poor baby, he couldn't help that his vocals had been damaged in a fire, but it didn't help the effect that sent a chill down everyone's spine.

Olivia threw open the door. "It's about time."

Harley launched himself at Kendra. She saw a flash of one blue eye, one brown eye, and curly brownish face and body hair before his paws hit her shoulders. The dog was part German shepherd, part mystery mutt, and totally adorable.

But that big tongue licking her chin was not, and neither was the liver smell Olivia had mentioned. "You're right, try another breath mint for him." Then she knelt down and started stroking and crooning to him. He instantly rolled over on his back and presented his belly for attention.

After a moment Olivia said, "That's enough." She bent down and snapped her fingers and made a downward motion.

Harley quickly rolled back over and jumped to his feet.

"Good boy." Olivia turned away. "Kendra, I poured glasses of wine for us when I heard you in the hall. You can sit down at the kitchen bar and keep me company while I finish the salad."

Harley was now calmly sitting next to the island and gazing happily at Olivia. He was completely ignoring Kendra. Night and day, she thought suspiciously "Could you have stopped that attack before it began?"

"Of course. Harley's training is going along splendidly. But both barking and displaying affection are vitally important to dogs. If I keep it within limits, I'll raise a healthy dog." Her lips twitched with mischief as she got down the salad bowl. "I decided that since you hadn't been around lately to contribute to his health and well-being, you'd certainly want to help out. Isn't that right?"

She sighed. "Right."

Olivia's smile had disappeared. "Then we need to talk."

"About what?"

"About why you've turned your back on me and stopped being my friend."

"What?"

"You heard me." Olivia turned toward the salad ingredients on her kitchen counter. "Have a seat."

Kendra was still trying to recover from the shock as she sat on a barstool on the other side of the counter. "That was a hell of a thing to say. What did I do? Look, I know you were upset about me missing dinner, but I didn't think you'd go that far to punish me. After all, I had work to do up at Oceanside. You're usually very understanding about professional engagements. Heaven knows, you have enough of them yourself."

"Yes, I do." She was expertly tossing the salad. "And I let all the excuses go for a little while because I thought there might be a smidgen of truth in them. But then I decided that it was time to clear all the crap away."

"Crap?" She frowned. "What are you talking about? And smidgen of truth? I was telling you the truth about working late at the school."

"Smidgen," Olivia repeated precisely. "You wouldn't lie to

me, but if you didn't want me to worry, you'd spend more time than needed on a project to avoid telling me about a problem. You've done it before. Sometimes I think you're not even aware you're doing it. But I *am* beginning to worry. Because it's stretching on too long..."

"And you want to clear the crap away?" Kendra said. "Did it occur to you that you could be wrong?"

"No, I know every nuance of your voice and phrasing. I'm terrific at it. I realize when I'm getting smidgens." Her expression was sober. "What's going on? I have to know. You're my best friend. You've never hidden anything from me before. Are you working on a new case? You haven't mentioned Griffin or Metcalf, but they've asked you to keep cases confidential before. I won't pry, but I want to be there when and if you need me. You live right upstairs, and I should at least know that much."

"You think a homicidal maniac is stalking me?"

"It's happened before." She drew a deep, relieved breath. "But judging by my infallible ability to read your voice, I gather that it's not happening now."

"No, it's not." She chuckled. "I haven't been called by anyone at the FBI for weeks. No serial killers knocking on my door or following me to the school. You screwed up, Olivia."

"No, I didn't." She finished the salad and leaned back against the counter. "The smidgen was there. I just exaggerated the threat. For which I'm grateful. I instinctively go for the worst-case scenario when I believe something's not right with you."

"Actually, I'm admiring how good you were to listen and

identify a possible problem. Your audio abilities might be better than mine these days."

"You've just gotten lazy since you got your vision. I have to work harder. I went after what I wanted, but I just took the wrong path."

And this wasn't going to be over until Olivia had everything clear to her satisfaction, Kendra could see.

"Then turn around and start over." She took a sip of her wine, trying to read Olivia's expression. "Don't wait and let it simmer. Come right out with it."

"Are you certain? I was trying to be diplomatic."

"That's always a lost cause between us."

Olivia shrugged. "If it wasn't a life-or-death situation, it has to be Lynch. I didn't think that was possible, because you usually do such a great job of guarding yourself from him. But maybe something has changed lately..."

"It could hardly have changed, since I haven't seen him for two weeks."

"That sounded a bit barbed," Olivia said. "Is he still in Tibet?"

"As far as I know." She added warily, "And I don't have any right to be barbed. We don't have that kind of a relationship. We're friends and partners, and anything else that occurs between us has to trail behind."

"Bullshit," Olivia said. "It would be nice if we could all keep our emotions in those neat little boxes, but it doesn't happen. They all get jumbled up together and who the hell knows where they'll land." She took a sip of her wine. "I've known you since the day you met Adam Lynch years ago and you're even more jumbled than most. You've both been moving cautiously around each other, but it was inevitable that you'd come together. Who could blame you? You're both brilliant, and you match each other. Then add sexual tension, respect, admiration, and a number of other emotions that are guaranteed to drive you around the bend."

Kendra forced a smile. "It sounds very uncomfortable."

"You'd have to tell me. I'm on the outside. From what I've been able to judge, it's like two fencers fighting a championship match. Sharp. Thrusting. Exciting. I have an idea you both draw blood on occasion." She shrugged. "But I can't let myself care, because you'd tell me to mind my own business. Which I will do, as long as you clarify that it's Lynch with whom you're having a problem and not some mystery serial killer." She added softly, "Because I'll always know a problem is there, Kendra."

Kendra nodded ruefully. "Acknowledged." She lifted her glass. "Between you and Harley, I don't have a chance, do I?"

"Hell, no." She turned toward the oven. "Now take Harley for a short walk, and then set the table while I finish dinner."

◆

Paul Fantinelli exited the elevator and strode across the rooftop patio of the London Hotel. The sun was setting over West Hollywood, and the poolside bar was packed with young entertainment industry professionals. There were the agents, the lower-level studio execs, and the impossibly good-looking stars- and starlets-in-the-making.

And a man who didn't fit in any of those categories. Nick Parillo stood on the pool's far side, nursing a drink as he stared at the lights of Sunset Boulevard. Parillo was a handsome man, maybe fifty, who obviously felt no connection to anyone or anything on that patio. He was dressed in an expensive suit, no tie, and a close-cropped hairstyle that almost appeared to be a military cut. He turned and waved Paul over.

"Nice hotel," Fantinelli said.

Parillo shrugged and finished his drink. "Any problems this morning?"

"No, I blended in with the paparazzi. There were probably ten of them there at the school. No one suspected a thing. I was just another member of the pack."

"Good. Anyone at that concert that I should know about?"

He shook his head. "It was only for the kids." He held up the fingers of one hand. "That hotshot Congressman Dalborne who wants to be the next president, Delilah Winter, Jessie Mercado, and Kendra Michaels."

"Kendra Michaels?" Parillo repeated. He swore softly. "And you didn't think I'd be interested in her? Are you an idiot? Even you must have heard about her background."

"It doesn't mean anything. She teaches classes up there at the school."

"Everything means something in this game. Particularly Kendra Michaels. Count on it." He suddenly stopped as a thought occurred to him. "But it's obvious you weren't worried about anything that happened this morning. So why did you call and ask to meet me?"

"I just thought we needed to have a talk." Fantinelli

hesitated. He was already having second thoughts. Parillo wasn't a man to fool with, and his contacts with the mob were legendary. But the stakes were high enough for Fantinelli to risk probing a little. He smiled ingratiatingly. "This deal is going to be a huge score. How much do you think you're going to make off it?"

Parillo stiffened. "Don't concern yourself with that. You're not paid to do anything but obey orders. I chose you because the word on the streets is that you're smart and your team couldn't be traced back to me. Just do your job and you'll get every dollar you've been promised."

"Maybe I should have asked for more," Fantinelli said softly. "Come on, I'll do a better job for you than those Las Vegas guys you usually hire. Like I said, you must be making a fortune. Share a little."

"Talk like that could be very dangerous for you." Parillo's eyes were suddenly fierce. "We made a deal. I'd advise you not to try to change it." He took a step closer, and his voice deepened into a tone that sent an icy chill down Paul's spine. "This isn't only about money for me. You know nothing about how I operate or what other contacts I might have. Trust me, my friend, it's about something far, far more important than that..."

# CHAPTER

# 2

"Where are you?" Special Agent Michael Griffin's voice was distinctly annoyed when Kendra picked up his call the next day. "You're safe, aren't you? You're not in a hospital or being held by terrorists at gunpoint?"

"What on earth are you talking about?" she asked. "I'm just leaving my condo on the way to L.A. to attend a concert at the Hollywood Bowl with Jessie Mercado. And you're the one who sounds like you should be in a mental hospital."

"You're right, I should be committed for ever paying attention to Lynch."

"He told you I was being held by terrorists?"

"No, I just added that into the scenario because I was so pissed off at him for thinking he could use me to run his errands for him. He said that he was being held up in Tibet and I should check in with you occasionally to make sure everything was going well."

"He *called* you? That's more than I've gotten from him since he left here."

"He didn't call me. I received a visit from some special Tibetan envoy, Chodan Ki, who gave me his message. The bastard was very insistent I obey Lynch's orders." He growled. "I wanted to strangle him, but I had to bow and be polite. I could see that damn Metcalf trying to keep from laughing at me."

She'd probably have laughed herself if she hadn't been so pissed off at being the center of Lynch's action, which spoke of his sheer arrogance and interference in her life. "I sympathize. Ignore Lynch as you usually do. I don't know what got into him."

"I *can't* ignore him. Now if anything happened to you, it would probably trigger an international incident. Knowing Lynch, I can see him deliberately setting it up to cause me the most grief possible."

She couldn't blame him for that suspicion. On occasion Lynch could be positively brimming with catlike mischief. However, that remark was very cold.

"I'm sorry if my possible demise might cause you inconvenience," she said dryly. "I assure you that I'll do everything I can to prevent it. Are we done?"

"Evidently not. But I guess that's all for me right now." His voice was silky with malice. "But I decided our fine Special Agent Metcalf was enjoying himself a little too much at my expense, so I gave him the task of delivering a present to you. I don't think he's going to like that at all. He should be waiting downstairs in your parking garage right now. Have a nice evening and make certain you take very good care of yourself." He cut the connection.

A few minutes later Kendra had left the apartment and was in the elevator on the way to the parking garage. All she wanted was to see Metcalf and get this encounter over with. She'd known Griffin and Metcalf too long to ever feel embarrassed at the hijinks that Lynch had thrown at her, but it still annoyed her. What on earth was he doing even hinting that she couldn't take care of herself and needed the FBI in the background to rush to her defense? It had to be some kind of practical joke, and it was one she didn't appreciate.

The elevator door opened, and Metcalf was standing there in front of her. "Stop frowning." He held up his hands. "It's not my fault. This is the last thing I wanted to do. And Griffin knew it and wanted to punish me."

Metcalf was a tall, good-looking man in his late twenties who was usually very efficient and confident. He didn't look either at this moment, and she felt a rush of sympathy for him.

"You shouldn't have laughed at Griffin."

"I didn't." He added glumly, "I just almost did. If you could have seen that envoy staring down at Griffin as if he was a first-year recruit at Quantico..." He was smiling at the thought. "Lynch and I sometimes have our differences, but it was a stroke of genius to bring in that Tibetan envoy."

"I don't agree. So far it seems to have brought me nothing but trouble." She added impatiently, "Griffin said you had some kind of gift for me?"

He nodded as he took a black leather box from his jacket pocket. "The envoy gave it to Griffin and said he must take care to guard it for you. It's a dagger given to Lynch by a lama whose life he'd saved, and it's supposed to be filled with magic. He chose you as temporary custodian until he returns." He carefully opened the velvet-lined box to reveal the silver dagger. "I got the whole story, and I'm supposed to tell it to you so that you'll be properly impressed." He tapped the eight-inch triangular blade with its steel tip. "It's a Lhasa Tibetan phurba. Its magic comes from the effect that the dagger has on the realm of the spirit. The tantric use of the phurba encompasses the curing of disease, exorcism, killing demons, blessings, meditation, and consecrations; it can even have an effect on the weather."

"Is that all?" Kendra asked ironically.

"No. But the envoy included a wider list that you can study at your leisure." He paused. "One thing you should know is that some of those phurbas are cheap souvenirs that can be found for sale at a bazaar. This is not one of those phurbas. It's over two thousand years old, and in order to maintain its magical value it must remain with the owner."

"Who is now Lynch," she said flatly. "I'll stick it in a bank vault and let him decide what to do with it whenever he comes back."

"But you're the temporary custodian." Metcalf was now grinning. "How do you know you're not destroying its power to fight demons?"

"I'll take the chance." She looked down at the dagger. It did look very, very old. "It's probably a priceless antique and Lynch just sent it to torment me with finding out what to do with it."

"Or to protect you from demons. Like he did when he sent that envoy to Griffin." Metcalf's smile faded. "I wouldn't mind giving you a gift like that."

And since she was always trying to avoid encouraging Metcalf thinking in that vein, it was even more frustrating to have Lynch do something to trigger this response. "Careful," she said lightly. "Or I'll put you in charge of being custodian and you can house-sit that dagger yourself."

He shook his head. "Sorry. You're the designated custodian of the phurba. We can't even lock it in the vault at the office."

She shrugged. "Rats. And right now I don't have time to find a bank to deposit it in. I-5 heading for L.A. is always a nightmare at this hour. I'd be late meeting Jessie. I guess I'll just have to lock it in my car and deal with it tomorrow." She headed for her Toyota. "Security is pretty good at the Hollywood Bowl."

"Better take good care of it," Metcalf called after her. "Maybe that Tibetan lama had a reason to give that dagger to Lynch. Black ops isn't the safest line of work. He can always use a little luck."

"We all can. But Lynch does just great at demon fighting on his own. Though he could probably use the weather app on that dagger with all those avalanches in Tibet." She didn't let Metcalf see her expression as she got into the driver's seat. She didn't want to think about that idiotic dagger, or black ops, or the fact that Lynch had sent her a message through Griffin instead of contacting her himself. It was all pure Lynch, whimsical, enigmatic, amusing. But she didn't feel amused right now. So don't think of him at all. Tomorrow, before she deposited the dagger, she'd take it up to Oceanside and show it to the kids in her class. They'd love all that magic stuff. She'd read them the directions and laugh with them about the weather app on a demon fighting weapon.

And don't think about what Lynch was doing on those mountains, and why he'd had to save that lama's life.

Kendra ran through the crowded plaza to the box-office windows, where after a brief wait in line she was given her ticket. She continued through the turnstiles and climbed another upward stretch to the Garden Box entrance. She stepped through and smiled. The Hollywood Bowl. If there was anything that would make her consider living in L.A., this was it. Nestled in the Hollywood Hills, this beautiful outdoor amphitheater was a hundred-year-old institution that attracted the biggest names in classical, jazz, and rock music year-round. She made it a point to drive down for at least one concert every summer.

Jessie waved to her from a box just a few yards from the stage. Kendra made her way over as Jessie raised a plastic cup filled with red wine. "You're late!"

"Sorry, I underestimated the Bowl traffic."

"No skin off my nose. More for me." Jessie gestured toward a massive basket of food and two carafes of wine on the box's small foldout table. "A gift from our hostess."

Kendra slid into the box and plopped into a canvas chair

facing the stage. She selected a fried chicken leg from the basket. "Wow. Dee is spoiling us."

"Yep." Jessie gestured to a large box filled with guests nearby.

"There's Matt Dalborne and several of his constituents. He stopped by to say hello and was clearly jealous and trying to impress his super PAC." Jessie sipped her wine. "But Dee spoils everyone in her orbit. Maybe to a fault. She wants the people in her life to know they're appreciated."

"Exactly how long did you work for her?"

"A little over two years. She was only sixteen when I started there. She saw me competing on the *American Ninja* TV show and heard about my military background. So she hired me to be a part of her security detail. I worked with eight guys, and they were almost all useless. Within six months, she made me head of security. I toured with her all over the world. It was quite an experience."

"Why did you quit?"

"I told you before, it's easy to burn out in that environment. I don't see how Dee does it. There's almost nowhere in the world she can go without people hounding her. I was exhausted by the end of my time with her."

Kendra grabbed a carafe and poured herself a glass of wine. "She seems grounded, though."

"Yes. Amazingly so. Especially since this has been her life since she was fifteen years old." Jessie shook her head. "She's had to deal with scumbag record company executives, crazed fans, a string of deadbeat boyfriends, and two parents who seem to care only about themselves. Dee is always surrounded by people, but she's probably the loneliest person I know."

"Is that why she haunts your office so much?"

Jessie nodded. "And it's another big reason why I quit her. I thought she needed me as a friend more than as an employee." She made a face. "Even though hardly a week goes by that she doesn't try to get me to come back to her organization."

Kendra chuckled. "Is that story really true about how she once showed up at your office with a million dollars in cash?"

Jessie smiled. "Yep. She carried it over in a knapsack and dumped it all over my desk. A million dollars in stacks of hundreds and fifties, all in exchange for heading up security for her ten-month world tour. She thought seeing it all in cash would tempt me."

"Did it?"

Jessie laughed. "A little, especially since I was still trying to get my private investigator business off the ground. It was *really* good salesmanship on her part."

"I'd say so. Hard to resist."

"Yeah, until I remembered that it might be good for Dee to have *one* person in her life who doesn't want anything from her."

Kendra raised her plastic cup and tapped it against Jessie's. "You're a good friend."

Jessie tapped Kendra's cup back. "To good friends."

The house lights went down, and the stage lights rose on a breathtaking set that Kendra could only describe as part steampunk, part early-twentieth-century industrial. A dozen backup dancers marched onstage, followed by the star attraction herself. The crowd roared.

For the next two hours, Delilah Winter held the eighteen thousand audience members in her thrall, putting on a spectacular show that was at turns exuberant, heartbreaking, and ultimately triumphant. The songs were catchy, but not simplistic; steeped in heartbreak, but also radiating an optimism for life and love.

At one point, Dee walked on top of the low wall separating the Pool Circle from the Garden Boxes, pausing to sing to the children in wheelchairs in the handicapped section. What could have been corny and manipulative was, to Kendra, the emotional highlight of the show, carried by the star's sheer charisma and obvious sincerity.

At the show's end, Dee and the backup dancers disappeared backstage while the crowd shouted for the inevitable encore.

After a full minute, there was still no sign of the performers. The audience's cheers grew even more frantic.

Jessie leaned close to Kendra. "Costume change. Wait'll you see this one."

Kendra waited another full minute. Still no sign of Dee and the dancers.

Jessie wrinkled her brow. She stood up in the box and turned toward the thousands of screaming fans, clamoring for another song. She turned back toward Kendra. "I don't like it."

"Neither do I." Kendra nodded toward a black-garbed security man standing over the stage right staircase. He tapped his finger over a hidden earpiece as his facial expression registered panic. He suddenly bolted into the concert shell and ran into the wings.

All over the Garden Box area, security agents mimicked the gesture and ran for the stage.

"Jessie..."

"I see it." Jessie cursed under her breath and jumped out of the box. "I've got to see Colin Parks, her head of security. Follow me!"

Easier said than done, Kendra thought as she and Jessie ran through the exclusive Pool Circle section and used an empty chair as their launch pad onto the stage. Kendra had never tried to keep pace with her friend, but it didn't surprise her that Jessie's athleticism put her almost immediately several paces ahead. With the crowd's roar still pounding in her ears, Kendra followed Jessie through the stage right wings and down the corridor.

They flew past a row of mirrored dressing rooms and turned left into another short corridor occupied by the stars' deluxe dressing area. The hallway was lined with flowers and large unused stage speakers, competing for space with a crush of security agents, backup dancers, and members of the stage crew.

"Where's Dee?" Jessie shouted.

A tall black-clad man, obviously in a position of authority, turned. "Get out of here, Mercado. We're handling it."

"You may be her security chief, Colin, but she's my friend. Are we sure she's not in the can?"

A stage manager wearing a headset shook her head no.

Jessie glanced inside the dressing room. "Her encore costume is still on the rack. That's it, isn't it? The yellow one with the wings?"

One of the backup dancers nodded.

Outside, the Bowl audience cheered even louder, now chanting "encore" in one thunderous voice.

"No one's seen her?" Kendra shouted above the din.

The stage manager stepped forward. "She came down this hallway for her costume change. No one's seen her since."

Jessie spun back toward the security chief. "Colin, you're telling me your guys didn't have eyes on her?"

"I had two men assigned to this hallway. No one else is permitted in her dressing room during costume changes."

"Which men?"

"Two of my best. Henner and Krabbe."

"Where in the hell are they?"

"Stop firing questions at me. Do you think I'm not searching for them?" He was swearing as she continued to glare at him. "Okay, missing. Just like Delilah Winter."

Jessie turned back toward the group. "They couldn't just vanish. There's no way three people could step out of this hallway without fifty crew members seeing them."

The crowd's chant had morphed: *"Delilah! Delilah! Delilah!"*

Kendra looked down at the floor, the walls, the flowers, traces of glitter from Dee's sparkly costumes...

*"Delilah! Delilah! Delilah!"*

Kendra closed her eyes.

Detach. Concentrate.

The smells. Cologne, perfumes, body odors from the sweaty dancers...

And something else. Soybeans?

*"Delilah! Delilah! Delilah!"*

Kendra opened her eyes. "Propofol."

"What?" Jessie said.

"Propofol. It's an anesthetic with a soybean emulsifier. Very distinctive odor. It was used here just in the last few minutes."

"Oh, God," one of the dancers whispered.

Kendra looked down at the unused stage speakers. Each about four feet tall, they were sprinkled with glitter, spread evenly over their top surfaces.

Except...

"Someone's been handling these since the last costume change." Kendra crouched by one of the speakers and pulled on its black grille. "Help me with this."

Jessie and two of the security agents pried off the front grille.

As they pulled it away, a body tumbled from the speaker enclosure.

"Henner!" Colin Parks knelt beside him and felt his agent's chest. He pulled his hand away. It was covered with blood. "Dead."

Kendra was already at work on the other speaker grille. Within seconds she had it off.

Another body tumbled out. Blood pooled on the concrete floor.

"Krabbe!" Colin moved to the other body. "Dead. Stabbed or shot, I can't tell."

Jessie's jaw clenched. "But where's Dee?"

Kendra stared at the floor between the two speaker enclosures. "There's nothing here..."

"What are you saying?" Jessie crouched next to her.

"There's glitter all over the place. But not here. An empty

space, the same dimensions as . . . " She lifted her head sharply. "There was another speaker here."

*"Delilah! Delilah! Delilah!"*

Jessie cursed. "That's where Dee is. These speaker enclosures are on casters. She was rolled away."

"Rolled away where?" Colin asked.

Jessie jumped to her feet. "The loading dock. Hurry!"

The group ran down the long hallway that ran behind the Bowl shell until they reached the loading dock. The small driveway was empty save for Dee's waiting limo and an eighteen-wheeler that stood ready for the loading of tour stage and lighting equipment.

Colin spoke to the truck driver as Jessie ran toward a uniformed LAPD officer. She pointed to the tall Hollywood Bowl marquee sign on an island in the middle of Highland Avenue. "There are people in there, aren't there? Controlling the traffic signals?" Before he could answer, Jessie continued, "Radio them and ask if a truck or van left this driveway in the last couple of minutes. We need to know which direction they're headed."

"Ma'am, I need to know why you're—"

Jessie, a good head shorter than the cop, raised her chin and got in his face. "Do it. *Now.*"

The cop nodded. He swallowed hard and raised the walkie-talkie to his mouth.

Colin had turned away from the truck driver and was shouting to the cop on the walkie-talkie. "We're looking for a black Ford Transit van, no windows. Two men in coveralls loaded a speaker into it. It just left!"

The cop nodded and repeated the information. Then he listened to his walkie-talkie before nodding to Jessie. "The van got on the 101 heading south toward downtown. Anyone care to tell me what—?"

"Later." Jessie grabbed Kendra's arm. "Come with me."

Kendra instinctively obeyed her. "What are we doing?"

"Stealing that limo over there that was waiting for Dee. Go around and get in."

Kendra did as she was told.

Jessie opened the driver's side door and pulled out the startled driver. "Sorry about this, but I don't have time to get my car."

The driver, stunned, looked dazedly toward the police officer for help.

Jessie didn't wait for him to decide whether or not to make that plea verbal. She climbed in, started the limo, and peeled out of the driveway. She ignored the red traffic light and roared across Highland to the U.S. 101 entrance ramp.

"Think maybe we should have brought some muscle?" Kendra asked.

Jessie squinted at the cars ahead of them. "No, I'll have to be the muscle," she said absently. "I didn't want to wait for the cops to get their act together. Every minute we spent back there increased the risk of losing them."

"If we haven't already."

Jessie shook her head. "Don't say that."

"One way or another, we'll find her, Jessie."

An ocean of brake lights appeared on the freeway in front of them.

Jessie drew a relieved breath. "L.A. traffic. This could work for us." She cut the wheel hard right and sped down the shoulder. "Keep on the lookout for a black Ford van."

Kendra had already risen in her seat as she scanned the six lanes of traffic. "I'm on it. So far I've only seen two white Toyotas and a Subaru."

Jessie cursed. "Damn, I wish I had my motorcycle."

Kendra pointed ahead. "See that?"

Jessie's gaze flew a few hundred yards in front of them, where a van had abruptly cut into the shoulder. It peeled out and roared into the distance. Jessie jammed hard on the accelerator. "It's a Ford Transit 250. Call 911 and make sure the police know. Late model, high roof option. Tell them the suspects are taking the Santa Monica Boulevard exit."

Kendra was already speaking into the phone before Jessie finished talking. She left the connection open and dropped the phone into the cup holder.

"Hang on," Jessie said. She spun the wheel as they swerved down the Santa Monica Boulevard exit ramp. There was no sign of the van. "Shit. Where is it?"

Kendra leaned forward as they reached the bottom of the ramp. There, less than half a block to their left, were the familiar taillights of the Transit van, frantically weaving in and out of traffic.

"There!"

"I see it." Jessie turned the wheel and gunned the engine, roaring down the street. "Keep your eyes on that van. I need to play some bob and weave here."

"Got it."

Jessie raced through the cars, at one point even jumping the curb and taking the sidewalk for a half-block stretch.

"It's turning right at the light," Kendra said. "Onto Sunset Boulevard."

"I'm on it." Jessie spun onto Sunset, now only a few yards behind the van. She put on an extra burst of speed and pulled even with the heavily tinted driver's side window. The window lowered slightly, and the streetlights caught the glint of a gun barrel.

BLAM!

But Jessie had already dropped several feet behind. The van swerved and sideswiped the limo's front right panel, pushing them into oncoming traffic. Jessie pulled back into her lane.

The van picked up speed.

"Don't lose it," Kendra shouted frantically.

"No way." Jessie gripped the wheel harder. "Those guys are *really* starting to piss me off."

They followed the van down Sunset until, without warning, it cut a hard left.

"Silver Lake Boulevard," Jessie said as she followed. "Where in the hell are they taking her?"

The streets narrowed, and the traffic thinned, leaving them almost alone with the speeding van.

Suddenly a blinding shaft of light struck the van from above, startling both Jessie and the van's driver. Both vehicles swerved as they continued down the street.

A helicopter roared overhead, its searchlight locked on the van.

"It's a police chopper," Kendra said. She nodded toward the phone. "They've been listening."

"Good. Now if they'll just get some police cruisers here to cut these guys off."

A black void had suddenly appeared to their left. "What the hell is that?" Kendra asked.

"The Silver Lake Reservoir. It goes on for almost a mile."

They were now on a two-lane road, with a chain-link fence bordering the reservoir on their left, and single-family homes on their right. The helicopter dipped lower, its rotors blowing the trees on both sides of the road.

The van put on an extra burst of speed as if trying to break free of the helicopter's searchlight. But as the road curved, the van appeared to lose control. It swerved one way, then the next, then finally crashed through the reservoir fence. The van went airborne, launching over and into the dark water below.

"No!" Jessie screamed. "Dee!" She slammed the brakes, and they jumped out of the limo. The police helicopter now hovered over the reservoir, its searchlight trained over the bubbling, churning water where the van had plunged.

Jessie ran around to the limo's trunk and pulled out a tire iron. "That van could be twenty feet down. How good are you in the water?"

"Good enough." Kendra grabbed a jack handle and hefted it. "Let's go get her."

They ducked through the opening in the damaged chain-link fence and ran to the reservoir's edge. Wind from the helicopter blades whipped around them, blowing up loose dirt and churning the water even more. A garbled voice spoke from the helicopter's P.A. system.

"I can't hear him. What did he say?" Jessie yelled.

"He's telling us not to go in."

"That's what I thought." Jessie shed her jacket and leaped into the water.

Kendra jumped in behind her.

Cold. Freaking cold.

Didn't matter, Kendra thought. They had to get to Dee.

She took a deep breath and dove beneath the still-churning water.

The helicopter searchlight cast a shimmering glow on the reservoir's bottom. Kendra and Jessie descended toward the discharging pockets of air until they finally reached the van, which, true to Jessie's estimate, was almost twenty feet down.

Jessie swam around to the driver's side door. The window was shattered, and there was no sign of the driver. Kendra looked inside. There was a built-in metal barrier behind the two front seats, shielding the rear compartment from view. Even in the dim underwater light, Kendra could see the frustration on Jessie's face.

They swam around to the van's rear doors. Kendra tapped on them with the jack handle.

*Tap-tap-tap.*

No response.

Jessie began prying the door open.

Kendra tried again. *Tap-tap-tap.*

*Come on, Dee. Let us know you're okay.*

But she might not be okay. She might be unconscious.

Kendra tried again. *Tap-tap-tap.*

Again, no answer.

Jessie was working frantically with her tire iron to pry open those doors. Kendra followed suit, inserting the jack handle in the gap between the doors and bracing her feet on the rear bumper.

The doors weren't budging.

Dammit.

Kendra's lungs ached, and she knew she had only another few seconds before she'd have to return to the surface.

She pulled even harder.

*Open, you son of a bitch...*

CRACK!

The lock broke and the door swung open.

Get her out!

They both surged forward—

No!

Kendra and Jessie stared in horror at the sight that awaited them in the van's rear compartment.

Nothing.

Absolutely nothing.

The van was empty.

———◆———

Kendra and Jessie pulled themselves out of the reservoir to find four police cruisers now waiting for them on the road. Eight officers had their guns drawn and aimed at them.

The helicopter's P.A. system sounded another garbled

message that neither Kendra nor Jessie could understand, but the cops understood it well enough to lower their weapons.

A tall, bald officer stepped forward. "Delilah Winter," he said grimly. "Is she..."

"She's not down there," Kendra said curtly. "This van was a decoy. They pulled us away right after we exited the 101 onto Santa Monica. The van with Delilah Winter could be anywhere by now."

"What about the driver?"

Jessie gestured out toward the dark reservoir. "Out there somewhere. They planned for this to distract us and buy time to get away with her. The driver is out there with scuba gear."

"How do you know?"

Jessie reached into the pocket of her wet jeans and produced a white plastic cap. "This fits over a regulator. I found it floating in the driver's compartment. You might want to get that helicopter patrolling the edges of this reservoir. If you're lucky, you might be able to catch him coming out of the water."

The cop nodded. "Will do. You ladies sit tight. We'll get you some blankets. We'll need full statements from you."

Jessie shook her head and started back for the still-running limo. "We're heading back to the Bowl."

"Ma'am..."

"No!" Kendra followed her. "We need to find out how in the hell this happened. If you need statements, you can get them from us there."

# CHAPTER

# 3

On the way back to the Bowl, Kendra and Jessie stopped at a twenty-four-hour pharmacy to pick up towels, sweatpants, and T-shirts so they could quickly dry themselves and change.

"It's a mob scene." Kendra gave a low whistle and shook her head as Jessie drove up the driveway toward the Bowl's parking area, which was still ablaze with lights. "It looks like we might have to fight our way back down to the crime scene."

The audience had obviously been cleared from the premises, but the parking lot was still full of vehicles. Kendra noticed innumerable cars from the LAPD and FBI as well as forensic and coroner's vans, but the majority of the vehicles were obviously media-related. TV crews were setting up all over the parking lot; there were even three TV vans pulled to the far side. Of course there would be media, she thought bitterly.

Dee was a mega-star, and this was a gigantic story. Journalists always had sources ready to clue them in on potential breaking news. They had probably arrived here before she and Jessie had even pulled out in pursuit.

But the reporters themselves seemed to be milling out here in the parking lot and weren't being permitted to enter the Bowl itself. There was an LAPD officer checking a clipboard at the front barricade for people to be allowed entrance, but he was looking harassed and being bombarded. "It's going to take us time to even get close enough to talk to that officer about letting us get down to the crime scene."

"The hell it is. I'm not in a mood to have to go through this bullshit." Jessie's tone was clipped as she parked the limo with a screech of brakes squarely in the middle of the parking lot. "I'm going to see Parks *now*. If that cop wants to try to stop me, we're going to have a discussion."

And that discussion wouldn't be pleasant, Kendra knew. Jessie was usually cool and reasonable and got her way by persuasion and cleverness. But she'd been stretched to the limit tonight and she was as frightened about Dee as Kendra. "Give me a couple minutes." Kendra reached for her phone. "Those are FBI vans over there. FBI is usually in charge in a kidnapping. Let me see if I can get someone to call off that LAPD cop."

"Do it." Jessie was looking straight ahead. "Hurry."

Kendra *was* hurrying as she dialed Metcalf's number. He picked up immediately. "God, I'm sorry, Kendra. Any news?"

"All bad, so far. I need your help."

"It's not our jurisdiction. L.A. cases are handled by an assistant director in charge up there. You'll have to go through him."

"Don't give me that bureaucratic bullshit. *Help* me."

"What do you need?" he asked quietly.

"Right now, not much. Just contact one of the FBI guys at the stadium and have him come up to the entrance gate and order this LAPD cop to let us go down to the crime scene. Jessie's in no mood to deal with any more delays. You have to know someone there you can ask for a favor. From the look of this parking lot, half the local FBI office must be here tonight."

"Probably close. I hear they're pulling out all the stops trying to locate Delilah Winter. I'll do what I can. Jessie is with you?"

"Yes. Hurry." She cut the connection and turned to Jessie. "Complications. San Diego jurisdiction doesn't apply to L.A. But Metcalf is working on helping us where he can."

"So I heard." She was swearing beneath her breath. "That's all we need is to have the local L.A. office getting in our way instead of helping us."

"We'll work it out," Kendra said. "We both know that there are ways to get around every problem. No one wants anything to happen to Dee. We'll just make sure it doesn't."

"But if those kidnappers think that she's too hot to handle and becoming a liability, the first thing they'll do is kill her."

"Not the first thing. They'll try everything else first and you know it. She's too valuable to them. And that will give us time to get her back." She opened her car door. "Come on, let's go up to that barricade. Stop being negative. I have faith in Metcalf. He'll pull those strings and we'll have you down there at the crime scene with Parks in no time."

"You're being a little too Pollyanna for me at the moment, Kendra," Jessie said grimly as she followed her. "Have I ever told you how I *hate* Pollyanna?"

"Now, that's truly negative. Though in most cases I agree with you. I was just trying to—"

"Dr. Kendra Michaels!" The LAPD officer was bellowing at the top of his voice, his gaze on his clipboard. "Ms. Jessie Mercado!"

"Shit!" Kendra grabbed Jessie's arm and pulled her through the crowd of reporters. "This is the last thing I wanted." She pushed her ID in front of the officer's face and then ducked through the barricade as the reporters started closing in to fire questions at her. "They'll latch on to every name, every person connected to the case."

"Particularly Kendra Michaels," Jessie said as she started to run down the steps toward the backstage crime scene. "How do you feel now, Pollyanna?"

"Low blow." But Kendra stopped as she saw a remarkably good-looking auburn-haired man whose sleek dark suit and air of authority were very familiar to her. "I think that has to be the FBI agent who's coming to follow up his call to that LAPD guy at the gate. I'll talk to him. You cut across the stage and go find Parks."

"I wasn't going to do anything else," Jessie said. "I'll see you later."

She was gone.

But the FBI agent had been taking the steps two at a time and was suddenly standing in front of Kendra. He was just as good looking as Kendra had first thought, with dark brown eyes, a golden tan, and a flashing smile that was very warm and personal. "Kendra Michaels?" He held out his hand. "Special Agent Nate Kelland. I'm delighted to have been able to help you. I've been looking forward to meeting you for a long time. Your reputation precedes you."

She shook his hand. "I appreciate you cooperating. I know the first few hours of a kidnapping investigation are so important. You and Metcalf are friends?"

He shook his head. "We've worked a few cases together and we've met at conferences. I respect him as an agent. But I'm sure he realized he was calling the right person when you said you needed help. We've spoken of you a few times, and I've told him how I much I admire what you've accomplished." He smiled. "I believe I even mentioned how I envied him the opportunity of working with you."

"That's very kind." Her eyes narrowed. "But does that mean you'll be willing to let Jessie and me have access to information and possibly contribute to the case as it progresses?"

"I'll have to see what I can do." He smiled that charming smile again. "I do have a certain amount of pull with the assistant director, but he might be stubborn where this is concerned. It's a tremendously big case and very high-profile. The outcome could affect his career...or mine." He added quickly, "Not that it would make a difference to me. I'm concerned only with the safe return of Delilah Winter."

"So are we," Kendra said quietly. "She's our friend and nothing is more important to us than getting her back."

"You're already doing that according to the reports I have from LAPD on-site at the reservoir." His gaze was on the wet hair clinging around her face. "It must have been quite a chase. I'm sorry you weren't successful in apprehending them. I hope we'll get another opportunity to go after them together." He added brusquely, "We'll need a detailed statement from both of you regarding the events that transpired on that chase in the city. All information is essential right now. You're welcome to question any of the witnesses yourself as long as an agent is present. I'll be glad to discuss the case with you at any time if you believe you have anything to contribute."

"We'll need to know when you get a ransom demand."

"That will be a little dicey. But I'll try to persuade the assistant director to share." He gestured to the stairs. "Now may I take you to meet my fellow agents and the LAPD officers who will also be working the case? The governor has requested it be a joint operation until we find the victim."

*Victim.* Kendra shivered at the thought of that term applied to Dee. That vibrant, glowing young woman who had lit up the stage only hours ago... "I'm glad. I wish he'd call in the state militia."

Kelland smiled. "I promise we'll put so many agents in the field, you'll think he has." He started down the stairs. "And since I'll be one of them, I have to get back to work myself. But I'm sure that's exactly how you'd want it."

"Yes, I would." She wasn't quite sure what to think of Nate Kelland, but she recognized he might be a force with which to be reckoned. All that charm and warmth and yet his actual commitment to helping them had been minimal. But this wasn't the time to tear apart the intentions of someone who might be of use to them.

He'd responded with support when Metcalf had asked him. She'd take that as an encouraging sign and worry about how to handle any other interaction later. She followed him quickly down the steps. "I'll make sure that you get our statements before we leave here tonight. And I'll be happy to meet everyone on your team a little later. But if you'll excuse me, I need to go see if Jessie Mercado was able to get any more information from Colin Parks."

As she hurried past him, she added dryly, "And to make sure she hasn't done him bodily harm in the process. She wasn't at all pleased at how careless he'd been to allow this nightmare to happen."

———◆———

But Jessie hadn't even started to speak to Parks yet when Kendra reached her a few minutes later. "He's giving a statement," she said curtly as she nodded at Parks sitting at a desk across from an agent typing into a computer. "He said he'd get to me as soon as he could. He's probably trying to avoid me." She crossed her arms across her chest. "I'd sure as hell want to avoid me right now."

So would anyone, Kendra thought ruefully. Jessie had been uptight before, but it was clear she was very close to explosion. "Maybe he's just trying to cooperate with the FBI. Special Agent Kelland seems to be a stickler about getting those statements right away." She nodded toward the agent. "Remember? We have to give one of our own before we leave here today."

"Stickler? I don't like that word." Jessie gave him a brief glance. "Good grief, he looks like a damn male model. Are we in trouble?"

"I'm not sure. He seems cooperative. We'll have to see how he follows through." She frowned. "If we have a problem, maybe we can work around him with Metcalf and Griffin."

"Who will have limited access and information now that they're out of the loop. We don't have time for that, Kendra." Her gaze was back on Parks, who had gotten up from his chair and was signing his statement. "And this should never have happened."

"You keep saying that," Kendra said impatiently. "But it did happen, and we have to accept it and just find a way to get her back. You know that as well as—"

But Jessie was no longer listening; she was crossing the stage to stand in front of Parks. "It shouldn't have happened," she repeated fiercely. "What did you do that was different from your regular routine, Parks?"

"Nothing," he said curtly. "Get off my back, Jessie. We had a schedule and routine that we went through every evening she had a performance. My men were as well rehearsed as Delilah. They wouldn't have changed the plan."

"But they ended up dead, and she ended up kidnapped. If they didn't change it, it must have been a lousy plan."

His hands grabbed her shoulders. "Yeah, they ended up dead, and I had to spend an hour tonight trying to explain to their families why that happened. And when I get through here, I have to go and face them in person." His lips were tight, his eyes liquid bright. "And I'm going to have to tell them the same thing I'm telling you. That they did their job, and nothing should have happened. But sometimes the bad guys are smarter or quicker than we are, and then we fail. All we can do is our best." He looked her in the eye. "And no one knows that better than you. You're just hurting because you care about the kid."

"Get your hands off me or I'll break your damn neck," she said hoarsely. "If you'd cared more about her, then she wouldn't have been taken. I *trusted* you."

"I'm done here." Parks released his grip on her shoulders and took a step back. "When I get through with dealing with my guys' families, I'll be back and try to find out exactly what happened. Maybe it will give us a lead. At any rate, I'm not going to stop until we find her. Because I *do* care about her. Ever since I took over from you, she's been a pain in my ass. Do you think it was easy following in your footsteps? She thought you walked on water. But I've always liked her, and I've always done my best to keep her safe. Believe it or not, that's the truth."

Jessie opened her lips to speak and then closed them again. She was silent a moment. "I believe you," she finally said wearily. "But something went wrong, and we've got to find out how it could have happened. How did they just whisk her up and take her? I taught her to always be careful. She was smart, Parks. Those scumbags couldn't have fooled her."

"Like I said, sometimes the bad guys turn out to be smarter than us." He strode across the stage toward the exit. "I'll see you later, Jessie."

"I could tell you were ready to take a machete to his head

61

when you stomped down here," Kendra murmured as she watched him leave. "You were easier on him than I thought you'd be."

"Because he was right," she said unsteadily. "No matter how hard we try, sometimes the bad guys are going to try harder and they're going to win. I knew Dee wasn't going to be easy for anyone to handle. That's why I was so careful when I chose Parks to take over my job with her. He had all the qualifications and discipline, and I knew he was flexible enough not to make her rebel. I thought he'd be perfect. It's hard to find that kind of balance."

"But you told me Dee had been rebelling lately," Kendra said. "Maybe someone out there was watching and decided it was time to step in and take advantage."

"Maybe. But as I said, she's smart. I don't think she'd do anything careless that would cause anyone to be able to snatch her. It would take something to fool her."

"Because you taught her," Kendra said softly. "And that will be to her benefit. She has those years of training with you and she'll remember them."

She nodded. "You're damn right." She cleared her throat. "Now let's go talk to Parks's crew and see if they remember anything. Then we'll go schmooze with those FBI and LAPD guys and impress them enough to squeeze information out of them if we need to." She shrugged. "Most of them are careful around private investigators, but I think a couple of those LAPD officers have helped me out before. And you shouldn't have any trouble." She looked over her shoulder with a smile. "Everyone wants to cozy up to a superstar like you. Who knows? They might even get their picture in the paper. Do you want me to go up to the parking lot and bring down a couple of those reporters?"

"Don't you dare." But she was glad that Jessie wasn't quite so much on edge. Jessie always bounced back from every blow. She wasn't bouncing now. She was too worried and sick and angry. But she was thinking, healing, working on the problem. "If you're talking to LAPD, I'll take the FBI agents. Agent Kelland wanted me to meet them..."

———◆———

KENDRA'S CONDO
11:40 A.M.

Kendra was back in her condo and starting to pack an overnight bag when Metcalf phoned her. "Did Kelland come through for you?" he asked. "I didn't expect a problem, but you didn't call me back."

"We were swamped from the minute Kelland pulled rank to get us down to the crime scene. You know how it can be on a case like this." She went to the bathroom and grabbed her toiletries. "Yes, Kelland was fine and did what we needed. Other than that, he seemed too busy to pay any attention to us. Which was great with Jessie and me. All we wanted to do was establish contacts with the LAPD and Kelland's fellow agents and listen in on any conversations they were getting from operators in the field. Then I grabbed breakfast with Jessie and hit the road back to San Diego to grab an overnight bag and call the school and tell them I'm taking a few days off."

"A few days? That sounds optimistic. Are you?"

"I don't know what I am," she said wearily. "Except I'm scared, Metcalf. I was telling Jessie not to be negative, but we're going at this blind. We don't know anything yet. Right now, Kelland just seems to be sitting and waiting for that damn ransom note."

"That's not what he's doing. If he's as good as I think he is, Kelland has already alerted his agents to stake out the phones of all possible sources who might be contacted by the kidnappers. That includes everyone from Dee's record company to her mother in Europe. It wouldn't surprise me if they've even staked out Jessie's phone since she's so close to her. He's probably also ordered all of Dee's bank accounts monitored in case they try to make her move the money herself." He paused. "That's what we do the minute we realize a victim has been taken. That's what I'd do, Kendra."

"I guess I knew that. As I said, I'm just scared and frustrated." She tried to keep her voice from shaking. "There are all kinds of bad statistics about kidnap victims. It's so much safer to kill a victim than return her after they have the ransom. That would probably go double for someone as famous as Dee."

"But there have been quite a few cases where a victim has been returned after ransom has been paid. John Paul Getty's grandson, Julio Iglesias's father, Frank Sinatra's son." Metcalf rattled the names off quickly. "And there have been a lot of CEOs and industrialists who have been kidnapped and then released in South America. It's practically a national pastime down there. Hell, there hasn't even been a ransom demand yet. Maybe she was taken by one of her fans. Remember that Miss Venezuela who was kidnapped several years ago? Her captors released her a few hours later after she agreed to sign fifteen autographs for them. Maybe it will be—"

"Shut up, Metcalf." She couldn't take any more. "I appreciate that you're only trying to keep my spirits up. But do you think I didn't mentally go over all those cases that gave me hope as I drove back down here? I was even smiling when I thought about that Venezuela beauty queen and wondering how Dee would have handled those nutcases." She swallowed hard. "But I'm not laughing now, because whoever did this was very clever and more than likely a professional. Which means I have to assume that this is just as bad as we thought it was when we found she was missing. So now tell me the other side of the coin. What's the worst-case scenario?"

He didn't speak for a moment.

"Answer me. You're FBI and you've worked kidnap cases before. Who should I hope doesn't have Dee?"

"Probably someone who has a political or fanatical reason for the abduction. You can't reason with groups like Isis." He added quickly, "But they don't generally go after celebrities like Dee. They want to make a statement."

"That's comforting," she said dryly. "Next."

"Revenge."

"She's too young to have chalked up much in that column. And she's probably one of the most popular entertainers in the world."

"Maybe too popular."

"Next."

"Money. And that's a big umbrella and can hide multiple spokes. Maybe someone so dedicated to a project that they consider she has no right to those enormous paydays?" He added, "Or maybe a plain blue-ribbon psycho. I could go on, but I'm not going to do it. You're the smartest woman I know. You'll find out who did this yourself. I just wish I could help you do it."

"Who says you can't? Ordinarily, I wouldn't ask you to break protocol when I know that the director assigned this case to L.A. But this isn't ordinary times. I can't promise I won't ask a favor now and then. I don't know what I'm facing dealing with Kelland. Feel free to turn me down."

"You know I'll help when I can. I'll just have to keep it quiet around Griffin." He paused. "You're feeling uncomfortable with Kelland?"

"He's an unknown factor. We were definitely the outsiders. It's a different world up there in L.A., Metcalf. What do you think of Kelland? He said you weren't really friends, but he jumped when you asked that favor."

"Because the favor was for you. He pumped me about you at a hotel bar one night. He'd heard I worked with you and he probably liked the idea of getting an introduction. I blew him off."

"That doesn't sound very friendly. What's wrong with him?"

"Nothing, I guess. He seemed like a pretty good guy. Everyone likes him."

"Except you?"

"I told you, he's a good guy." Then, at her puzzled silence, he burst out, "Okay, he's one of those golden boys you come across now and then. You saw him. He's good looking and polite and does everything right. He's a really good agent and was even given the FBI Medal of Valor two years ago when he took a bullet for another agent. Everyone knows that he's going straight to the top and will probably someday end up as director."

"So?"

"He has it all. I didn't like the idea of him trying to weasel his way into meeting you and maybe trying to work with you."

"What? He didn't impress me as the weasel type."

"Perhaps not. I guess I don't trust anyone who does everything right. Hell, I'm even the one who managed to get the golden boy what he wanted this time."

"He seemed polite but not that eager to work with me. I only hope that he lets us get our foot in the door when the action starts."

"I do, too. You know I'll be there for you," Metcalf said sincerely. "What's next?"

"I've just finished packing my bag, so I'll go down and say goodbye to Olivia. Then I'll head back to L.A. to Jessie's house. We'll probably both grab a nap and then set out to retrace Dee's steps for the last few weeks. This kidnapping was too well planned not to have been heavily researched. Which means that she had to have been followed, and there's a chance someone will have noticed who was doing it."

"That may mean a lot of legwork. I could do some of it on my own time."

"Hey, I may take you up on that." But not unless she found it absolutely necessary. She was very touched by the offer, but she wanted to use Metcalf only in an emergency. "I'll let you know." She headed for the front door. "I have to leave now. I'll stay in touch."

"You do that." He paused. "Does Lynch know about Dee?"

"I told you, I haven't talked to him since he left. Was I supposed to send up a flare? It's not as if he could do anything from some mountain in Tibet."

"I just thought you'd want to let him know," he said quietly. "He's always been there for you during the rough times. I think this is one of those times."

"Well, this time he's otherwise engaged. We're both adults with our own careers and I can't expect anything else. Jessie and I will do fine without him. Bye, Metcalf." She ended the call.

Everything she had said was true, she thought as she went down the staircase to Olivia's condo. But it didn't stop her from feeling a little lost without Lynch. No, a lot lost. The sadness and panic when she thought about Dee were there every moment, and being with Lynch usually seemed to ease any loneliness or pain.

Which meant she was entirely too dependent on him. This might be the learning experience she needed. What she'd told Metcalf was correct.

She and Jessie would get along fine without Lynch.

Kendra followed Jessie to her home in Venice, a beach community within sight of the Santa Monica Pier. Jessie's small two-story house was a comfortable distance from the tourist-plagued boardwalk, situated along one of the community's many charming canals. The waterway was lined with tufts of tall grass and a variety of colorful plants, each chosen according to the whims of the individual homeowners.

Kendra looked up at the house as she climbed out of her car and joined Jessie on the sidewalk outside. "I can't believe I've never been to your place before."

Jessie shrugged. "You've been to my office. That feels more like home to me."

"I don't believe that. This is amazing. Right on the canal. How did you find it?"

"It found me. Or its previous owner did, right before he was killed by his girlfriend and her Zumba instructor."

"Seriously?"

Jessie nodded as she unlocked the front door. "Yep. And after I cracked the case, the man's son gave me a sweetheart deal on the place. Trust me, I couldn't have afforded it any other way."

Jessie pushed open the door and punched the entry code on her alarm keypad. Kendra looked around the foyer and living room. The open layout gave her a view all the way back to the floor-to-ceiling windows that perfectly framed the small yard and canal outside.

"Beautiful."

"Thanks. By the way, the previous owner's body was found just about where you're standing now."

Kendra looked down at the Italian tile. "FYI, if you ever decide to sell this place, you should let the listing agent do the talking."

"Probably a good idea." She was suddenly grinning. "Nah, I was just kidding you. He was killed outside, near the beach. Though it probably wouldn't have bothered me. That only happens when it's someone I care about. I've lived side by side with murder and death from Afghanistan to the Hollywood Hills since I was a teenager. I'm not callous about it, but I accept it."

"Particularly when you decide you want to freak me out?" Kendra asked dryly.

"Yep, particularly then."

Jessie flipped on the lights, giving Kendra an even better view of the place. While her office had a 1940s retro vibe, the house was funky chic, with tasteful splashes of color accenting adventurous furnishings and artwork.

"Well done," Kendra said. "Your taste or the dead man's?"

"Mine. I totally gutted the place and started from scratch. I did it pretty much all myself."

"Impressive. I can't even seem to find the time to replace my drawer pulls."

Jessie pointed to her sleek galley kitchen just off the living room. "You'd probably think I was bragging if I told you I made all the cabinets, too."

"I hate you."

"Yeah, I thought so."

Kendra looked at a wall of photos in the living room, accented by colorful frames that somehow complemented rather than overpowered the pictures. Kendra had seen some of the same shots in Jesse's office, surveying her past as an Afghanistan army vet, a popular contestant on the *American Ninja* television show, and her stint as Delilah Winter's security director. Several shots pictured Jessie with a strikingly handsome man who occasionally wore horn-rimmed spectacles and tailored jackets.

Kendra pointed to the man. "Who's this guy?"

"Oh. Him." She shrugged. "No one to speak of."

"That obviously isn't true. You have half a dozen pictures of him on your wall, spanning at least..." Kendra looked at the photos a moment longer. "...nine years."

Jessie pulled her away from the wall. "Don't pull that Kendra Michaels shit on me. There will be zero pictures of him as soon as I get some new frames."

"Sounds like there's a story there."

"Trust me, there isn't," she said curtly.

Kendra couldn't help being curious. The way the man in the photo was regarding Jessie was very...intimate. And why not? Some of those photos revealed how beautiful Jessie was when she wasn't being the fiery dynamo Kendra knew her to be. Those high cheekbones, that wonderful mouth that was so expressive. Usually Jessie was frank and open regarding the multitude of interesting men who moved in and out of her life. But she clearly didn't want to talk about this one, so Kendra decided to let it go. "Okay. Whatever you say."

Her gaze wandered to another wall where ceiling spotlights showcased an odd collection of objects: a bicycle horn, a matchbook, an eight-track tape, a set of keys, and a thermal coffee mug, among other things. The items were arranged artfully, but Kendra spent a long moment trying to figure out their meaning.

Jessie smiled at her obvious confusion. "It's a souvenir collection."

"Souvenirs of what?"

"Of my cases. Each one of those things played a part in my cracking an investigation. I've spent so many nights wanting to beat my head against that wall that this seemed like a healthier way to go. They remind me that the solution is always out there waiting to be found. Even if I don't recognize it at first."

Kendra nodded. "When we find Dee, you'll put something else up there."

Jessie nodded firmly. "I will."

"We *will* find her, Jessie."

Jessie stepped away from the wall and looked out at the canal. "I'd feel better if we knew why she was taken. A ransom note, a manifesto, anything. You know?"

"I know."

"Until then, we don't even know if she's still alive."

"She's alive. If they wanted her dead, they would have killed her at the same time they killed the members of her security team."

"I keep telling myself that."

"Believe it."

Jessie nodded, but Kendra knew that she was still worried out of her mind. Words weren't going to help. Try to distract her. "Come on." She motioned toward a pair of white wooden beach chairs out on the back patio. "Let's sit down and take in that million-dollar view. I can tell you what I learned from Kelland on the way down here."

"Kelland? You talked to him?"

"He took my call right away, believe it or not." Kendra opened the sliding glass door and stepped out onto the patio. "And I don't think my friends at the San Diego FBI office even had to lean on him to do it."

Jessie joined her outside. "Why are you surprised? I think you impressed him last night. And he's probably heard how much his colleagues have benefited from your help over the years."

"Maybe." Kendra sat down and gazed at the canal. "Anyway, they got some info on those speaker cabinets backstage. They were delivered about one thirty in the afternoon, shortly before the sound check. Delilah's crew thought they belonged to the Bowl, and venue staff thought they were part of Delilah's show. No one paid attention to the speakers, but there's some thought that the people who took Delilah may have been hiding inside them all day."

"I had the same thought," Jessie said. "Did cameras get the truck making the delivery?"

"Yes. Looks like the same van that took her away last night. The big speakers were rolled off, and the van left immediately. The two guys pushing the speaker shells don't pop up on any other surveillance cams until last night, when they were rolling the speaker back during the show. The FBI is swabbing the hell out of the remaining speakers. If those guys left so much as a drop of perspiration in there, we'll soon have their DNA."

"Good. In the meantime, I want to talk to her crew."

"Which ones?"

"All of them. Every single one."

"You think it was an inside job?"

Jessie shrugged. "It's hard to pull off this kind of thing without some intimate backstage knowledge. You never know."

Kendra pulled out her phone and started typing. "I'll send Kelland a text and see if he'll help set that up. They'll probably be questioning the crew themselves, and maybe they'll let us tag along."

"Most of her tour crew have been with her from the beginning. I know them. They're a great bunch of people. They were always very protective of Dee."

"She was fifteen when she started, right?"

"Professionally. But she actually started singing when she was thirteen. She recorded dozens of videos of herself singing songs in her family's little apartment up in Lancaster. A lot of the songs were originals. Within a couple years, she had a million followers. She landed the Disney Channel show, then a recording contract, and everything else came pretty quickly after that."

"Has anyone notified her mother?"

The subject brought a sour look to Jessie's face. "I called her this morning. She's in France with the latest in a long line of loser husbands."

"Is she coming back here?"

"I don't think so."

"Really?"

"She said there's nothing she can do for her daughter here

that she can't do there. She seemed more concerned about her monthly check than anything else."

"Touching."

"Yeah, Gina Winter is a piece of work. Incredibly selfish and overbearing. Dee became a much happier person when she got her own place and encouraged her mom to move to Europe. Trust me, we're all better off with that woman staying exactly where she is."

"Got it." Kendra's phone rang in her hands, and she checked the screen. "It's Kelland. That was fast." Kendra pressed the button to answer. "Hi, Kelland. I'm here with Jessie. You're on speaker."

"Hello, ladies. I just got your text. We've actually already spoken to most of the stage crew."

Jessie leaned closer to Kendra's phone. "So you won't mind if I take a crack at them?"

"Free country."

"Good."

"But let me ask *you* something, Jessie. What can you tell me about Adrian Nash?"

Jessie frowned, thinking. "Sound guy. Small build, longish blond hair?"

"Sounds like him."

"He's been with Dee's stage crew for years. I can't tell you much more. Why? Did he set off alarm bells for you guys?"

"You could say that. He's missing."

Kendra and Jessie glanced at each other.

"Since when?" Jessie asked.

"Since immediately after everyone left the Bowl early this

morning. His live-in girlfriend said he never came home. No one's heard from him."

Jessie thought about this. "It wouldn't be the first time a roadie went home with someone else after a show."

"She says he isn't like that. He missed a doctor's appointment and a lunch date. I'm about to run over and talk to her. If you'd care to join us..."

"What's the address?" Kendra said.

"It's in Palms, just off National. I'll text it to you."

Jesse nodded. "Right. We'll be there in twenty minutes."

"See you there."

Kendra cut the connection.

# CHAPTER

# 4

Kendra and Jessie rolled to a stop in front of a one-story Spanish-style home in the West L.A. community of Palms, on a street uncomfortably close to the din of the 405 freeway.

Kelland was already there. He climbed out of his Ford Explorer, pulling a dark suit jacket over his broad shoulders.

Kendra and Jessie joined him on the sidewalk. "Thanks for letting us in on this," Kendra said. "We appreciate it."

Kelland shrugged. "You're welcome. According to my boss, we should be the ones grateful to you. He got an earful from the special agent in charge of the San Diego office."

Kendra asked, "Michael Griffin?"

"Yes. He said we'd be complete idiots not to include you for whatever extent you choose to be involved in our investigation. After seeing you in action last night, I tend to agree." A warm smile lit his face. "Griffin says he's been trying to get you to join the Bureau for years."

"I value my sanity far too much for that."

"Yet you've been involved in the office's most high-profile cases of the past few years."

Kendra grimaced. "I guess I just don't value my sanity enough."

"How many cases has it been? Twenty-eight, twenty-nine?"

"Don't remind me. Not all of them have been for the FBI. And I've turned down ten times that number."

"So I've heard. There are days I wish I could do that."

"Like today?" Jessie said.

Kelland shook his head. "No. Believe me, I want to find Delilah Winter as much as you do. And we will." He gestured to the house in front of them. "But I'm not sure if this will help us do that."

Kendra strode quickly toward the front door. "Let's find out."

Kelland and Jessie had barely caught up with her when she rapped on the door. It opened to reveal a small woman in shorts and a tank top. She eyed them nervously. "Yes?"

Kelland stepped forward. "Katy Wynn?"

"Yes?"

"I'm Special Agent Kelland. FBI." Kelland flashed his ID. "And these two women are helping us on the case. We want to talk to you about Adrian Nash."

She cast a wary glance at them. "Did you find him?"

"Afraid not," Kelland said. "That's why we're here."

"I don't have anything more to say." She stepped back from the door and moved to close it.

Jessie slapped her palm against the door and pushed back. "Let's give it a shot. You want to help Adrian, don't you?" She cocked her head. "Or maybe you don't."

"Of course I do," she answered quickly.

"Then talk to us."

"I've already talked to another FBI agent and a cop."

"Which is why we're here," Kelland said gently. "Just following up. Okay?"

Katy nodded reluctantly.

"May we come in?"

She pulled the door open wide and walked back into the house.

Kendra glanced around as they followed her inside. The small house was decorated with framed concert posters, many autographed, that she assumed must have come from Nash's previous tour jobs. The décor and furnishings had a definite masculine vibe, suggesting that Katy had only recently moved in.

"Your boyfriend is Delilah Winter's sound guy?" she asked.

Katy nodded. "Second audio engineer."

"He works in the booth?" Kelland said.

"No. On the stage. He manages the microphones for the instruments and vocalists."

Kelland looked at several framed photographs of Adrian, posing with such rock luminaries as Tom Petty, Bruce Springsteen, and Paul Simon. "I remember him. We spoke to Adrian briefly at the Bowl before we let the crew go."

Kelland pulled out his phone and swiped his finger across the screen.

Kendra leaned over and saw he was scrolling through photos he'd taken of the crew members. He finally stopped at what was clearly Nash. "Yeah, I remember him. He said he assumed the big speakers were there for another show this weekend." Kelland glanced up at Katy. "We released everyone by four thirty A.M. You're sure he didn't come home while you were sleeping?"

"Positive. He would've had to turn off the alarm, which would have woken me up. I've been here all day. I'd know if he was in the house."

"Have you tried calling him?" Jessie said.

"About fifty times. It just goes to voicemail."

Kendra scanned the room, looking for something, anything that would give her insight into the missing man. She paid special attention to the cluttered foyer table and the kitchen's overflowing trash can. "Has he behaved or spoken in a way you might call unusual?"

Katy shook her head. "He's been on tour with Delilah Winter. I joined him two or three weekends a month, and things were the same as always. He seemed happy to be back home. We're supposed to drive up to Big Sur together next week." She looked down. "I thought he might be going to propose there."

Kendra smiled. "He may still." She was still glancing around the room. She stiffened. Yes, that might be it. Now pull it all together...

"Maybe," Katy said. "I don't want to talk about it now."

"Is there anyone else who may have an idea where he went?" Kelland said. "A friend, a coworker..."

"He'd tell me before he'd tell anyone. But I did check with a couple friends of his. I'm so upset. No one has any idea where he is."

"Really?" Kendra asked softly. "Aren't you laying it on a little thick, Katy?"

Katy's gaze flew up to meet her. "What?"

"You heard me." Kendra tried to sound threatening. It was hard to do because there was something vulnerable about the woman that reminded her of a lost kitten. "I don't have to tell you that it may appear suspicious that he went on the run just hours after Delilah Winter was abducted on his stage."

"Suspicious?" Katy recoiled at the word.

"Yes," Kendra said. "Even more suspicious than it is for you to stand there and lie to us."

She could tell Jessie and Kelland were almost as surprised to hear this as Katy. "I know Adrian was here this morning," she said. "He packed a rolling bag and left. I think you even helped him. Maybe you carried another bag out to his truck. Or maybe a large van or camping vehicle?"

Katy stepped back and raised her hands in an almost-defensive posture. "What in the hell is going on here?"

Kendra moved toward her. "You tell us, Katy. But be careful. You've already lied to the FBI. That alone can get you jail time. How deep do you want to bury yourself?"

Katy's eyes widened as she tried to think frantically. "One of my neighbors told you, didn't they?"

"Does it really make any difference? Start by telling us where he went."

"I don't know. He said he parked his pickup on the street a couple blocks from here. He left in an old RV he inherited from his parents. I have no idea where he went."

Kendra shot her a skeptical look.

Katy's eyes were tearing. "Really, I have no idea!"

Kelland gave Kendra the faintest nod of approval before turning back to Katy. "Okay, let's back this up. I want to hear about every second you had with him this morning. Don't leave one word out. What you say next could mean the difference between spending the night in jail and not. Do you understand?"

Katy nodded.

"Good. So when did he get home?"

Katy was silent for a long moment, as if weighing her options. Finally she replied, "About five this morning. He came straight from the Bowl. He was freaked."

"About what?" Jessie said.

"Delilah's kidnapping. He said some security guys had been killed."

Kelland nodded. "What else did he say?"

"He said he had to get the hell out of here. Right away. Like at that very moment."

"Why?" Kendra said.

"He wouldn't say. He said the less I knew, the better."

"He used those words?" Jessie said.

"Exactly. He was scaring me. He wouldn't even let me go with him."

"Okay, so where was he headed?" Kelland asked.

"He wouldn't tell me."

Kelland clicked his tongue. "You wouldn't be holding out on us, would you?"

"No. I'm telling you, he was here only long enough to change clothes and pack a bag. Then he was gone." Katy crossed her arms in front of her. "I've never seen him like that. He was scared."

"Scared of what?" Kelland said. "The police?"

She shook her head. "I don't think so."

"Then what was he afraid of?"

"I . . . don't know. He'd been acting kind of strange since he got back into town."

"You said he was happy to be back."

"He was. It's just that sometimes he was kind of . . . distant. He was on the phone a lot."

"Was that unusual?" Jessie said.

"Not by itself. Whenever he finished a tour, he was trying to line up his next one. But in the last few days . . ." Her voice trailed off.

"If you want to help him, you need to talk to us," Kendra said.

Katy looked away, then back. "He left the room when he was on the phone. He didn't usually do that. I joked that he was having an affair, but he said he needed to concentrate."

"Did you believe him?" Jessie said.

"I don't know. I didn't really think he was having an affair. He really cares about me. And a couple times I could hear that he was talking to a man and he's definitely not gay. I think Adrian met him for breakfast on Tuesday or Wednesday."

"Now, why did you lie to us?" Kendra asked.

Katy nervously ran her fingers through her hair. "Adrian told me not to tell anybody that he'd left town. I don't know why. It was important to him. It was the last thing he said to me before he left."

"We're going to need you to call him," Kelland said. "We'll have a better chance of him picking up if he sees it's you."

"That won't be possible." She held up her hand. "I'm trying to cooperate, dammit."

"Then why won't you call him?"

Katy walked over to a coffee table and pulled open a drawer. She picked up an iPhone and showed it to them. "It's Adrian's. He didn't want to take it with him."

"Did he say why?" Kelland said.

"No. He just said he bought a new one."

Kelland extended his hand. "May I?"

Katy handed it to him.

Kelland tapped the screen and flicked his thumb over it.

"Password-protected?" Jessie said.

"No." Kelland furrowed his brow as his thumb flew across the screen. "Not at all. This phone has been wiped clean. There are no apps, contacts, call history, or email accounts. It looks like a total factory reset." He looked up at Katy. "Did you know he'd done that?"

"No. He must have done it before he got back here this morning. He said he'd call me with his new number."

Kelland pulled a plastic evidence bag from his jacket's breast pocket. "Do I have your permission to take this?"

"I thought you said the phone had been erased."

"It has. But there's erased and there's *erased*. It could still be helpful to us. May I take it?"

Katy wrestled with this before finally nodding. "Okay."

Kelland bagged the phone. "Please do not dispose of or otherwise remove anything from the premises. Do you understand me?"

Katy seemed disturbed by this. "That's what they say on all the cop TV shows. Is Adrian in trouble?"

"That's what we're trying to find out. It may be nothing. A big part of our job is to clear potential suspects."

"Look, Adrian adores Delilah. He told me once that she took less on her last contract so that they'd up the money to the musicians and crew. You can't think he had anything to do with what happened to her."

"The sooner we talk to him, the sooner we can clear all this up. Can we count on your help?"

She responded with a weak nod.

Kelland handed her his card. "Call when you hear from him. Try and get him to come back. I guarantee it would be for his own good."

Katy looked shell-shocked, Kendra thought. Her face was red, and she was on the verge of tears. No lost kitten, but she was scared, and Kendra had helped to make her that way. She put a hand on Katy's arm as she passed her. "Do as he says," she said quietly. "You'll be okay. One more thing. Have you left the house at all today?"

Katy shook her head no.

"We'll be in touch." Kendra followed Kelland and Jessie down the short driveway and stood on the sidewalk near their cars.

Kelland turned toward Kendra and spoke in a low voice. "How in the hell did you know that stuff about Adrian coming back here and leaving with the suitcase? That was too much detail for a bluff."

"I don't bluff," Kendra said.

"Too bad," Kelland said. "It can be a useful investigative tool."

"Not my style." She motioned down the street. "There's a lot of ragweed in this neighborhood. That's the cause of the fine dusting of pollen on this sidewalk and the driveway. Look for yourself. You can make out a tire tread that almost has to be an RV or large truck."

Kelland and Jessie turned to look at the driveway.

Kendra walked over, crouched, and pointed to two thin parallel lines. "A two-wheel rollaway suitcase. A man's footsteps, and what I believe to be a woman's. A barefoot woman, probably Katy."

"How did you know it was Adrian who came here, and not somebody else?" Jessie asked.

Kendra stood. "The interview video that Kelland was looking at on his phone. Adrian was wearing a gold chain and an earring. The same gold chain and earring that were in the blue bowl in the foyer. It's possible that he had exact duplicates, but it's more likely that he took them off after he came home and left them there."

"Shit," Kelland said. "I walked right past that bowl."

Jessie shook her head. "We all did." She turned to Kelland. "So do you think your techs can get anything off that phone?"

"Hard to say. Sometimes it's easier to get data off a supposedly wiped phone than off one that's still password-protected. We'll see."

"Again, thanks for including us," Kendra said. "I feel as if we made a little progress."

"Thank *you*." Kelland smiled. "You're living up to the San Diego office's hype. Listen, I'm going to drop off this phone at the office and take care of a few other things, but if you ladies would like to join me later for dinner in Westwood..."

"I'm exhausted," Kendra said. "Jessie probably is, too. I think we're going to head back to Jessie's place and crash."

Kelland looked mildly disappointed. "No prob. But if you're ever in the mood for an FBI-expensed meal, I'm your guy."

"We'll keep that in mind," Kendra said. "Thanks, Kelland. Keep us in the loop, okay?"

"Will do." Kelland climbed into his car and drove away.

Jessie smiled. "Hey, you've made a fan."

"At least he thinks we're of some value to the investigation."

"Oh, it goes a lot further than that. You should have seen the look on his face when you were on that driveway doing your thing with the footsteps, tire prints, and rollaway luggage tracks. A combination of being so moony-eyed and so respectful, I thought I was going to lose my lunch. He's obviously crazy about you."

"*You're* crazy."

"Then there was the after-hours dinner invitation..."

Kendra walked back toward the car. "He invited both of us."

"Because he's a gentleman and couldn't think of any other way to do it. But he was looking at you."

"I'm no longer listening."

They both climbed into the car, and Jessie started it up. "For someone so damn observant, you sure can be obtuse about some things. It took you ages to admit that Metcalf has a thing for you." Jessie frowned. "Oh, poor Metcalf. He's not going to be happy with this development."

"There's no development."

"But I don't feel sorry for Lynch at all. It'll be good for him to have such a gorgeous-looking rival for your affections. This is going to be interesting."

"Stop it."

"Just commenting. I don't get the opportunity very often to give you a hard time about your love life. You're so damn discreet."

"And you're not? Privacy is important. And I don't have a love life. I'm too busy."

"Hmm. What would you call it then? Your relationship with Lynch is definitely combustible." She held up her hand. "Never mind. You're right, I don't want to become involved in the fireworks between you and Lynch." She added wearily, "You're both too complicated, and I have enough complications in my life right now. Maybe I was only looking for a distraction."

"That's probably it," Kendra said gently. "I can see it. I'm feeling the same way. But don't use my relationship with Lynch to do it. Whatever is between us is a very delicate balance, and I don't know where the hell it's going. Probably nowhere." She made a face. "But I should mention that even if I wanted to have fireworks, it would be extremely difficult when half of the equation is saving the world on a snowy mountain in Tibet."

Jessie laughed. "All the more reason to bring in a pinch hitter. Though I've seen Lynch perform harder tasks if he set his mind to it. So have you."

"But I don't want to be another project he has to set his mind to accomplishing. Talk about distraction." She kept her tone light. "Governments could fall. Revolutions erupt around the world. Bombs fly. I don't want the responsibility. So could we drop this discussion about him?"

"Sure." She shrugged. "I've forgotten him already. Now all you've got to do is convince him to forget about you . . ."

"That's no issue at the moment." She was looking back at the door of Katy's place and frowning. "The only thing I'm worrying about right now is that I have a nagging feeling there's something that I missed back there with Adrian's girl-friend." She rubbed her temple. "And I'm just too tired to know what it is."

"It will come back to you. Don't be so hard on yourself."

"But I want to know *now*." She saw Jessie shaking her head and sighed. "Right. Okay, rest and then see what happens . . ."

Jessie nodded. "Now you've got it."

Her phone was ringing...

Kendra drowsily reached out to the bedside table. It seemed as if she'd just gotten to sleep, but the light streaming in the guest room window was twilight-dim. She must have been even more tired than she'd thought...She glanced blearily at the face of the phone. No ID and she was tempted not to answer, but she couldn't risk that it might be Kelland or one of his men with information. "Kendra Michaels."

"You sound delightfully sleepy," Lynch said softly. "I've always loved to hear that froggy hoarseness in your voice when you first wake up. It reminds me of Kermit. But since it's only seven in the evening your time and you're always too alert for naps, I'm suddenly very curious."

She sat up straight in bed. She could almost see Lynch there before her, the piercing blue eyes, those movie-star good looks, that mischievous sense of humor. "I don't sound froggy. And it took you long enough to be curious about anything concerning me, Lynch."

"No more Kermit." He sighed. "I startled you out of it. How pissed off are you with me?"

"Not at all. I have no right to be upset. You don't owe me anything...except courtesy."

"*Very* upset. The mission was top secret, and I did the best I could to make contact when I sent Chodan Ki with your gift. Did you like it?"

"It was completely unique. But it caused problems that you went through Griffin. And I'm sure it cost a fortune, and then I got busy and forgot to put it in a bank vault."

"Really? That's not like you."

"I was busy," she repeated.

"Doing what?"

"It doesn't matter."

Silence. Then a gentle nudge. "Kendra."

She changed the subject. "If it's so top secret, why are you calling now?"

"I've managed to ease the pressure a bit. I'm going into the final phase, and I thought I'd call and see if Chodan Ki was right about everything being as peaceful with you as he made it out to be. He's sharp, but he doesn't know you and might have trouble recognizing the signs of trouble on your horizon. Plus I thought he was a little too eager to give me what he thought I wanted. He wants this mess here cleared up. How are you?"

"Fine. I'm sure that envoy was honest with you. There was no trouble when he showed up to make Griffin's life difficult." She added impatiently, "And if there had been, what could you do? You're thousands of miles away. You couldn't help if you wanted to."

"Not fair. You know I'll always want to be there for you." He paused. "You didn't answer me. Why are you napping at seven in the evening?"

He wasn't going to give up. Lynch was nothing if not persistent, and he knew her too well not to be able to read her. Just this small change of her routine had set off alarm bells. "I was helping Jessie and I didn't get much sleep. I'm staying at her place for the time being." She added quickly to stave off the next question, "Look, I appreciate the concern, but I don't need you. I admit there's a problem, but it's nothing I can't handle. And I have plenty of help. As a matter of fact, I thought it was an FBI agent just now when I answered the phone. So you go on with whatever you're doing in Tibet and let me take care of my own business. It's not as if you have to hold my hand."

"What if I like to hold your hand?"

"The Justice Department might not understand the concept."

"Screw Justice."

"I'm going to hang up now. I'm sorry if I was curt. I had no right to be." She tried to laugh. "It must have been that crack about Kermit. Not what a woman wants to wake up hearing."

"You should. I'm nuts about Kermit."

"Because you're weird. Bye, Lynch. Take care of yourself." She cut the connection.

She drew a deep breath before she swung her feet to the floor and got out of bed. The discussion hadn't gone as well as she'd hoped, but she'd held her own and, if Lynch was as busy as he seemed, he might not be able to follow up and interfere as he usually did. All she needed was to have to play phone tag with a black ops expert who was trying to balance his mission with Dee's life-and-death problems.

"Lynch?" Jessie stuck her head in the door. "I was about to come in and wake you when I heard you on the phone. Is he done with Tibet?"

"Yes, it was Lynch. You must have been sending him vibes by talking about him earlier. And no, he's still in Tibet. But it's winding down. He just had to make certain that he still had control of everything in his world."

"Particularly you," she murmured. "Too bad. I would have liked to have a little Lynch razzle-dazzle on the scene. I'll take all the help I can get at this point."

There had been many moments since this nightmare had started when Kendra had felt the same way. She was sick with worry when she thought about Dee. So don't think about her until they could do something productive to free her. Until then they could only count on themselves.

"Not available. We're on our own. And having Lynch trying to tell us what to do might be unbearable in spite of any advantages."

"You've never had problems with him that you couldn't handle."

"Situations change. So do people." She shrugged. "And Lynch can make ebony black look white as the driven snow." She changed the subject. "Now tell me that you made coffee when you were being so diplomatic about not disturbing us."

"I did. And I was just about to start cooking dinner to go with it."

Kendra shook her head. "The coffee will have to do. Because when I was bracing myself to deal with Lynch, I suddenly realized what was nagging me this morning that I couldn't quite remember." She turned back and headed for the bathroom. "But it turns out it might be time-sensitive. So while I wash my face and throw on clothes, suppose you make a couple of travel cups for us to take on the road."

Son of a bitch!

Lynch leaned back in his chair after he slipped his phone back in his jacket pocket. He should have known better than to trust Chodan. He'd been fighting for years in these mountains to lure his brother back to his village and away from Beijing's influence. Now that he could see how close Lynch was to negotiating a settlement where he'd failed, he wasn't about to let him leave. Chodan might not have lied, but he wouldn't have balked at turning away and presenting a more pleasant view of Kendra's situation if it was more comfortable for him.

Which left Lynch not knowing what the hell was happening with Kendra, but realizing it wasn't good. He'd been lucky that she'd told him even this little she had. It would be useless to probe to get more out of her when he was obviously not one of her favorite people at the moment. Better to go around her and get the full picture. Griffin? Metcalf? She'd mentioned FBI, but she would have referred to them directly if she was receiving help from either of them. What else did he know? The only other clue she'd given him was that she was not in San Diego but in L.A. where Jessie lived.

Why L.A.? Call Jessie?

Think about it, but right now he had to wind up these negotiations here in the mountains before they blew up in his face. The chances were he wouldn't be able to get out of Tibet alive if he didn't finish what he'd started. So go top speed and still do what he had to do here while working to find out what was happening to Kendra in L.A. Strike the balance as he'd done so many times before.

But none of it was going to get done by him sitting here. He got to his feet. Move! He threw open the front door and strode out into the driving snow.

———◆———

Jessie handed Kendra her coffee when she jumped into the passenger seat fifteen minutes later. "One time-sensitive cup of coffee for the road," she said as she backed out of her driveway. "But since you declined my offer of a meal, have you got a better suggestion where we can pick up a sandwich or doughnut to go with it?"

"Maybe." Kendra took a sip of her coffee. "How about the 7-Eleven on National Boulevard?"

"Interesting choice."

"Adrian's girlfriend said he'd bought another phone, one that presumably couldn't be traced."

"A burner phone."

Kendra nodded. "Everything else about his departure was in a last-minute panic. I'd say it's likely he bought his phone between the Bowl and her place. Between four thirty and five thirty in the morning, options are limited."

"Not so limited. This is L.A., remember? There are hundreds of convenience stores and gas stations open at that hour."

"But we know he went to 7-Eleven, probably one very close to his house."

"How do we know that?"

"There was a 7-Eleven coffee cup in the kitchen trash can, translucent enough that I could see it was still about two-thirds full. He probably bought it nearby and brought it inside with him. I didn't see any cell phone packaging in the trash, though."

"Maybe he hadn't opened it yet."

"Possible. Or maybe he opened and activated it before he left the store."

Jessie nodded. "Are you proposing a dumpster dive?"

"If the packaging gives us the phone's serial number, we can track his location with the carrier."

"Oh, it's definitely worth trying. I'm just saying, I hope the parking lot trash can hasn't been dumped yet today."

"I told you it was time-sensitive. I tried to call 7-Eleven to find out, but they kept putting me on hold. If I'd had my wits about me, I would have been able to put this together before I left the house this morning," she added in disgust.

"Maybe we'll get lucky. Did I ever tell you about the time I found a human hand in a dumpster?"

"Seriously?"

"Yeah. Funny thing was, it wasn't even connected to the case I was working. We never got an ID on that thing. I did find the ammo cartridge I was looking for, though. It helped break the case."

"Did I see that on the wall of your living room?"

"Yes. Probably looks better than the hand would've."

"I'm sure it smells better."

"Most likely."

Jessie pulled onto National Boulevard and two minutes later turned into the 7-Eleven parking lot. They parked in front of a brown cylindrical trash receptacle at the far end of the store's front sidewalk. Kendra saw with relief that the huge can was still practically overflowing with trash. "Pickup must be every other day."

"Yep." Jessie reached into her center console and pulled out latex evidence gloves. She threw a pair to Kendra. "You'll want to use these. Watch out for diapers and needles."

Kendra made a face as she pulled on the gloves. "Great. Let's get this over with."

They pulled out the trash can and dumped it on the pavement. Receipt time stamps told them it hadn't been emptied since at least early the previous day. As Jessie warned, there were indeed used diapers and hypodermic needles amid numerous coffee cups, snack wrappers, and discarded lottery tickets. But soon Kendra spotted the distinctive pink-and-white packaging of the prepaid mobile phones carried by the store.

She picked up the torn cardboard packaging and held it up to show Jessie. Affixed to the carton with sticky blue Slurpee juice was a store receipt.

Jessie cocked her head to read the receipt. "Paid in cash. Five sixteen A.M."

"Promising..."

"And he also bought a large coffee."

Kendra smiled. "It has to be him."

Jessie pulled out her phone and snapped a shot of the carton's underside. She inspected the photo on her screen. "Perfect. We have a serial number and the bar code."

"Shall we call Kelland?"

"We *could*. But then we'd have to wait for a warrant, then wait for the carrier to send along tower data."

"Got a better idea?"

"Yeah. I know a guy."

"Naturally."

"It'll be faster." Jessie was already tapping a text into her phone. "He'll give me a full readout first thing in the morning. Maybe even earlier."

"Good."

A shadow fell over the pile of garbage in front of them, and Kendra and Jessie looked up to see a pimply-faced counter clerk dressed in his polo-style 7-Eleven shirt. He was staring at the mess they'd made on the sidewalk.

Kendra gave the kid a sheepish look and shrugged. "Lost earring."

———◆———

"Rimrock!"

Kendra sat bolt upright on the living room sofa, startled awake by Jessie's yell. It was still dark outside, and she felt as though she had just drifted off. She checked her watch. Five fifteen A.M.

Jessie held her phone in front of her. "I heard back from my friend. That burner phone has been connecting to a cell tower out in the desert. It hasn't moved since yesterday afternoon."

Kendra sat up and wiped the sleep from her eyes. "Where?"

"I told you. Rimrock."

"I've never heard of it."

"Me neither, until I just looked it up. It's out in the middle of nowhere, near Joshua Tree. According to Google Maps, the town doesn't even have a traffic light."

Kendra thought for a moment. "If he's still in that RV, he shouldn't be too hard to track down there." She stood up from the couch. "Let's go."

# CHAPTER

# 5

K endra and Jessie slowed as they rolled into downtown Rimrock, which was even smaller and dustier than it had appeared on the satellite image. The town mostly consisted of a mile-long stretch of homes and small ranches, with street names that included Tumbleweed Trail and Apache Pass.

"There isn't much place to hide an RV around here," Jessie said. "Maybe in one of those barns or behind a house."

They reached the end of the town in less than two minutes. "Maybe he's already left," Kendra said.

"My friend said he'd call if his phone started connecting to a different tower."

"There's another possibility." Kendra looked around. "It wasn't Adrian who bought that phone after all."

"I'm not prepared to admit that possibility."

"Me neither. But if we don't find him here, then..." Kendra's gaze locked on something ahead. "Wait a minute. Drive forward a little bit."

"What do you see?"

"Just go."

Jessie drove until they were alongside a shallow ridge that rose a few feet over the roadway. Large tire tracks curved from the shoulder and over the ridge.

"I'd say someone may have gone off-roading," Kendra said. "But those don't look like jeep treads to me."

"Gotcha." Jessie pulled over and killed the engine. "Let's take a look."

They climbed out of Jessie's SUV and walked up the short embankment. Jessie reached the top first and froze. "Shit."

Kendra was half a second behind her. There, in an empty field just fifty feet in front of them, was a Vita Class C Winnebago.

"That's it," Kendra whispered.

Jessie nodded.

They quietly walked toward the RV. Wind whistled across the deserted landscape as they drew closer.

Jessie pointed to the rear of the vehicle, and Kendra followed her as she walked around to the other side.

"Aughhhhhh!" a man yelled and jumped from behind the RV. He swung a tire iron toward Jessie's head, but she grabbed it and punched the man in the throat and torso. He dropped to his knees and gasped for air.

Kendra crouched beside him. "Hello, Adrian."

Adrian's face was bright red. He had shoulder-length hair

and a full beard. He wore cargo shorts and a faded Tom Petty tour T-shirt.

Jessie held up the tire iron. "Is this any way to greet your guests?"

The man finally caught his breath and looked at Jessie. "It is when you're scared shitless. But I know you . . . You're Jessie Mercado. You used to run security for Delilah Winter."

"Once upon a time."

"You're working for her again?"

"No. Just helping out an old friend. I'm hoping you can help her, too."

Adrian stared at her for an instant before getting to his feet. "We can talk inside." He walked around toward the RV's side door, opened it, and climbed inside. Jessie and Kendra followed.

The Winnebago had obviously not seen an interior update since it was purchased twenty-five or more years before. The well-dinged oak cabinets and countertops were complemented by the linoleum floor and burnt orange cooktop.

Adrian cracked open the curtains and stole a quick glance outside. "I wish it hadn't been so easy for you to find me."

"It wasn't exactly easy." Jessie hefted the tire iron she'd taken from him. "Who'd you think you were going to use this on?"

"I don't know."

"Stop lying, Adrian," Kendra said.

"I'm serious. I have no idea who could come walking through that door at any minute."

"Second question. Where's Delilah?" Jessie's grip tightened on the tire iron. "That's all we need to know right now."

Adrian shook his head. "I don't know."

"Wrong answer." In one motion, Jessie leaped behind him and snapped the tire iron over his throat. She pulled it back, cutting off his airway. "Do better."

He rasped something unrecognizable.

"Where is she?" Jessie pulled harder on the iron.

"Don't...know."

"Who does?"

"Don't know...his name."

"Bullshit." Jessie's knuckles went white as she squeezed even tighter.

Adrian's eyes rolled back into his head.

Kendra put her hand on Jessie's arm. "You're going to kill him."

"It's a distinct possibility." She practically hissed into his left ear, "You're going to tell us everything you know about what happened to Dee. Because that knowledge is your only worth on this planet."

His face was purple. "Please...I'll tell you...what I know."

Kendra gripped Jessie's forearm. She could see that her emotions were getting the better of her. "Give him a chance. Let him talk."

Jessie finally pulled the iron away.

He staggered away and rubbed his throat. "I guess I deserved that."

"Glad you agree," Jessie said. "You most certainly did. Now start talking."

He took a moment to catch his breath, then leaned back against the tiny kitchenette counter. "I got into debt with some bad guys. *Really* bad guys."

"Gambling?" Jessie said.

"I wish. Narcotics. Just oxy at first, but then some harder stuff. It wiped me out. I needed money bad."

Jessie glared at him. "That's your excuse for kidnapping Dee?"

"I didn't kidnap her. But I...may have helped the people who did."

"*May* have?" Kendra repeated.

He looked down. "Look, I like Delilah. She was great to all the crew. No one was supposed to get hurt."

Jessie bit her lip in anger. "If you only knew how many times I've heard some dumbass tell me that. Who said that to you?"

"He said his name was Arthur Cabot." He made a face. "I guess that was a phony name. I met him at a diner in Denver a couple weeks ago. It wasn't an accidental meeting. He said he'd been watching me. I think he and his partners had been watching a lot of us, maybe looking for the perfect..."

"Dumbass?" Jessie snapped.

"I was gonna say 'sucker,' but yeah, 'dumbass' works, too." Adrian shook his head. "He knew how desperate I was, and he zeroed right in. He said he had a way for me to make half a million dollars. All I had to do is give him some information and loan him my access badge for a few hours. I guess he cloned it."

"What information did he want?" Kendra asked.

"Just our travel and sound-check schedule. I talked to him maybe five or six times between then and the night Delilah was taken."

Jessie's face flushed with rage again. "You knew they were going to kidnap her, and you *helped* them?"

He looked ill. "He seemed like a nice enough guy. And they said they wouldn't hurt her. They told me they wouldn't hurt anybody."

"Tell that to those two dead security guys."

"I know." He let out a long breath. "That's when the shit got real."

"It got real the second you put Dee's life in danger," Kendra said. "And those men might still be alive if it hadn't been for you."

"Don't you think I know that?" He pounded his fist on the counter with sudden violence. "He said she'd be home for dinner safe and sound, less than an hour after the ransom was paid."

"No one's even asked for a ransom yet," Jessie said. "We haven't heard a thing."

"Shit," he whispered. "It's not the way this was supposed to go down. None of it."

"Why'd you leave town?" Kendra asked. "The police had no reason to suspect you until you left."

"It wasn't the police I was worried about." Adrian's face tensed. "When I saw that these people were willing to kill two security officers, I figured what in the hell would stop them from killing me? Then Arthur called and asked me to meet him in Griffith Park at five A.M. the day after the abduction. He said he wanted to give me a cash advance for my good work."

"Out of the kindness of his heart," Jessie said caustically.

"It didn't sound right to me, either. So I went home, threw some things together, and got the hell out of town."

"We found you quickly enough," Kendra said. "If Dee's kidnappers want you dead, they'll find you, too. You can identify one of them. If the FBI can link him to known associates, their whole scheme falls apart. That's pretty good incentive to silence you."

"That's why I'm living in this thing." Adrian gestured around the RV's shabby interior. "So I can keep moving."

"You're not going anywhere except back to L.A.," Jessie said flatly. "You're going to tell your story to the FBI."

Kendra nodded. "We'll sit you down with a sketch artist and get a good drawing of this Arthur. We'll spread it everywhere and see if anyone recognizes him. If you're really sorry about what happened to Dee and those security men, it's your only option."

"I can't go to jail. I'd go nuts in there."

Jessie crossed her arms and leaned against the small stovetop. "Maybe you won't have to."

"Don't bullshit me."

"I'm not gonna lie, this is bad for you. If you don't play this just right, you could go down for two murder accessory counts and one for kidnapping. You could be serving hard time for a long while."

He looked down. "Shit."

"But you have another path. You come with us to the Federal

Building in Westwood and talk to the FBI. You tell them everything, and you help them every way you know how."

"I've already told you everything. What else can I do?"

Kendra thought for a moment. "Maybe you can convince this Arthur and his crew that you're still in and want the money you've been promised. You'll arrange to meet him."

He shook his head. "I could get killed."

"The FBI will have your back," Kendra said. "If he or anyone else makes a move against you, they'll be on it. In the meantime, we'll keep you safe."

"What could they do about a sniper's bullet?"

"The FBI is smart. They'll be watching out for that. We wouldn't let you meet them anywhere that would be unsafe for you."

"I don't believe you."

"You can trust us."

"I can't trust anyone."

"We're your only chance. Even when we do get Dee back, we'll need you to testify against those scumbags," Jessie said. "You can get your life back if you just do what's right."

He slowly shook his head. "It's too risky. Pay the ransom. Maybe she'll be okay . . . like they told me."

Jessie stepped toward him with a bearing that even Kendra found surprisingly intimidating, especially given her small size. "Just so you know, this isn't a negotiation. You're coming with us."

He tensed with alarm. "You're not cops. You can't make me do shit."

In one lightning-fast motion, Jessie grabbed his left wrist, wrenched it behind his back, and slammed his face onto the cooktop. He howled in pain.

Jessie leaned over and spoke into his ear. "Ever hear of citizen's arrest? That's a real thing, asshole. If you'd like to ride back to L.A. with plastic zip ties cutting into your wrists and ankles, we can make that happen."

A high-pitched whine escaped his lips. "I think you broke my arm."

"Trust me, you'd know if I'd done that. Wanna see what it feels like?" She pulled on his wrist, and he screamed. "Kinda like that, but about fifty times worse."

His eyes were wild. "You're psycho!"

"I've been called worse, buddy." Jessie grabbed his other hand, pulled it back, and slapped a zip tie around his wrists. She pulled it tight. "Did I mention how much I like that sweet kid you sold to those scumbags?"

"Owww." He wiggled his fingers. "You're cutting off my circulation."

"Your hands will be a nice shade of purple by the time we get to L.A. I wouldn't worry unless they turn black."

"Can't we . . . discuss this?"

She shoved him toward the open side door. "Sure. We can talk all the way back to the FBI L.A. regional office."

Kendra followed as Jessie steered him to her SUV and practically threw him into the backseat. Adrian gazed pleadingly up at Kendra. "Jessie doesn't believe that I'm really sorry about Delilah. It's true. But I've been so scared and desperate ever since this began." His eyes were frantic in his pale face. "I'm not a bad guy, and I can see how wrong I was to let them take her. Maybe I can make it up to her somehow. You guys were right, I have to try to change it. I'll do whatever you want to save her. Just don't let anyone hurt me."

She could see he was terrified. Not only from his dealings with those kidnappers, but Jessie must have thoroughly intimidated him. And what was more encouraging was that he also seemed sincere about wanting to save Dee. What he'd said about her had held the ring of truth. "All you have to do is cooperate and you'll get through this okay. But you have to help us or we can't do anything. Do you understand?"

"I told you, anything you want. Anything I can do to save her." His voice was shaking. "If I do that, will you promise I'll come out of this alive?"

"I promise. All we want is to save Delilah. Just give us a chance to do that, Adrian." She slammed the door. "And it would help if you'd avoid irritating Jessie on the way back to L.A."

She glanced at Jessie as she climbed into the passenger seat. "We can get him to help us to find Dee," she said quietly. "I believe him."

"I can see you do." Jessie shrugged. "I hope you're right. Better let Kelland know we're on our way."

But Kendra was already on the phone to Kelland. "We got Adrian."

He sounded surprised. "By 'got' you mean..."

"Hands zip-tied behind his back, stuffed into the backseat of Jessie's SUV."

"You're not joking."

Jessie started the SUV and peeled out.

"Definitely not joking." Kendra turned around and held up the phone. "Adrian, say something to the nice FBI man."

"I want a lawyer and protection the minute we pull up in front of your office."

She pulled the phone back to her ear. "That's Adrian."

"Can't wait to meet him. What's his story?"

Kendra filled Kelland in on the information they'd gathered from Adrian, emphasizing his meetings with the mysterious Arthur Cabot.

After she finished, Kelland paused for a moment. "Good work. But did it even occur to you to loop me in when you got your lead on him?"

"Actually, no. If you really wanted to tag along with us for every lead that may or may not pan out, you wouldn't have time for anything else. I think you have better things to do with your time."

"Maybe so. Especially if you believe my contribution would be limited to 'tagging along.'"

"No offense. We all have our strengths, Kelland."

"Nice. I'll make sure the team is here when you arrive with Adrian."

"Good. We'll be there inside of two hours." Kendra cut the connection and turned to Jessie. "He's only slightly annoyed."

Jessie didn't respond. Her eyes were focused on the rearview mirror.

"What is it?"

"Not sure. Maybe nothing."

Kendra leaned forward to look in the side mirror. The highway behind them was deserted except for two men on motorcycles. As she watched, the men exchanged hand signals.

"See that?" Jessie said.

"Yes."

"Any idea what they're saying to each other?"

"No."

"Me neither. But they've been making those signs to each other for the past half mile."

Kendra watched them for a moment longer. "It's not sign language for the deaf."

"And they're not motorcycle group riding signals, at least none that I've ever seen."

Kendra looked at the men for a moment longer. They wore black leather jackets and matching black helmets that looked as menacing and stylish as their identical Ducati motorcycles. The riders were now facing forward.

Kendra called back to Adrian. "Get down. Now."

Adrian spun around to look out the back windshield.

Kendra grabbed him by his back collar and yanked him down so that his face slammed onto the car seat. "What did I just say?"

Adrian made a choking sound. "Okay, okay. I just wanted to see."

"Friends of yours?"

"No."

"Maybe your buddy Arthur?" Jessie said.

"Hard to say. These guys look bigger than he was."

"They're both loaded down with padding and tactical vests," Kendra said.

The two riders split and raced toward Jessie's SUV, advancing on it from either side.

Jessie gripped the wheel harder. "Shit. Both of you get down."

Kendra slid lower in her seat. "What about you?"

"Someone needs to drive this thing." She checked her side-view mirror. "I think this one is wearing a holster underneath his jacket."

Kendra tilted her side-view mirror down so she could see the motorcyclist on her side. "This one, too. Major artillery, by the looks of it."

The rider next to Jessie sharply pointed to the side of the road, indicating for her to pull over.

Jessie put on an extra burst of speed, leaving the riders slightly behind. She reached under her jacket, pulled out a small handgun, and placed it barrel-down in a cup holder.

Kendra stared at it. "What are you doing with that?"

"Depends on what *they* do."

Kendra moistened her lips. "Got one for me?"

Jessie gave her a sideways glance. "I didn't think you liked guns all that much."

"I don't. But desperate times..."

"I'm good with guns. My uncle in Texas taught me," Adrian piped up from the back. "I'll take one."

"Forget it," Jessie said. "No more guns, at least none that are handy. Both of you just stay down." She turned to Kendra. "If I ask you to take the wheel, grab it."

"From over here?"

"Keep us in a straight line, no matter what happens. We're not slowing down for anything."

"Not even that?" Adrian said, pointing out Jessie's window. The rider had a submachine gun aimed at her head.

Jessie spun the wheel hard left, and the rider swerved into the opposing lane. She stepped hard on the accelerator.

"They both have guns out now." Kendra looked into her side-view. "Looks like Uzis."

Jessie nodded. "Mini Uzi carbines with forty-round mags. Matching."

"Gotta like murderous thugs who know how to coordinate accessories," Kendra murmured.

RAT-AT-AT-AT-AT-AT-AT-AT-AT-AT-AT! A barrage of gunfire pounded the back windshield, which in seconds became a translucent white.

But the glass was still intact.

"What the hell?" Adrian glared in astonishment up at the window.

"Bulletproof glass all around," Jessie said.

RAT-AT-AT-AT-AT-AT-AT-AT-AT! Another hail of bullets hit the back windshield.

"Bulletproof?" Kendra looked at the window. "Just another day at the office for you?"

"Not quite. I sometimes use this vehicle when I'm working as bodyguard, and it makes the client feel safer. But each pane is only rated for five shots. That back one's already taken a couple dozen."

RAT-AT-AT-AT-AT-AT-AT-AT-AT-AT! The rear passenger

side window exploded in another gunfire bombardment. Adrian cut loose with a distinctively girlish scream.

The rider, with gun still extended before him, pulled closer to Kendra's window.

Kendra slid up slightly and unlocked her door. She gripped the handle and nodded to Jessie.

Jessie nodded back.

The motorcycle's roar filled her ears, and its shadow slowly moved across her dash...

"Now!"

Kendra pulled the handle back, swiveled in her seat, and kicked the door open.

It struck the motorcycle, catapulting the rider over his handlebars. He hit the pavement in a heap. His gun went flying, and the motorcycle spun crazily on its side on the pavement, its motor still roaring.

"One down," Jessie said. "Now if we can just—"

RAT-AT-AT-AT-AT-AT-AT-AT-AT!

The back windshield finally gave way, falling apart in several large chunks.

The remaining rider raced behind them, his Uzi now fortified by an even larger ammo clip.

"Sixty fresh rounds," Jessie said, looking at the rearview mirror. "He's coming to play."

Jessie grabbed her handgun from the cup holder.

Kendra looked at it and shook her head. "What good is that going to be against a machine gun?"

"It's not going against a machine gun. It's going against one flesh-and-blood man. Big difference."

RAT-AT-AT-AT-AT-AT-AT-AT-AT!

The SUV shook and a low grating sound roared in their ears.

"He's going for the tires," Jessie said. "They're run-flats, but they aren't bulletproof."

Kendra listened as the vehicle shook even more violently and loose tread flapped on the roadway. "The left rear tire is shredded."

RAT-AT-AT-AT AT-AT-AT-AT-AT-AT-AT!

"There goes the right." Kendra looked at the desolate highway ahead. "Nobody for miles. We're on our own out here."

"I know. We have to do something fast."

"Got any ideas?"

"One. Hang on. And stay down."

Jessie cut the wheel hard right, and the back rims fishtailed across the pavement in a shower of sparks. She stepped on the accelerator. They were now facing the rider, charging toward each other as if in a medieval joust.

RAT-AT-AT-AT-AT-AT-AT-AT-AT-AT!

Bullets sprayed across the front windshield and grille. Before Kendra could recover, she was jolted by a different sound.

BLAM-BLAM-BLAM-BLAM!

Jessie's left arm was protruding from the window, and she was returning fire on the motorcyclist. As two of her shots appeared to make contact, his body jerked and twisted, but he managed to stay on the bike. He cut across the car's right side and fired again, this time toward the shattered rear passenger side window.

RAT-AT-AT-AT-AT-AT-AT-AT!

Jessie spun off the road, kicked open her door, and jumped

out. She took a position behind the bullet-riddled hood and took aim.

But the rider wasn't coming back.

The motorcycle sped off into the distance, back in the direction from which it had come.

Kendra straightened in her seat and turned see the rider, about half a mile down the road, stop to allow his limping partner to climb on behind him. The motorcycle sped away with the two men.

Kendra looked down to the backseat. "You're safe now, Adrian."

No answer.

Oh, God.

Adrian.

Jessie stood up and walked toward her. "What is it?"

Kendra jumped out of the car and threw open the rear door. "Help me."

Adrian was a bloody mess. Kendra could see he'd been shot at least twice, once in the head and once in the chest. He wasn't breathing.

Kendra tore open his shirt and started chest compressions.

Jessie grabbed her arm. "Kendra..."

"Do you have towels or any kind of clothing in the trunk? We need to get pressure on these wounds."

"It's too late."

Kendra pushed his chest with the heels of her hands. "One-one-thousand, two-one-thousand..."

"Kendra..."

Tears stung her eyes. "We have to try. He was so scared. He

said he'd do whatever I wanted him to do. I promised I'd take care of him. Help me!"

Jessie reached down to stop her. "Stop it. The back of his head is gone." Jessie looked down the highway, where the motorcycle had disappeared into the rippling waves of heat. "Adrian is who they wanted. They didn't care about the two of us at all."

Kendra finally backed away from Adrian's body. Her hands and sleeves were covered with blood. "He was right to run," she said numbly. "If we hadn't found him, he'd still be alive."

"You don't know that. They could have found him on their own."

"He was scared out of his mind. He was making mistake after mistake. He was just waiting for someone to save him. Then we found him and told him what he wanted to hear."

Jessie grabbed Kendra's lapels and leaned close. "He was a scumbag. He helped them take Dee, remember? He made the choice to get mixed up with those people. What did he think was going to happen?"

"I don't know. He said he didn't think they'd hurt her. Maybe it was the truth." Kendra looked down at Adrian's bullet-ridden body. "Whatever he thought was going to happen, it wasn't this," she said hoarsely. "He didn't bargain for this."

———◆———

"You're lucky to be alive."

Kendra nodded and turned to face Kelland. It had been over two hours since Adrian's death and the scene was now swarming with police cars, uniformed officers, and a van from the San Bernardino County Medical Examiner's Office. Kelland had just arrived with a few agents from the FBI L.A. regional office.

"Adrian wasn't so lucky." Kendra gestured toward Jessie's bullet-ridden SUV. "He's still in there."

"I know. But at least you and Jessie are safe."

"We're no closer to finding Dee than we were before."

"I wouldn't say that. He told you where and when he was approached by this Arthur character. We already have our Denver office tracking down every bit of security camera video around his hotel there, including the coffee shops. We'll turn something up." He nodded at the wrecked motor-cycle down the road, which was now surrounded by bright orange pylons. Jessie was standing over the bike, taking photos with her cell phone. "Were you able to get anything from that?"

Kendra shook her head. "The VIN has been removed, and there's no plate. The make and model are rare enough around here that we may still be able to track ownership, particularly since it may have been purchased at the same time as an identical model with the exact same option package. The bike is clean, too clean to have been ridden very far. So it was brought here in a covered vehicle, probably a truck. The other bike is probably back in it now. You might check freeway cams for a truck like that."

"I thought of that. I'll get right on it."

"Of course you will. You know what you're doing." Her lips twisted bitterly. "I was so cocky before, wasn't I? I was just happy that we'd caught Adrian and had a chance to find Dee. You should have slapped me down instead of being that polite."

"No, I shouldn't. I like the idea that you were that excited. Every now and then something happens that makes this job worthwhile. You were having one of those moments. You did a good job, and it could have gone either way."

"That's very generous of you." She was no longer listening. Her gaze had returned to the SUV, where they were preparing to extract Adrian's body. She was visualizing that last sight of his broken, torn body after she'd tried to save him.

But she hadn't been able to save him. She'd failed him. And in failing him, she'd also failed Dee.

And she didn't want to see that bloody failure again no matter what Kelland said about her doing such a "good" job. She turned on her heel. "Look, I'll give you a full statement later. Could we borrow one of your vehicles? I've got to get out of here."

He looked startled. "Where are you going?"

"I'm not really sure." She was walking toward Jessie. "Just away from here."

◆

"You're too quiet." Jessie glanced at Kendra's face when they were almost back to her house. "You haven't spoken more than two sentences since we got on the road. No one is blaming us. We did the best we could."

"That's what Kelland said. It wasn't good enough."

"And there was no way you could have kept that promise to Adrian. So stop blaming yourself. If you want to blame anyone, I'm here and I'm the one who was forcing Adrian into going to the FBI."

"Which is what you should have done," she said wearily. "And I realize that everything you said about what Adrian did was true. I was angry with him, too. But for that little while, I thought we could turn it around. I thought that maybe all this horror surrounding Dee could be erased. That if I gave him my word, Adrian would miraculously remember how much he cared about Dee and do whatever he could to save her. I wanted that so much, Jessie."

"I know you did," Jessie said gently. "But miracles are few and far between."

"And those people who took Dee are damn smart. Look how they found Adrian and twisted his life to suit their purpose. Nothing we could do to stop that from happening. They seem to know what they're doing every minute and plug up every hole we find."

"We'll find others. Tomorrow we'll go down to the FBI office and make our statements, and Kelland might already have a breakthrough."

Kendra nodded. "Lord, I hope he does. But those bastards sure aren't in any hurry. They have to see we're pulling out all the stops to find them. Why wouldn't they want to negotiate quickly so that they could get away with the loot?"

"Maybe they will after what happened today. We didn't make it easy for them." They'd reached her house, and she pulled into the driveway and turned off the FBI van. She added grimly, "Until then all we can do is to keep on searching and hope for a break that will stir them to *move* their asses."

---

NEXT DAY
9:45 A.M.

Kendra's phone rang just as she and Jessie were leaving the house to go to the FBI field office.

"Have you left yet or are you near a TV?" Kelland asked when she picked up.

"We were walking out the door." She tensed. "Why? Something to do with Dee? Is it bad?"

"It depends on how you look at it. As far as I'm concerned, it might be a nightmare. Hell, but I'm probably scaring you. It's about Dee, but it's not about her being hurt or killed. Just turn on the TV and see what's all over the news. I'll talk to you later about what it might mean to the case." He cut the connection.

"TV news," she said over her shoulder to Jessie as she ran over to the set and grabbed the remote. "Something about Dee."

"Of course I'm sincere," a good-looking young man who looked to be somewhere in his twenties was saying to the group of reporters and TV journalists surrounding him. Kendra saw the name NOAH CALDERON—SILICON VALLEY below the shot. "Why would I have called you all here to my headquarters if I didn't want to spread the word so that I could bring my good friend Delilah safely back home?"

He was staring directly into the cameras. "I've been in touch with law enforcement, and I'm worried that they don't seem to have any clues. I thought it might be better to go to the people who love her most to see what they can do to help her. That's why I'm offering five million dollars to anyone who can secure the safe return of Delilah Winter. I'm also offering the services of my own company for the search."

His expression was sober, but his voice was intent and very persuasive as he said softly, "Come on, all of you out there, I'm offering you a lot of money. But what I'm really offering you is the opportunity to save Delilah whose music has meant so much to all of us over the years. Who could resist that? My phone lines will be staffed twenty-four hours a day. Now let me hear from you."

Kendra was aware that Jessie was muttering a curse as the rest of the interview was drowned by the journalists' onslaught of questions. She pressed the MUTE button. "You're not pleased. Neither was Kelland. Why not?" She frowned. "Noah Calderon...I've heard of him."

"Of course you have. Everyone's heard of Calderon." Jessie made a face. "Or maybe not you. You may be the only one on the planet who isn't involved with social networking."

"I don't have the time." She looked back at the face of the man on the screen. "But I've heard he's some kind of billionaire, isn't he?"

"He made his first billion at the age of twenty-one creating Hookup, which is still the most popular dating site in the world. He followed up with Friendz, the social network now used by a fifth of the world's population including almost everyone you've ever known."

"He seems very appealing. Why did he make you so angry?"

"Because he could be getting set to cause us a big headache. Look, Calderon *can* be appealing, and that little speech he gave, coupled with the millions he's tossing out, will make everyone want to run out and save Dee."

"And that's what they should be wanting to do. Even if they don't find her, this might be the way we get those kidnappers' attention."

"Possibly. But when you turn hundreds or thousands of detectives and wannabe investigators from all over the world loose on a single case with that much money and notoriety involved, they'll get in the way. From accidentally destroying evidence to interfering with a ransom delivery, it will increase the threat. I don't like it."

"I didn't think about that." But Kendra could see the difficulties now. "Could you explain to Calderon and get him to cancel the reward?"

"Not a chance. He's probably liking the idea of being a hero who saves the day. He's made his decision and he won't back down. Noah Calderon believes he's smarter and knows better than almost anyone who walks the earth. Why else would he be a billionaire with the whole world fawning over him?"

"But he's a friend of Dee's?"

"They were an item a few years ago. They were both superstars in their own fields, but evidently there wasn't much else there to hold them together. They came from completely different backgrounds, and that probably initially attracted them to each other." She shrugged. "Dee spent most of her childhood in a mobile home or on a TV soundstage. Noah was a trust-fund baby whose parents traveled the world and left him in the hands of servants most of the time. He went to school in England for a few years and then quit when his website took off. The only thing they had in common was the fact that they barely knew their parents and were both aware that's the way their parents wanted it."

"That could be a strong bond."

Jessie nodded. "Evidently not strong enough. But Dee told me when they broke up it was amicable, and he was dating some Parisian supermodel two weeks later. He even still sends flowers to Dee's concerts."

"Including this one. Five million will pay for a very fancy bouquet."

She made a face. "Maybe he liked her even better than I thought. It's hard not to like Dee, and they both lived in a world I'd never want to inhabit. It could be I don't understand the rituals."

Kendra nodded. "You know them far better than I do." She turned off the TV and turned toward the door. "I'll call Kelland back while I'm on the road. Though I'm certain he's going to tell me exactly what you did." She shrugged. "Too bad. I thought for a moment it might be good news."

"It could be. Maybe someone out there knows something and is just waiting for Noah to offer them five million. Or maybe one of the bad guys will be tempted to turn traitor and turn Dee over to us for that same five million."

"But you don't think so."

"I wish I did." She locked the front door behind them. "I really want Noah to just throw some money down and suddenly Dee will be safe and free. I really wish I did, Kendra."

"I'd settle just for knowing where she is right now," Kendra whispered. "Give me that one thing, and I'll be willing to work to find out everything else."

# CHAPTER

# 6

S he couldn't *swallow*, Dee realized, panic-stricken!
She struggled desperately but only felt as if she was
choking. She was panting, and that only made it worse.

"Open your mouth, you stupid girl. I'm trying to help
you." It was a woman's impatient voice as a straw was pressed
to Dee's lips. "Do you think I like babying you as if you aren't
the spoiled brat we both know you are? But I won't get the
blame. It wasn't supposed to be like this. Now suck on the
damn straw and drink the water."

Straw...

Liquid...

Dee was already frantically sucking down the ice water, and
it was gradually easing her dry throat. But after only a few
minutes the straw was taken away. "Enough," the woman said
sourly. "You don't need any more. I won't have you throwing
up and making me clean you. That drug they gave you caused

dehydration, but the saline solution was supposed to take care of that. I might have given you a little too much. I'll probably get blamed for that, too."

Drug...

What drug? Who was this woman?

"Okay, my orders are to make sure that no permanent damage was done to you yet. Open your eyes and say something, Delilah." She laughed harshly. "Whatever possessed you to choose a stage name like that? You sound like a porn star or a stripper."

"I never liked...it, either." Her throat was still a little sore and the words came out huskily. "But my mother did...when she named me. It's not a stage name..."

"Then she must have been as stupid as you are. She probably had an idea what you'd become."

Ugly. So much bitterness. Why?

"Now open your eyes and look at me. I'm going to have to give a report, and you'll be unconscious again in another few minutes."

Unconscious. Drug. All this ugliness...She was fighting to understand through this haze and confusion. What was happening to her?

And then it was all whirling back to her! Backstage. The crowd roaring. But something wasn't quite right. Two security men crumpled on the floor...

Her eyes flew open and she was staring up into the woman's face. It was a long, thin face, and the dark eyes that were looking down at her were large and fierce beneath pale white arched brows. She was vaguely aware the woman must be at least in her sixties with sleekly coifed salt-and-pepper hair. "You took me prisoner," she whispered. "Kidnapping? You kidnapped me?"

"Yes, but I really had nothing to do with it. I wouldn't have you if you were delivered gift-wrapped. I'm just the caretaker until we get what we need from you."

Dee didn't speak for a moment as she tried frantically to gather her wits about her. Jessie had always told her that if she was ever in a bad spot, she should assess her surroundings, then do anything she could to escape them—but always to wait for the right time. Assess her surroundings. She looked down at what she was wearing and found that someone had changed her out of the scarlet sequined mini-dress she'd been wearing for the finale to jeans and a loose white tunic. She glanced around her and tried to get a clue to where she might be. But it was too dim, and she could only make out a stand next to her with a plastic IV bag, along with the impression that the room was long, the walls curved. As far as escape was concerned, she seemed to be bound with metal restraints, and she couldn't move. Besides, there was only this one very rude woman here with her, and she had little hope that she'd be of any help. Still, Dee tried to talk to her. "Look, I'm not going to cause you any trouble. My security team always told me in a situation like this I was to cooperate and just let them handle the ransom. You don't have to drug me again."

"You don't tell me what to do with you." Her lips curled. "I have my orders. Do you think because you're this big super-star, you can control everything and everyone around you?"

She was spitting out the words now as she reached over and turned on the IV. "You're nothing. You'll learn that soon."

Dee wanted to strike back in any way she could, but she could already feel the drug taking hold and making her drowsy again. Now wasn't the time to antagonize, not when she was soon going to be helpless. Just try to find out as much as possible before she slipped into unconsciousness. She could act on it later when she was able to fight off that damn narcotic. "Who…are you? You said you…don't like my name. Is yours any better?"

"Oh, yes. It's a fine, sensible name and I'm not afraid of your idiotic tricks to make me reveal who I am. It won't make the slightest difference in the long run." She bent closer. "You can call me Charlotte. It's Charlotte who is doing this to you. It's Charlotte who is in control of whether you live or die."

Dee felt a chill go through her. Nothing she was saying was reaching the woman. She was brimming with venom and actually seemed to hate her. She might not be in charge, but there was no doubt she was a dangerous enemy. "For some reason you appear to be angry with me. I just wanted to assure you and your partners that whatever you want, I can give it to you."

"Oh, can you?" She leaned forward and murmured, "But that's not the way it's going to work, Delilah. It's not what you give, but what we take. You're done with setting the rules." She leaned even closer, her smile pure malevolence. "And though I hate to make you feel helpless, my dear, money is only a small part of the equation."

———◆———

JESSIE'S HOUSE
NEXT DAY
4:05 A.M.

"Come on, get up." Jessie burst into the guest room and turned on the lights. "We have to get out of here and on the road, Kendra. We might have gotten the break you were talking about. I just got a call from an officer I know from LAPD who's repaying a favor. He's letting me know about it before all hell breaks loose and the media gets hold of it."

"What break?" Kendra jumped out of bed and started throwing on clothes. "At four in the morning?"

"You take breaks when and where you can find them," Jessie said. "And once Kelland gets hold of this info, he'll be very careful about releasing it to anyone but top FBI officials. That's protocol in kidnap cases. Everything is always top secret if connected to the money. But if we're already on-site when he gets there, he won't have any choice but to include us in the negotiations." She grimaced. "Maybe. I hope."

"Gets where?" She grabbed her handbag and ran after Jessie. "Where the hell are we going, Jessie?"

"The ransom note. It's been delivered, the LAPD has it, and we have to be there before it's turned over to Kelland."

"At the FBI regional office? The LAPD?"

"The cemetery," she said over her shoulder. "We're going to the cemetery..."

———◆———

HOLLYWOOD FOREVER CEMETERY

It took them only forty minutes, but it was still almost too late by the time they arrived at the cemetery.

Kendra and Jessie walked through the tall iron gates facing Santa Monica Boulevard, where police had already set up a mini-barricade. Journalists had taken positions on the sidewalk outside, and two news copters circled overhead. They passed a series of elaborate headstones that, in the Russian tradition, featured detailed etchings of the departed.

Jessie pointed ahead. "We're headed down there and to the left."

Kendra was still bewildered. "You seem to know your way around."

"I bring a lot of my out-of-town guests here."

"Yeah, right."

"I'm serious. This place is a big tourist attraction. A lot of the old-time Hollywood stars are buried here. Valentino, Cecil B. DeMille, Douglas Fairbanks, and lots more." She pointed to the right. "And there's an amazing statue of Johnny Ramone on his grave over there."

Kendra glanced around. "Still . . . Strange place for a ransom note."

"I won't argue with that."

They approached the south end of the cemetery, where a small group of uniformed officers were clustered.

"I guess it's over there," Kendra said. "But I don't see how—"

She froze.

"Oh, my God," Jessie whispered.

Dee's face, twenty feet high, was projected on the flat white surface of a tall mausoleum. A brief message was superimposed over the image:

Delilah Winter is our guest in a place you will never find her, not even if you look AMONG THE STARS.

She will be released INTO THE WIND only when we receive twenty million dollars, in unmarked, non-sequential bills that can fit in a box 1 x 2 x 2 feet. COUNTDOWN for instructions 8:30 A.M. in Pershing Square day after tomorrow. Don't be SO WRONG, SO SAD. One mistake and she will be gone in the BLINK OF AN EYE.

Kendra immediately recognized the capitalized words as titles of Dee's most popular songs. She turned toward Jessie. "This could be a hoax."

"It's no hoax," a police detective called out. He was standing near a cluster of cops in the middle of a sprawling lawn with no graves.

"What makes you so sure, Weller?" Jessie replied as they walked toward the group. Kendra noticed she was speaking with an ease that suggested some measure of history between them.

There was an intent frown on Weller's full, ruddy face. He pointed down, where a small white projector sat atop a cardboard box. "The message is coming from here, Jessie.

Battery-powered. One of our techs says it can run for at least six hours without a recharge."

"So?" Jessie knelt beside the projector. "Any idiot can walk into Best Buy and get one of these."

Weller held up a clear plastic evidence bag. "Could the idiot get one of these, too?"

Jessie's face fell. "Oh, shit."

"Recognize this?"

Jessie took the bag and held it up so Kendra could also see. Inside was a platinum bracelet with the words FACE FORWARD engraved on a tiny ID bar.

"This is Dee's," Jessie said.

"Are you sure?" Kendra asked.

"Positive." Jessie swallowed hard. "I gave it to her. It was my way of telling her to keep looking ahead and not get hung up on things in her past. Dee loved it. She always wore it when she performed."

Weller took back the evidence bag. "The bracelet was on the list of things Delilah Winter was wearing when she was taken. It was resting on top of the projector."

Jessie nodded. Seeing the bracelet had obviously knocked her for a loop, but Kendra could see she was managing to recover. Her gaze was still on the bag. "It belonged to her, and they couldn't have picked anything better to show us they have her."

Kendra stepped back and looked at the large projected image again. "Whatever happened to ransom notes made from cut-up newspapers?"

Kelland's voice sounded from behind them: "This is getting

134

a hell of a lot more attention, if that's what the kidnappers want."

They turned to face him. Kelland was accompanied by a pair of agents Kendra recognized from her meetings at the L.A. FBI office.

"True," Kendra said. She motioned up to the hovering news helicopters. "This will be all over the world in the next few minutes, if it isn't already."

"Who was the first to see this?" Jessie asked.

Weller pointed to a man giving a statement to a pair of uniformed officers. "Landscaper. He didn't see anybody else around."

Jessie stepped behind the projector. "You know what gave them the idea, don't you?"

Kelland nodded. "The Hollywood Forever Cemetery summer movie series."

Kendra looked at Jessie as if he'd just made a sick joke. "What?"

"They show movies here during the summer," Kelland said. "Thousands of people are on this lawn every weekend. This cemetery used to be terribly run-down, but you can see how beautiful it is now. They use the movies to get the funds to make sure it's kept that way. The movies are projected against that mausoleum, and they sell booze and food. I once saw *Die Hard* here."

"I came for *When Harry Met Sally*," a female cop said.

"*Moulin Rouge* for me," Jessie said. "With fireworks."

"Fireworks in a cemetery," Kendra said in disbelief.

Jessie nodded. "Welcome to L.A."

Kendra shook her head and turned back to the cops. "I don't suppose this place has security cameras that may have seen who set this up."

"There *are* cameras," Weller said. "But only a few, and it would be easy enough to avoid them, if you were so motivated. We're already trying to get our hands on the recordings. And there are some businesses on the street that we're reaching out to see—" His eyes flicked past them. "Ah, shit. Who let that guy in?"

The rest of them turned to see a police officer escorting a slight young man toward them. After a moment, Kendra realized she was looking at Noah Calderon. Even though she had just recently seen him on television, he appeared much smaller and younger in person. He was definitely good looking, but his sweatpants, tennis shoes, and T-shirt added to his high-schooler vibe, one that was a closer match for a member of the AV club than a captain of industry.

Weller glared at the uniformed officer. "Is there a reason you let him in here?"

The officer stammered. "Well...We thought, since Mr. Calderon made his offer, he would have some part in, uh, well..."

Noah smiled. "Don't blame your men. I probably gave them the impression that I was part of your operation. I felt as if I should be here with you."

Weller still looked annoyed, "Oh, I'm definitely blaming my men. They've seen you on *60 Minutes* and the cover of *Time* magazine, and they're starstruck. Not a good quality for a law-enforcement officer to have in Los Angeles."

The officer started to grab Noah's arm, but he awkwardly stopped himself. "Uh, do you want me to escort Mr. Calderon back...?"

"We'll take care of it," Weller said. "Just get back to your post. And if Brad Pitt wanders up, try not to let him in, okay?"

The officer turned and headed swiftly back to the gate.

Noah Calderon smiled at Jessie and moved in to embrace her. "Good to see you, Jessie. It's been a long time."

Jessie held up her hand. "Still not much of a hugger, Noah. But I'm glad things are still going so well for you." She gestured to Kendra. "My friend, Kendra Michaels."

"Ha! Right." Noah stepped back and extended his hand to Kendra. "Dr. Michaels, it's a pleasure. I've been wanting to meet you for a while."

Kendra shook his hand. "Me? Why?"

"You've trended on my platform several times in the past few years. Pretty much every time you've cracked a high-profile case. I make it my business to know who my customers are taking an interest in."

"Your customers?" Kendra said. "All five hundred million of them?"

"Closer to six hundred fifty million now. But only a hundred million are in the U.S."

"Congratulations...I guess."

"I just give them what they want. And they give me what I want." Noah suddenly sobered as he looked up at the projected ransom note. "Wow. So this is what it's all about."

"Twenty million in cash," Jessie said.

"Does Dee even have that much?" Kendra asked.

"Of course. She's probably made that in the past three months. Maybe double that if you count her last Netflix special."

"I probably made that yesterday," Noah said. "The money isn't a problem."

"Okay," Kelland said. "If you're all through making a bunch of government-salaried law-enforcement personnel feel absolutely worthless, we need to get real. No one's paying this creep twenty million."

"What if we don't have any other choice?" Noah said. "What if Dee's life depends on it?"

Kendra turned to Kelland. "It's a discussion we need to have." She waved to the larger-than-life ransom note. "We have our instructions. We *have* to show up day after tomorrow."

"Of course we'll show up. But we need to do it in a way that's smart. In a way that will lead us to Delilah Winter. This isn't the FBI's first rodeo. Kidnapping cases have been our specialty since before Lindbergh's baby was snatched."

Kendra rolled her eyes. "Poor salesmanship to bring that case up, Kelland."

A young uniformed officer wrinkled his brow. "Who's Lindbergh? Is he a rapper?"

Kelland sighed. "No. Not a rapper." He pointed to the projector. "We're taking this. Break down the scene. This circus has gone on long enough."

"I don't want to be pushy," Noah said. "But I want to make it clear that I'll front the twenty million for Dee's ransom and work with you in any way you choose to make certain it's accepted."

"I'll think about it. Thank you."

"I can't see why you're hesitating. It seems ridiculous for you to make it so difficult for me to give you the twenty million to save Dee." He turned to Jessie. "Don't you agree, Jessie?"

"It won't be difficult," Jessie said as she turned away. "Everyone wants Dee away from those scumbags, Noah. I'm sure Kelland will get back to you."

"I'm sure, too," Kelland muttered as he headed for his vehicle. "I might as well accept the offer if he gives me complete control, or he might be on the phone to one of his political cronies complaining of lack of cooperation."

"What's the next step?" Kendra called after him. "And how can we help?"

"The next step is to keep trying to find these sons of bitches before we have to pay this ransom. That hasn't changed. We'll keep investigating. And we'll have a meeting tomorrow to go over every bit of evidence we've gathered and see what we can put together."

"And can we be there?" Jessie asked.

He looked impatient and then shrugged. "Why not? You two seem to get to most crime scenes before I do." He smiled crookedly. "To hell with protocol. Who knows? Maybe you can help me keep Calderon in check."

---

FBI REGIONAL OFFICE
NEXT DAY

"The meeting is in conference room two," Kelland said curtly when he ran into Kendra and Jessie as they were getting off the elevator. "I'm running late but I'll join you as soon as I can. Things aren't going as well as I'd like."

Kendra and Jessie both stopped short. "Why not? Dee? Something's gone wrong with the ransom delivery?" Kendra asked. "But they're still going to go through with it?"

"As far as we know. We haven't received any word to the contrary since the cemetery. I'm surprised they allowed us this much time for delivery. Evidently they realize twenty million can't be found on every street corner and we'd need a little time." He grimaced. "Sorry. I didn't mean to scare you. It's just that this is such a big case, I'm running into all kinds of bureaucratic interference from the director's office."

"Well, you did scare us," Jessie said coldly. "And I feel like decking you. Next time I might do it. Don't talk to me about your office politics when we don't know from minute to minute whether Dee is still alive."

"I apologized, and I'll do it again if you like," Kelland said. "But I live in a world where I have to occasionally bow to bureaucracy, and I won't apologize for that. It allows me the power and influence to get my way when I want to invite people like you here who ordinarily would never be permitted to attend a closed meeting like this." He nodded down the corridor. "Conference room two. Noah Calderon has already arrived. If you want to make yourselves useful, you can stall him until I get this problem sorted out and can start the meeting. I'm sure you've noticed that he believes the sun rises and sets to please him and he can be difficult. But you'll probably only have to listen to him tell you how wonderful he is to keep him in line." He punched the button for the elevator. "All I'd need is for him to withdraw the offer to front the ransom and have to scramble to get it from the banks."

"He wouldn't do that," Kendra said. "Even if he didn't care anything about her, he values what the public thinks about him."

"Sharp," Kelland said as he got on the elevator. "Good thinking, Kendra. I agree, but it never hurts to soothe the beast on a day when everything else is going wrong."

"He's in a nasty mood." Jessie watched the elevator door close before she turned and started down the hall with Kendra. "Not that I helped. I'm used to him being all smooth and diplomatic, and that remark terrified me. I didn't expect him to let loose on me." She made a face. "Though I actually respect him more for it."

"So do I. It was honest. And we should have expected that reaction. Metcalf said he was the complete agent, and everyone was betting on him to become director someday." She shrugged. "Dealing with the political bullshit connected to the job would become second nature."

"Not one that pleased him today," Jessie said dryly. "I wonder what ticked him off." She opened the conference room door. "Beside the fact that his turf is being invaded by Noah. Though that might be enough to—" She broke off as they saw Noah Calderon sitting at the conference table surrounded by three of his executives buzzing around him. Papers and documents were spread out in front of him. He was on the phone and as he caught sight of Jessie and Kendra, he didn't stop talking but beckoned to them imperiously to come to him. "Never mind," Jessie murmured. "He's turned this official FBI conference room into his own corporate boardroom. I can see why Kelland might be annoyed with him." There was a reckless smile on her face as she started across the room. "Shall we go and see what the great Calderon requires of us?"

"Easy," Kendra said quietly. "There's a reason Kelland is putting up with him. We need everything to go smoothly until we get Dee back. And you said yourself that Calderon seems to be doing his best to make that happen."

"I'm not going to explode. I just don't have much patience for arrogant assholes right now." She stopped before Noah. "You summoned, master?"

He stopped talking on the phone, took one glance at her expression, and pressed the disconnect. "I guess it seemed that way." He smiled ruefully as he jumped to his feet. "Sorry, Jessie. I'm just swamped trying to pull this deal together so that nothing will happen to Delilah. We only have another twenty-four hours to deliver, and I showed up here almost an hour ahead of time this morning to show my support and eagerness to help." He shook his head. "But Kelland didn't appear to appreciate the urgency and is dragging his feet. He kept saying that we had to wait until he was able to talk to his superiors before we could make any plans. I almost got up and walked out."

"Which would have accomplished nothing," Kendra said. So much for her cautioning Jessie to be discreet. For a moment she'd been drawn back into that same warmth and appeal that she'd experienced that first time she'd seen Noah on TV. But his last remark had been too similar to that of a small boy who had wanted to take his toys and go home because he hadn't gotten his way. "I vote we wait and see why the FBI thinks we should let them consult to find the best way to do this. Do you suppose it might even save lives? Wouldn't that be amazing?"

"I don't appreciate your sarcasm, Dr. Michaels." He actually sounded hurt. "Jessie realizes that Delilah is my very dear friend, and I'm only trying to do what's best for her. It's obvious you have a relationship with this Agent Kelland and these other FBI people, and it's getting in the way of your objectivity."

"Yes, you mustn't let your objectivity be put in question, Kendra," Kelland said from behind her. He was at the door and entering the room with several agents trailing behind him. "Sorry to keep you waiting, Calderon. But we're ready to go forward now. We had to come to an important decision about the handling of the ransom and then we had to wait for the courier."

"Courier?" Kendra repeated. "What courier?"

"I told you that this is a big deal to the director." His expression was totally noncommittal. "There were several strategies from Quantico about how it could be brought to a successful conclusion. I thought we were doing very well and making progress keeping it within the Bureau. But the director let himself be influenced to go in a different direction. He wanted to indicate to the media and public that we were going all out in every department with no holds barred."

"What do you mean?"

"He involved the Justice Department. They brought in a black ops expert to do the delivery of the ransom." He gestured to the door. "He just arrived. Naturally we're very eager to work with him. I believe you know him, Kendra." He paused. "Adam Lynch?"

She froze in shock as Lynch walked into the conference room. She heard Jessie inhale sharply beside her.

For an instant Kendra couldn't speak. "Yes, both Jessie and I have worked with him before." She couldn't take her eyes from him. Lynch was smiling and nodding politely at her as he crossed the room to stand beside Kelland. "Though the last I heard he was busy in Asia. I had no idea he'd be available to take on an assignment like this."

"Always glad to go wherever I'm needed." He met her eyes. "I found I had a break in my schedule. I'll look forward to having you fill me in on all the details of the case later." Then he smiled gently at Jessie. "Good to see you again, Jessie. Sorry it's under these circumstances."

"I'm not sure I am," she said slowly. "Hello, Lynch."

"Mr. Lynch?" Noah was on his feet and reaching across the table to eagerly shake Lynch's hand. "Noah Calderon. I'm glad to meet you. I was getting a bit worried about how the case was progressing under FBI direction. I'm sure if the Justice Department is involved it will give us an even greater chance to rescue Delilah."

"I wouldn't be concerned," Lynch said. "As far as I can see, the FBI appears to be doing a very good job. And I've just been designated as a glorified errand boy at the moment." He turned to Kelland. "Now if you'll run down what you want from me, then tell me about my backup and how you want me to handle any snafus."

"There won't be any snafus," Noah interrupted. "I'll deliver the cash to you in an armored car tomorrow morning and you'll take it to the kidnappers. We should have Delilah free by evening."

"Really? But I've seldom run across any crime involving big money when I didn't run across a snafu or two. I understand that there have been a few problems with these kidnappers, and I'm wary of problems." He looked back at Kelland. "So let's pretend that snafus might occur and prepare for them. Then let's go step by step when we get the final directions and see if we've missed anything. Would that be okay, Kelland?"

"Absolutely. Exactly what I would do anyway." He gestured at the other agents who had followed him into the room. "That's why I brought my team to give their input."

Kendra couldn't take any more at the moment. Shock on top of shock, and now Lynch was in the process of taking over the investigation within minutes of walking into the conference room. "Well, this sounds as if you're in agreement, and so I believe I'll opt out while you get down to FBI strategy. I have something else to do." As she stopped at the door, she met Lynch's gaze. "And I'm sure one of you will let me know what's happening later if you think I can be helpful."

"Count on it," Lynch said quietly. "You don't need to be involved with minor details."

Then Kendra was out in the hall and taking a deep breath.

"Okay?" Jessie had come out in the hall and was standing behind her. "I thought you might try to escape being caught between Lynch and Kelland. There might be a little tension. Lynch can always read you."

"Don't be ridiculous," she said curtly. "There's nothing to read, and if there was, it wouldn't apply to this situation. I was just shocked and didn't want to deal with past history when there were more important things on the agenda. We both know I won't miss anything by leaving now. Lynch will make it his business to come after me and clarify and convince me he was right all along."

Jessie made a face. "I admit he can be very controlling, particularly when he'll be having those FBI guys agreeing with everything he says before the morning is over. But I can take it, so I'm going to go back and stick it out. I want to make certain I won't miss anything since Lynch won't be running after me with answers when this is over." She gave her arm a quick squeeze. "And you should go away some-where you can forget all this for a few hours. It's been a rough couple days. Clear your mind and maybe you'll come up with something brilliant that will bring Dee back to us. Will you do that for me?" She didn't let her answer but turned back to the conference room. "Get out of here. I'll see you later, Kendra."

Then she was gone, leaving Kendra to stare after her.

Clear her mind? Come up with something brilliant? Forget for a few hours? How was she supposed to do any of those things?

But Jessie had asked her to try and she would do it. Forget Lynch. Forget everything else and let herself drift away for these few hours...

The FBI meeting didn't break up until midafternoon and Lynch was in the center of everything. But if Jessie thought she was going to be able to slip away without a confrontation, it wasn't going to happen.

"Jessie! Wait!" She stopped at the door to see that Lynch had broken away from the other agents and was striding toward her. "No ducking out for you," he murmured as he took her arm and pushed her gently out of the room. "You hardly spoke all day in that meeting, and that's not like you. So I might have to mend fences with you before I even get to Kendra. Let's go pick her up at your place and I'll take you both out to lunch and we'll talk."

"I could hardly get a word in edgewise if I'd wanted to," she said dryly. "Between you and Kelland, you managed to dominate the conversation. Not that I felt left out. You saw that everyone who wanted a voice had one. But I wasn't there to chime in. I just wanted to make certain that I had a grasp on what was going to happen tomorrow." She added wryly, "And that you had control of the ransom drop. I don't want anything to go wrong and get Dee killed."

"Neither do I. Then I take it that you trust me to do my best for her?" He grimaced. "I know my showing up like this looks like an ego trip, but it was the only way I could do what I needed in the fastest possible time frame. After I was free to leave Tibet, I had to scramble to find out all I needed to know. I tapped as many sources as I could to bring me into the picture so that I'd be of value."

"I could see that by the way you were interrogating every-one in that room today. I don't believe anyone else realized

147

,

that you weren't totally knowledgeable about every facet of the case, and by the end of the session they thought you could walk on water."

"Except Kelland."

"Of course, you caught that. He might have a few issues on a personal level with you. Two alpha males who instinctively gravitate toward the desired female." She added dryly, "I even told Kendra it would amuse me to see you go up against such an attractive, intelligent guy who could give you maximum competition."

"Oh, did you? What did she say?"

"She said for me to mind my own business."

"Excellent idea."

She shrugged. "That sounded edgy. But I knew you'd be able to handle him. And he won't let it interfere with getting Dee back." She said coldly, "If it does, then I'll expect you to step out of the way and let me take care of him. I like him, but not enough to take a chance on losing Dee."

"I believe you can rely on me not to let that happen."

"That's what I'm counting on. I told Kendra that I wouldn't object to having you around to spread a little of your razzle-dazzle if it meant you'd help Dee."

"That's all I want to do, Jessie."

"I could see that today, and I wasn't sitting there judging you." She smiled. "If anything, I was admiring your technique. So I'm not one of the obstacles you're going to have to jump over to get to Kendra. That's her business. The only problem you're going to have with me is if you get clumsy and rush in and hurt her more than she's already been hurt by trying to help me find Dee. That would royally piss me off, Lynch."

He frowned. "What are you talking about?"

"The fact that you had to hurry so much that you might have gotten all the facts, but you didn't have time to examine them and realize what they meant."

"It wasn't that bad. Go on."

"Adrian."

He made the connection instantly. "The man who was killed when you went after him."

"Very good. Did any of those efficient FBI agents mention that we'd made a deal with him to try to get Dee back? That Kendra had promised to protect him? Did they tell you that she was still trying to resuscitate him even though I told her that the back of his head was blown away?"

"Oh, shit."

"I didn't think so. It wasn't something that would be important to the case. But it was important to Kendra." She stared him in the eyes. "And you know how it would affect her."

"Hell, yes."

"Because Kendra's not like either of us. She didn't go through two tours in Afghanistan as I did. And everyone knows your kill record is a complete cipher. Kendra can be tough. She's even had to kill the bad guys every now and then. But it was always the very bad guys, and there were no promises involved. Adrian was flawed, but very human. She thought she'd persuaded him to save Dee by making him that promise. It hurt her to realize that in the end she wasn't able to save either of them. It's still hurting her."

"And you couldn't talk her out of it."

"You know I couldn't. You won't be able to, either. She has to get over it on her own. Just don't be clumsy, and if you can find a way to make it easier for her, take it."

"I hear and obey." He smiled crookedly. "Now can we go to your place and pick up Kendra? I can hardly demonstrate my lack of clumsiness if I'm not allowed in the same room with her."

"You can go to my house if you like. But I'm sure she won't be there." She got on the elevator. "I asked her to go somewhere she could relax and clear her mind of all this business and maybe get some fresh ideas on the case. Since your appearance had obviously disturbed her, I believe she probably took my advice and is doing just that."

"So where is she?"

"You know her as well as I do." She punched the DOWN button as the door started to close. "Figure it out for yourself."

# CHAPTER

# 7

K endra should have known when she heard Harley's joy-ous howl.

Olivia had spent weeks training her dog not to give voice to that terrifying howl. Now he only lost control when he was confronted by special individuals. Adam Lynch was definitely in that category. Kendra tensed and then forced herself to turn on her bench to where Harley was raising such a ruckus. Lynch was standing several yards away with Harley's paws on his shoulders and a frown on his face.

"Down, Harley. Dammit, not *now*." But he gave the dog an affectionate rub on his neck before pushing him off. Then he quickly used the hand signals he'd taught the adorable mutt who'd taken over their lives when Olivia had first been having discipline problems. Harley obeyed immediately but gave one final joyous howl as he followed Lynch down the path toward Kendra.

She braced herself. "Olivia told you where I was? I'm surprised she didn't call and warn me."

"Why should she?" Lynch dropped down on the bench beside her. "Both Olivia and Jessie have far too much respect for you even to hint that you couldn't handle me with one hand tied behind your back." He grinned. "Though I prefer you have all appendages available and ready for action when we're together. It's much more enjoyable." He took her hand. "Besides, they both knew that we had to come to some sort of detente before going forward. So did we, or you would have made it much more difficult for me to find you. As Jessie said, all I had to do was tap into what I knew about you. When you're hurt or need healing, you always go to Olivia." He was toying with her fingers. "I've always been a little jealous of that aspect of your relationship. You've never shown it to me."

"Bullshit," she said bluntly. "If I had, you'd have run the other way. We both know you appreciate your freedom as much as I do."

"Do I?" He lifted her hand to his lips and brushed his lips on the palm. "Perhaps you don't know me as well as you think you do. I found I was feeling very vulnerable when Jessie was telling me about your encounter with Adrian."

"Vulnerable? Not likely." She should pull her hand away, but she didn't. His touch was making her feel safe and secure for the first time since the night Dee had disappeared. "I've never seen you vulnerable." But the fact that she was feeling this need for him showed just how vulnerable she was to him. It would be okay. She could allow herself to accept these moments of comfort for a short time. "And I wasn't trying to hide from you. I knew you'd be coming after me when I left that meeting this morning. The minute you walked into the conference room, I could see you were committed and nothing I could do would make any difference."

"Commitment isn't such a bad thing in a situation like this."

"No, it isn't. We're lucky to have you. I'd be the last person to slam the door in Adam Lynch's face when Dee's life is on the line."

"Even when you have such a dynamo as Kelland on the case?"

"He's been very helpful."

"I can imagine," he murmured, before reminding her: "And you did your best to keep me out of the investigation."

"Because you have your own life and career. Nothing could have shown me anything plainer than when I woke up one morning and found you'd left me without saying a word." She held up her hand as he opened his lips. "I know, top secret. Most of the time I can accept it. But this time for some reason it hurt, and it brought home that maybe I don't have the stamina for that kind of relationship. One thing became crystal clear: I can't keep running to you to solve my problems." She smiled wryly. "But here you are. So it seems I'll have to deal with handling it later."

"Then that's what we'll do. I do have to warn you that I'll be preparing battle strategy, but I can hold off for a little while." He leaned back on the bench. "In the meantime, it's a beautiful day and we'll try not to worry about what's going down with Dee until tomorrow. We'll talk and have dinner with Olivia, and I'll tell you what I can about Tibet." He reached out, and his fingers gently touched the hair at her temple. "And then you'll let me hold you until it's time for us to leave. No sex. No pressure. You don't need that right now. I just want to be with you. I've been looking forward to that since the minute I got on that plane for Tibet. I figure we can leave here at three in the morning and be at Pershing Square in L.A. by six. Sound okay?"

"It sounds very unusual for you." She looked at him curiously. "But very much okay."

"I was afraid of that." He sighed. "I'm being sensitive and trying to demonstrate a complete lack of clumsiness. But now I can't get out of it even if I wanted to." He chuckled. "And I don't." He kissed the tip of her nose. "Now should we take Harley around the dog park one more time before we head back to the condo?"

NEXT DAY

Kendra and Lynch arrived at Pershing Square shortly before 8:00 A.M., their journey delayed by hordes of journalists and fans lining the downtown streets.

Lynch cursed. "Crazy. This is what happens when you project your ransom note in letters eight feet high."

Kendra looked at the barricades lining the sidewalks in front of the Hill Street jewelry stores. "The kidnappers knew it would happen. They planned for this."

"Planned *what*?" Lynch said. "All of L.A. knowing I'm

carrying a suitcase packed with twenty million? How the hell is this going to work?"

"We're about to find out."

Pershing Square, an elevated concrete park in the heart of downtown, was now surrounded by police barricades. After a uniformed officer checked off their names on a printed list, he ushered Kendra and Lynch up the dozen short steps that would take them to the main plaza. Kelland was there with a dozen FBI agents and over fifty uniformed police officers. No one seemed to have any purpose, except for a small group of officers surrounding an armored car in the middle of the plaza.

"Glad you could make it," Kelland said. "Lynch, our command center is in the tent on the other side of the plaza there. We're going to put you in a Kevlar suit."

"That won't be necessary."

Kelland frowned. "We're not letting you make the drop without some kind of protection."

Lynch patted his jacket. "I'm already wearing my own protective suit. Custom-made for me in Abu Dhabi. It's made of Dyneema, much stronger and more flexible than Kevlar."

"I've heard about it." Kelland nodded approvingly at the clothing. "Ever been shot wearing that?"

"Twice. And only a cracked rib and a nasty bruise to show for it."

"We'll give you a helmet."

"No, thanks."

Kendra rolled her eyes. "Take it, Lynch. This isn't the time to be worried about helmet hair."

"Trust me, I wear the mussed-up look exceedingly well. I just don't want anything interfering with my hearing or sight lines."

Kelland shrugged. "Your choice."

Kendra glanced around the plaza. "Have we heard anything from the kidnappers yet?"

"Not a peep." Kelland checked his watch. "Eight thirty is still twenty minutes off, so they may wait until the last possible second."

Lynch looked up at three news helicopters buzzing around the plaza, then at onlookers watching from offices and building rooftops. "How in the hell are we supposed to get instructions?"

"Kidnappers' problem." Kelland motioned for them to join him in walking toward the blue tent on the plaza's far side. "We'll be here at the appointed time with the specified cash."

"We saw the armored car," Kendra said. "I take it that belongs to Noah Calderon."

"Yep. He and his security men are already in the tent. My guys are drooling at the sight of all that money. They've taken down some major drug lords, but I don't think any of 'em have seen that much cash in one place before."

They ducked into the tent and were immediately greeted by a row of six monitors cycling through views of and around Pershing Square. Agents wearing headsets staffed consoles in front of the monitor bank.

Several other FBI agents stood around a coffee-and-Danish

station, while others just stared at the stack of cash on a folding table.

"Good morning, Dr. Michaels."

Kendra turned to see Noah standing in the corner of the tent. Jessie stood next to him.

"Good morning, Noah," Kendra said. "You seem awfully chipper for someone who's about to put twenty million dollars on the line."

Noah shrugged. "All for a good cause." He extended his hand. "Mr. Lynch, I understand you'll be custodian of my money. I knew I could trust you the moment I met you."

Lynch shook his hand. "That's the plan. But there's no guarantee it'll still be your money at the end of the day. My job is to hand it over and stay alive."

Noah nodded. "And hopefully get Dee back."

"That's up to the kidnappers," Jessie said. "Who really thinks we can trust these people? They've already murdered three men."

"No one here trusts them," Kelland said. "But if Lynch and that pile of money can draw them out, we'll be better off than we are now."

Kendra turned back toward the cash, which was being closely guarded by two uniformed employees of the armored car company. The men sported identical mustaches, and for some reason Kendra found that bizarre under the circumstances.

She looked from one to the other. "Does the facial hair come with the uniforms?"

Neither man smiled.

"Tough crowd," she murmured.

Lynch looked at the money, separated into neat stacks and bound by blue paper bands. "Unmarked, nonsequential, untraceable?"

"Absolutely," Noah said. "You wouldn't believe what a pain in the ass it was to get that much cash without at least some of the serial numbers being consecutive."

"Pardon me if I don't tear up for you," Kelland said sarcastically. "The Bureau regrets putting you to such bother. May I remind you that you're the one who offered to help keep Delilah alive."

"And I'm here, aren't I? I don't deserve your rudeness, Kelland." Noah picked up a stack of thousand-dollar bills and rifled through it. "They specified that it must fit in a container one by one by two feet. So they obviously don't mind big bills."

Kelland picked up a black leather satchel and handed it to Lynch. "You'll carry it in this unless they instruct you otherwise."

Lynch looked inside the empty bag and felt its sides. "No tracking devices in here, right? They were very specific."

"No trackers," Kelland said. "But our agents will have eyes on you from rooftops all over the downtown area."

Lynch handed the satchel to another agent, who began loading the money into it. "Good. Because there's about a hundred thousand other people out there who will also be watching me. And thanks to that projected ransom note, they all know I'll be carrying twenty million dollars in cash."

Metcalf ducked into the tent, holding a tall cup of coffee. "Don't tell me the great Adam Lynch is getting cold feet."

"Assassins and soldiers of fortune have never worried me.

Greedy mobs are another matter entirely. I've seen riots break out over free doughnut giveaways. I can only imagine what twenty million will do to people."

Metcalf smiled as he watched the cash being packed. "You've been in tough spots before, Lynch. I'm sure you'll work your way through this one."

"Now I *am* worried, Metcalf." He smiled crookedly. "I'm not used to hearing words of encouragement from you."

"Be afraid. Be very afraid."

Kendra checked her watch. "It's almost time. Any guesses how they plan to communicate their instructions? Skywriting? Dropped leaflets? Another PowerPoint?"

"Some of the cops outside were taking bets when I came in here," Kelland said. "If you want a piece of that action, I'd hurry."

"Racketeering concerns aside, I'll pass."

"Your choice. I got twenty dollars on a messenger service delivery. I just hope that—What the hell!" His gaze was on two LAPD cops escorting someone through the crowd outside and then into the tent. "Surprise. Surprise. What's he doing here?"

It was Congressman Matt Dalborne, Kendra realized, and he looked very sheepish as he made his way across the tent toward her. "I apologize for getting in the way like this." He turned to Kelland. "I thought my presence might help to keep the media at bay while this circus was going on. Instead, thanks to the LAPD I seem to have become a part of the circus. Just tell me where to stand to keep out of your way."

"It's a little late," Kelland said sharply as he pointed to a corner. "And I won't appreciate it if politics has anything to do with you showing up here."

"Absolutely not," Dalborne said quietly as he obeyed the order. "I just wanted to help. Kendra will tell you that I was at that concert when Delilah was taken. We'd already formed a bond at the school. This shouldn't have—"

Kendra's phone rang. She looked at her screen, and the caller ID lit up: DELILAH SAYS HI.

Jessie gasped. She'd seen it, too. "They spoofed the caller ID display."

Kendra held up her still-ringing phone and showed it to everyone in the tent.

"Shit," Dalborne murmured.

Kelland snapped his fingers and pointed to Kendra's phone. One of the techies said, "We've got it. We're recording."

Everyone else had fallen silent.

Kendra answered the call and hit SPEAKERPHONE. "Hello."

"Hello, Kendra Michaels." The low, masculine voice sounded heavily synthesized.

"Who is this?"

"I have Delilah Winter. That's all you need to know."

Kendra spoke in an even tone. "How do I know you're who you say you are?"

"We left her bracelet at the cemetery. We could have left her ring. The silver one that has 'forever' engraved inside. She'll be wearing it when we return her to you."

Kendra glanced at Jessie, who nodded her confirmation.

"You've killed three people. How do we know you haven't killed her?"

"You're just going to have to trust me."

"Not good enough." Kendra held the phone closer to her mouth. "We have your money, but we're not authorized to give it to you without proof of life. You need to do better than a couple of her trinkets."

A long moment of silence.

Noah looked nervously to the FBI agents. He looked as if he was about to speak, but Lynch held up a hand to silence him.

The caller finally responded. "What do you propose?"

"Put her on the phone."

"Not possible."

"Right now," Kendra insisted. "Or the twenty million goes back into the armored car. It's a beautiful sight, believe me. It's a lot to kiss goodbye. Work with us."

The caller paused for a long moment. "You drive a hard bargain, Dr. Michaels."

"A reasonable bargain. We need to know she's alive."

"Give me a question for her."

"Excuse me?"

"A question for dear Miss Winter. Something that only she can answer. Something that will prove to you that she is very much alive."

Kendra looked at Jessie and held the phone in her direction.

"Answer me," the caller demanded impatiently. "That's as far as I can go."

Jessie quickly stepped forward. "The one thing Dee was afraid of when she was a little girl. She had nightmares about it. Tell us what that was."

"Interesting. One moment."

The line went silent, as if it had been placed on mute. A few seconds later, the caller returned.

"She says it was an orange ceramic cat in her mother's bedroom. It had green eyes, and it terrified her."

Jessie looked to Kendra and then the others. She nodded.

"Okay," Lynch said. "How do we get the money to you?"

"To whom do I have the pleasure of speaking?"

"My name is Adam Lynch. I'll be bringing the money."

"Very well. There's a trash receptacle just outside your command center. An LAPD officer standing next to it."

"You're watching us?" Lynch asked.

"The whole world is watching. CNN has a particularly good angle right now."

"Good to know."

"Bring in the contents of that bag. You'll need something in there."

Metcalf bolted out through the tent's opening. "I'm on it." He returned in less than fifteen seconds and dumped the contents out into the middle of the tent. There were several empty coffee cups, empty paper bags, and half a dozen cardboard food containers.

"What are we looking for?" Lynch asked.

"A dark blue zipper pouch."

Lynch found the pouch and unzipped it. It contained a small cell phone and a wired earpiece.

"Put the phone in your pocket and insert the earpiece."

Lynch did as he was told. A moment later, the phone rang and the earpiece lit up.

"Tap the button on your earpiece."

Lynch tapped the button.

"Do you hear me in the earpiece?"

"Yes. Loud and clear."

"Good. Leave your own phone, weapon, and any tracking device right where you are. You'll soon be scanned. If you're detected with a tracking device, Delilah Winter will pay the price. Do you understand?"

Lynch pulled out his phone and semiautomatic and laid them on a nearby folding table. "I understand."

"There must be no one following you or walking with you."

"Got it . . ."

"Good. Then walk north on Olive to Fifth Street. I'm transferring you to someone else for the remainder of the transaction. The others will also be leaving the conversation at this time."

Kendra's phone went dead.

Lynch grabbed the money satchel and took one last look back at the group.

Kendra moved toward him. She'd seen him in some of the most dangerous situations imaginable, but for some reason she'd never been more frightened for him than she was at that moment.

Lynch gave her a reassuring wink. "It'll be okay." He looked toward the group and patted the satchel. "Anyone want coffee? I'm buying."

He ducked out of the tent.

Typical Lynch. Trying to defuse her worry with a wink and a quip.

It didn't work.

Kendra whirled toward the monitor bank. "Do you see him?"

One of the techies nodded. "Yep. We'll be able to follow him on almost any downtown street."

Kendra joined the others around the monitor bank. "*Come on, Lynch*," she whispered to herself. "*Make the damn delivery and get your ass back here.*"

———◆———

"Turn left." It was now an entirely different synthesized voice in Lynch's ear.

"Someone new," Lynch said. "Perhaps an introduction is in order?"

"We'll become quite well acquainted later. Just make the turn."

Lynch turned left onto Fifth Street. Police officers were attempting to keep a wide perimeter between onlookers and Lynch, but groups of people were gathering on the opposite side of the street. "I've already started attracting a crowd," he said quietly.

"Not a surprise, Mr. Lynch. Just hold on to that bag."

Lynch looked up as helicopters roared overhead. "And I'm guessing the news stations are giving you a good look at me."

"Again, all part of the plan."

Lynch walked past the Biltmore Hotel and crossed Grand Avenue. "Care to give me a hint where I'm headed?"

"Turn left again, Mr. Lynch."

Lynch stopped. He was standing in front of the Los Angeles Central Library. "Here?"

"Yes."

"Sorry to be the bearer of bad news, but the library isn't open yet."

"Never mind that. Walk across the main plaza. Ever been to this library, Mr. Lynch?"

"Can't say I have."

"Pity. It's quite beautiful."

Lynch looked up as another helicopter buzzed overhead. "Where are we going?"

"Step around to the left. You'll walk down a short flight of steps running down the side of the building. See them?"

"Yes." Lynch walked across the plaza and took the red brick stairs down, under cover of a row of cedar trees.

"You'll see a black door on your right. Step inside, Mr. Lynch. It's unlocked."

He pushed open the door and strained to see beyond. Only darkness.

The voice grew more insistent. "Step inside, Mr. Lynch."

He walked through the doorway.

"Tear the tape off the doorjamb and close the door behind you."

Lynch saw a slender piece of duct tape stretched over the doorjamb's locking mechanism. He tore it off and pulled the door shut. It locked behind him with a loud click.

Lynch took two steps forward and a light flicked on. He whirled around. He was in what appeared to be a landscaper's workroom, with several electric edgers, tree trimmers, yard shears, and a power mower neatly arranged against the wall.

"It's a motion-activated light," the voice told him. "You're still quite alone."

Lynch looked around. "I'm leaving the money here?"

"Oh, no. We're just getting started. Look for a dark nylon bag on the floor. Pick it up and look inside."

Lynch spotted the bag crumpled up in the corner. It was a medium-sized gym bag with a long shoulder strap. He lifted it and peered into the unzipped main compartment.

"You'll find a windbreaker and a baseball cap in there."

"I see them."

"Take them out and put them on."

Lynch put on the navy-blue windbreaker and matching hat. "Done. Not quite my style, of course."

"I'm sure those broad shoulders of yours fill it out quite nicely."

"How kind of you to notice."

"I'm not the only one. I think CNN's morning anchor has a bit of a crush on you. Now, Mr. Lynch, take the money out of your satchel and place it into the bag."

He transferred the bills into the gym bag, keeping the stacks piled neatly. He tossed aside the leather satchel. "Okay."

"It's time to go now. But not the way you came in. There's a metal door in the back of the room. See it?"

He walked toward the rear door, which was adorned by a rusty metal sign that read MUNICIPAL ACCESS ONLY.

"Grab the handle and give it a good pull. It will open. There's another piece of tape there on the doorjamb. Rip off the tape, step through the door, and close it behind you."

He pulled open the door, which groaned on its hinges. He tore off the tape and walked through the door. After it closed and locked behind him, Lynch froze. "I can't see a thing."

"That's why there's a small flashlight in the right pocket of that jacket. You'll need it."

Lynch fished out the flashlight and turned it on. A set of stairs descended into the darkness in front of him. "Where does this go?"

"Down. Way, way down. But you must hurry, Mr. Lynch. You have quite a bit of ground to cover."

———◆———

"Where in the hell is he?" Kendra looked frantically from one monitor to the other in the makeshift command center.

"We lost him after he left the library plaza," one of the techs said, still staring at his monitor.

A female tech, who was monitoring the news networks, pulled off her headphones. "MSNBC says Lynch went into a side door."

Kelland cursed. "Putting aside the fact that we're getting our surveillance info from cable news stations when we have half the freakin' law-enforcement officers in the city on the job... We think he's in the *library*?"

Jessie nodded. "Looks like it to me. He headed down those stairs and never came out the other side."

167

Kendra's eyes darted from one monitor to the next. "That explains why the kidnapper wanted this to be so public."

"What do you mean?" Kelland said.

"You said it yourself. Who needs the resources of the FBI and the LAPD when you can have half a dozen TV stations following him in real time? He's able to track every step Lynch makes."

"Well, we still have something the kidnapper probably doesn't," Metcalf said. "Infrared. Kelland, do you have a scope on that building yet?"

"Our helicopter is moving into position now," one of the techs said. "We should see any and all body heat signatures in the library. I should be able to superimpose it over building blueprints I just downloaded from the city planner's office. I'll put it up on monitor four."

The team huddled around and waited for the helicopter to lock in on its position. After a moment, the color HD image of the library was replaced by a black-and-white image peppered with occasional bursts of orange and red.

"Those are lighting fixtures," Kelland said. "But, dammit, where's Lynch?"

"He's not there," the tech said, his eyes darting over the monitor.

Kendra joined him in studying the image. "Are you sure?"

"Positive. No one's in that building."

"That's crazy. He has to be there," Kendra said.

A heavyset man in a white short-sleeved shirt stood up from another table. He was holding a large book. "Excuse me. I think I know."

Kelland stepped aside for the man. "This is Ken Delano, the city planner."

Delano held up the book. "He's in the pit."

"The pit?" Kendra said.

"An underground system of tunnels that allows access for electrical, plumbing, and traffic light maintenance in the greater downtown area. They run from the convention center on the south end up to the Music Center on the north and as far east as Union Station."

"What makes you think Lynch is in there?" Jessie said.

Delano pointed to a diagram in his book. "There's an access point on the east side of the library. Right where Mr. Lynch entered."

"Where are they taking him?" Kendra said.

"Anybody's guess." Delano pointed toward the pathways extending from the library. "It could be anywhere along the system."

Kelland turned back to his techs in front of the computer monitors. "I need you to put maps of these passageways onscreen. We'll redistribute our people along those routes. Now!"

———◆———

Lynch played the beam of his flashlight off the concrete walls of the subterranean tunnel. "I see lighting fixtures down here. You planned everything else...Couldn't you have flicked a few on for me?"

"So sorry," the voice said in his ear. "Not possible without alerting your friends to your location. You should be approaching an intersection any time now."

"I see it. But I can only go straight or turn right."

"Take the turn. You'll find a gift."

"For me? Aw, you shouldn't have."

He turned right and almost ran into a bicycle. It was leaning against the wall of the passageway.

"See it?"

"The bike? Yes. The handlebars almost buried themselves into my groin."

"It has an electric motor. It's very fast and very quiet. Climb on and switch on the headlight."

Lynch swung a leg over the bike frame and settled onto the narrow seat. He powered on the headlight and rotated the handle grip back toward him. The bike lurched forward and moved almost silently down the narrow corridor.

"I see some light ahead," Lynch said.

"It's just daylight filtering down from sidewalk gratings. No one will see you."

"Still no hint about where I'm going?"

"Still no hint. But if it's any consolation, you'll make far better time down here than you would at street level."

"I have no doubt." He sniffed as he passed the patches of daylight filtering down. "Hey, I wouldn't be in Chinatown, would I? I think I just caught a whiff of the spring rolls from Plum Tree Inn. Just heavenly."

"We're not going to Chinatown, Mr. Lynch."

"Too bad. There are very few disputes that couldn't be solved over a large platter of bok choy."

"We'll settle for the contents of that gym bag."

"Point taken. How much farther do I have to go?"

"I'll tell you when you're finished."

In the next nine minutes, Lynch tried to keep his bearings, but he was only certain of his location when he saw access signs for the Grand Avenue Music Center complex.

Soon the voice shouted out one last command.

"Stop!"

Lynch eased off on the throttle and rested his feet on the passageway's concrete floor. "What now?"

"Welcome, Mr. Lynch." This time the voice came from behind him, different from the one from his phone.

Lynch threw down the bike and spun around. Two men stepped from the shadows, wearing black tactical suits and face masks. Both men carried guns, and one walked with a distinct limp.

Lynch smiled. "You wouldn't have gotten that limp on Desert Route 19 a couple days ago, would you? Because if so, I know the young women who gave it to you. And neither of them is the least bit sorry."

Lynch could tell that he'd provoked a strong reaction. The man leaned forward and balled up his free hand. His tightening jaw was visible even through the mask.

Excellent, Lynch thought. The man was already having trouble controlling his anger. That would make him easier to take down if the situation demanded it.

The other man was still a question mark. He was tall, and he moved with steady, more deliberate motions. He bent over and picked up a large electronic wand.

"I'm not carrying a weapon," Lynch said.

"I'm not worried about weapons. We need to make sure you're not being tracked."

"I'm not."

"We'll see." The man switched on the wand and waved it in Lynch's direction. After a moment he put down the wand. "It appears you're telling us the truth."

The limping man pointed toward the gym bag Lynch was holding. "You have something that belongs to us."

"And you still have Delilah Winter. I was hoping to see her here."

"That was never a part of the deal."

Lynch shrugged. "Twenty million dollars is an awful lot to give away on faith."

The tall man chuckled. "You're talking as if it's your money."

"I just want to see an innocent young woman returned safely."

"She will be."

"Where? When?"

"When and where we decide."

The limping man stepped forward and snatched the gym bag. He unzipped it and shone his flashlight inside at the stacks of currency.

"Unmarked and nonsequential serial numbers," Lynch said. "Per your request."

The tall man adjusted his sensor wand and waved it over the bag. The device emitted a low-pitched tone.

The man inhaled sharply, every muscle tensing. "What are you trying to pull here?"

"It's your bag," Lynch said. "There's nothing in it but the cash."

The man pulled out a stack of bills and checked it with the wand. Again it emitted a tone. He rifled through the bills, then tore off the paper band. He held the band up and waved it past his wand.

Another low-pitched tone.

"You scumbag," the man said. "There are tracking chips in these paper bands." He glanced around. "Your friends could be here any second."

"You've got to be wrong. Check it again." Lynch stepped back warily as the two men turned on him. "I don't know anything about that."

"Like hell you don't. Your friends just signed that songbird's death warrant."

The other man smiled through the opening in his mask. "And yours."

BLAM!

Lynch ducked just in time to avoid the bullet as it whizzed by him and ricocheted around the passageway's concrete walls.

Lynch rolled.

BLAM! BLAM!

Two more misses.

Gotta put something between himself and these guys. Fast.

The bike. Lynch grabbed it and hurled it at the men, knocking them off balance. Before they could recover, Lynch punched the taller man and knocked the gun from his hand. He grabbed the man by the back of his neck and rammed his skull against the wall. Lynch spun toward the other man.

Too late. The guy was ready with his gun.

BLAM!

Lynch's ears buzzed and his vision blurred. He'd been hit. Maybe on the forehead, maybe on the temple. But in either case, why was he still conscious?

BLAM!

He flew backward as another bullet struck his protective jacket. It may have shielded his vital organs, but his insides still felt like they were exploding. He rolled into the darkness and moved his hands across the floor.

The gun.

Gotta find that gun. It was here somewhere.

But a fog was creeping over his forehead, matched by the warm stickiness in his hair.

Blood.

The fog was thicker now.

Fight it.

Stay awake.

Stay *alive*.

BLAM! BLAM! BLAM!

Both men fired indiscriminately into the dark passageway, but they were flying blind and none of the bullets found their mark. Lynch rolled over to hug the passageway's inside wall.

The gunfire stopped.

"Let's go," one of the men said to the other. Lynch was too woozy to know which one was speaking. "And leave the money."

"Leave it?"

"It isn't safe. It will lead them straight to us. Hurry!"

Their two sets of footsteps pounded away, echoing in the concrete corridor.

Lynch forced himself to stand.

His head buzzed even louder. If he wasn't careful, he was going to die in this hole.

Gotta get to the surface. There at least he had a chance.

He cocked his head. There was another sound, behind the buzzing. A distinctive clattering of steel wheels on rails. Trains.

Trains?

He staggered forward. He heard a P.A. system, blaring announcements of some kind.

He was beneath a train station. Of course. Union Station.

The sound was filtering down from a grate. He grabbed a rusty iron rung protruding from the wall and pulled himself up.

Damn. This wasn't going to be easy.

He climbed another step as blood drizzled over his forehead and eyes.

His head throbbed, but his bruised ribs pained him more.

Dammit!

Pain. Sharp, stabbing pain.

He tasted blood on his lips. Ignore it. Fight through it.

He climbed a few more feet. The announcements were now louder and more distinct. The Amtrak Pacific Surfliner was now boarding...

One more rung. Then another. And another after that.

He stopped. Everything was spinning, and he felt his grip loosening.

No. He couldn't pass out now. Not when he was so damn close...

He looked up and focused on the grating. Busy commuters walked back and forth over it. A luggage cart rolled over and momentarily darkened the narrow passageway.

*Focus. Climb.*

He pushed himself upward, racing against his receding consciousness.

Just a few more feet...

Made it.

No time to celebrate. He still had to get topside.

With his left hand gripping the rung, he shoved the fingers of his right hand through the crosshatch grating and pushed upward.

It didn't budge.

The iron grating was heavy, and his ribs weren't making things any easier.

Again.

He grunted and pushed with everything he had.

It was happening. He cleared the rim and pushed the grating over just enough for him to squeeze through.

He lifted himself up the three remaining rungs and emerged in the bustling art deco main terminal.

Success!

A woman screamed. Not that he blamed her. He knew he must've been a bloody mess.

He collapsed onto the floor. As consciousness left him, he was vaguely aware of two cops rushing in his direction.

# CHAPTER

# 8

"What the hell happened, Kelland?" Lynch shook his head to clear it and was barely able to make out the figures of Jessie and Kendra standing behind the agent. At the moment he was seeing two of each of them, and he had to keep his head still or risk blacking out again. "That ransom was supposed to be clean. Noah promised us it would be."

"I know he did," Kelland bit out. "And I can't tell you why it wasn't. All I know is that when I bolted up to that conference room to ask him all he could do was yell that it wasn't his fault and he wouldn't take the blame. I didn't have time to get anything else out of him before I ran here to see how badly you were hurt." He frowned. "You were unconscious when we got here. We should get you to the ER."

"I'm all right," Lynch said savagely as he pushed him aside. "There's no time for this. This was my job, *my* responsibility.

I'm not going to stand by and let Dee be killed because of this foul-up."

"Wrong," Kelland said. "It's my job. You're out of it now."

"The hell I am." He got to his feet. "You've got to contact them fast and tell them we want to renegotiate. If you don't reach them right away, it will be too late. I've dealt with ransoming prisoners in the past, and all kinds of motivations can drive them at a time like this. We don't want them to choose the first action that occurs to them based on anger or impulse. We have to give them a way to think they're still going to come out of this with what they want."

Kelland was swearing. "Do you think we're not trying to reach them? They broke contact the minute they realized the ransom might be a trap."

"Then find another way," Lynch said. "And damn quick."

"Suggestions?" Kelland asked sarcastically.

"The cemetery." Jessie stepped forward, her hands clenched into fists at her sides. "Use the cemetery. Put a message on the mausoleum that they used to send their message and tell them that a mistake was made and we're ready to deal and offer an even higher fee."

"The cemetery," Kelland repeated. "It could work..."

"It *will* work," Kendra said desperately. "We still have a chance of saving her. Just do it. Fast. And call in the media and get them out there to the mausoleum to publicize that message."

"I said it might work. Don't get your hopes up." Kelland turned on his heel. "I'll do what I can."

"Yes, you will. And I'll go with you," Jessie said grimly.

"I'll begin calling the media now so that they'll start broad-casting the story even before you get the message on the mausoleum. Like Lynch said, I want those bastards to know they have a chance of getting what they want. Any objections?"

He shook his head and said over his shoulder, "By all means, join me. Just stay out of my way. You're not the only one who wants your friend to come out of this alive."

Kendra watched them leave before turning back to Lynch. "Will you let me bandage that wound or am I going to get all kinds of flak from you?"

"Flak," he said curtly as he took out his handkerchief and dabbed at the cut. "I'll take care of it once I get back to FBI headquarters. I'm surprised you didn't want to go and help Jessie."

"I intend to do that as soon as I'm sure that you're not going to collapse and cause us more problems. It was entirely your fault that you've probably got a concussion." She was struggling to keep her voice from shaking. "You're the one who wouldn't wear any protective headgear to keep that from happening."

"That's absolutely correct."

"Yes, and since Dee's more important right now, I can't be bothered with you after I'm sure that you're not going to do something stupid. So tell me that's not going to happen and I'll leave you."

"I won't do something stupid." His lips tightened. "You all appear to be on the right track trying to save Dee, so I thought I'd go and see why the hell she needed saving." He met her eyes. "And there's only one place I can go to ask that question. Noah was in sole charge of the ransom until it was given to me. He was told not to put any markers on those bills. That mistake could cost Dee her life."

"I know. I don't understand it, either. But it had to be a mistake. He was so eager to get her away from them."

"I'm not in a mood for excuses." His tone was ice-cold. "He put her on the spot and he almost got me killed. I want to know why and then I still may break the son of a bitch's neck."

"That's really smart," she said caustically. "Particularly since you probably have a concussion and Noah's always surrounded by his executives and bodyguards."

"If I don't believe I can handle them, then we'll have a discussion...maybe."

She'd had enough. "Then do what you like. I have to go help Jessie try to keep Dee from being murdered. Why don't you stagger back to that conference room, confront Noah, and see how much satisfaction you can squeeze out of getting him to admit he was an idiot. That sounds like a real way to win the day."

She walked away from him. She would not look back. She might tell one of the officers to keep an eye on him to make sure he didn't black out again. But she wouldn't give him the satisfaction of knowing how worried she was about him when he wouldn't take care of himself.

"Kendra."

She hesitated and then glanced back at him.

He was smiling gently. "I won't be stupid about it. I just

can't let it go. Let me know as soon as you get an answer from that message. Okay?"

She nodded. "I don't know when that will be. Maybe they'll just ignore it."

"It's hard to ignore twenty million dollars. If we get lucky, they'll just up the ransom and make sure the safety restrictions are totally foolproof."

"If we're lucky." But they'd been lucky about Lynch not getting his head blown off, she remembered. Only an inch more and he would have been dead. Stop it. She was starting to shake again.

It might be okay. Maybe they'd be lucky about Dee, too...

She turned away. "I'll let you know the minute I get word."

———◆———

SECOND-FLOOR CONFERENCE ROOM
FBI HEADQUARTERS

When Lynch entered the conference room an hour later, it was full of noise and chaos erupting from several sleek executives plus Noah's two bodyguards.

Noah himself broke free of the people surrounding him the moment he saw Lynch. "Lynch, they told me you were hurt." He hurried toward him. He shook his head as he saw the cut on his temple. "That's terrible. But you were lucky to escape with only that wound. I'm sure it could've been much worse." He smiled tentatively. "Maybe they'll give you a Purple Heart or something?"

"Not likely. The mission was a failure. We'll be fortunate if we can get Dee out of this alive now." He took a step closer. "Most of the time, kidnappers feel they have an obligation to kill their victims if the deal falls through." His voice suddenly turned savage. "Maybe you didn't know that or didn't believe it. Why else would you deliberately cause it to happen?"

"It wasn't my fault." Noah nervously moistened his lips. "How could you think it was? Delilah and I are friends. At one point we were almost more than that. All I could think of was getting her away from those scumbags. The minute I heard this had happened, I started an investigation to find out how I'd been betrayed. They can't do that to me."

"*You've* been betrayed?" Lynch repeated silkily. "I'd think it was Dee who'd been betrayed, wouldn't you? She's the one whose severed head may end up being delivered to us because you let this happen."

"I meant that, of course. We were both betrayed." His lips pursed pettishly. "But I seem to be the one getting the blame and it's not what I deserve. I was trying to save her. I did everything right."

"Then how did right become so damn wrong? You have one minute to tell me before I take you apart."

"You might have difficulty with that." He glanced at his bodyguards across the room. "But I'll forgive your rudeness because of what you went through today."

"Thank you. You're too kind," Lynch said. "I'm accustomed to difficulty; sometimes I even embrace it. You're running out of time, Noah."

"I told you, I was betrayed." He lowered his voice to a

whisper. "You don't understand how a man of my means and influence can be constantly surrounded by people who want to catch the brass ring or punish me for having it. I suspect it must have been one of my executives who changed my orders."

"Why?"

"Well, when I was arranging for the money, my financial advisors kept telling me that we should hedge the bet, that there were all kinds of ways to save those millions and still keep Delilah alive. I listened to them, of course, who wouldn't? But naturally I turned them down."

"Naturally. Yet they still managed to get those trackable bands in my backpack."

"I believe one of my executives might have thought I was interested in what those financial advisors were proposing and arranged to do it for me himself. He probably thought that once the switch was completed successfully, I'd thank him...and it would put him first on the list for promotions." He frowned. "I was just attempting to start questioning my staff when you came bursting into the room."

"So you didn't know anything about it?"

"I told you that I didn't. It was done by someone who either wanted to please me, or wanted to ruin my reputation. Either way I'm also being hurt by this terrible injustice." He lifted his chin. "Now may I go back and continue interrogating my employees so that I can determine who is guilty?"

Lynch gazed at him appraisingly. Noah could be telling the truth, or he could be lying like a rug. He was inclined to believe the latter. But since he'd been in charge of the ransom,

183

he was still responsible for what had happened to it either way. "You mean who else is guilty?" He dropped down in a chair at the conference table. "Yes, feel free to question them to your heart's content. I'll just stay here and watch and listen. Then when you've decided who you think 'betrayed' you, I'll have my own turn at talking to him. I believe I've earned that right, haven't I?"

"It might go faster if you're not here." Noah was nibbling at his lower lip. "You might make them nervous."

"You think so?" Lynch smiled and leaned back in his chair. "Good. After what happened today, that's a response I'll definitely appreciate."

---

KELLAND'S OFFICE

FBI HEADQUARTERS

"This is crazy." Kendra gazed in frustration at the computer screen reflecting the wall of the mausoleum. "Why haven't we heard?" She couldn't understand why there hadn't been an answer to the message at the cemetery for the last four hours. The message had gone up on the mausoleum within forty-five minutes of when Kelland had called in the order to his men. The media had been having a field day, building suspense, then crushing it, then starting the process all over again.

"They have to have seen that message," Jessie said through set teeth. "Everyone in the damn country must know that we've been practically begging those scumbags to give us another chance."

"Yes, we have," Kelland said. "In the most humiliating way possible. The only reason I haven't been asked to turn in my badge yet is that the director is hoping desperately I might turn into a hero and save the day." He grimaced. "Not likely. There couldn't be a more public revelation of inefficiency than that message on the mausoleum."

"Yet you didn't bat an eyelash when we asked you to do it," Kendra said. She'd been in such a frantic hurry to try to save Dee that she hadn't realized what a career breaker this might prove for Kelland. "You only wondered if it would work."

"I couldn't do anything else," he said wearily. "I'm a good agent. My job was to save Delilah Winter's life. We'd just heard from the Denver office. They checked surveillance cameras in and around coffee shops in a sixteen-block radius of Adrian Nash's hotel, The Brown Palace. They got Nash walking south from his hotel one day, but he disappears from view pretty quickly. Naturally there's no footage of him meeting with that Cabot guy who solicited his help in the abduction scheme."

Kendra shook her head. "Damn."

"Yeah. So your idea to contact the kidnappers may be the best shot we have right now. It didn't matter that I ended up looking like an asshole bungler who let myself be manipulated." His lip curled bitterly. "No, I can't say it didn't matter. I'm mad as hell."

"So was Lynch," Kendra said. "He said he couldn't let it go."

"Neither can I. But I was busy here, so when Lynch called

and told me he was interrogating Noah and all his executives, I gave him permission. Not exactly protocol, but I knew Lynch was just as pissed off as I was. I want answers." He shrugged. "I figured Lynch would get them for me."

"You have amazing faith in him. Even though he was possibly suffering a concussion?"

"He refused treatment. He can take care of himself." He glanced at her face. "You must agree. You told me when you got here that you knew he was on his way to see Noah."

"I agree he thinks he can take care of himself in any situation." She was keeping her gaze fastened on the computer screen. "Have you heard from him since then?"

His brows rose. "I hardly expected him to check in. The director was happy just to get him to come here. Lynch pretty much told me that he expected to run his own show when he arrived. As long as he cooperated, I wasn't going to make waves." He paused, curious. "When you worked a case with him, were you accustomed to having him check—"

Kendra's phone vibrated, and a text appeared on her screen:

LAST CHANCE

FIVE MILLION MORE

INSTRUCTIONS 5/3

"Here it is!" Kendra showed them the screen. "They answered. Thank God."

"Tomorrow," Jessie murmured. She took the phone and typed. PROOF OF LIFE?

A long wait. Then:

PERHAPS 5/3

Message ended.

"Son of a bitch!" Jessie muttered. "They're keeping us on tenterhooks. Punishment for screwing up this delivery?"

"I guess that's it." Kendra moistened her lips. "Regardless, they have us over a barrel until they see fit to give that proof to us." She turned to Kelland. "What do you think?"

"I think that you're right," he said grimly. "And that I hope we got that message out to them in time."

She'd been afraid to put that last thought into words. "We've got to assume they did. What good would it do them to stretch this agony out if she wasn't still alive?" She drew a deep breath. "Lord, I'm tired of feeling this helpless. Is there anything else we can do?"

"We're already doing it. The phone calls," Kelland said. "Remember? I started trying to trace those voices on the phone from the first moment they began giving orders to Lynch. We've made incredible advances lately in the audio field and can do amazing things not only with tracing but also with voice analysis."

"How soon?"

"It depends. I made it a priority." He shrugged. "Tonight? Tomorrow?"

"Tomorrow might be too late."

"I'll get it as quick as I can," he said quietly. "No one wants to get those bastards more than I do."

"Wanna bet?" Jessie asked. "Could we go down to the lab and listen to the original tapes again?"

"If you promise not to get in the techs' way. I meant it when I said top priority."

Kendra hesitated. "You go ahead, Jessie. I promised to let

Lynch know when we knew about the mausoleum message. And I want to see if he's found out anything about why this ransom delivery went to hell. Do you want to go with me, Kelland?"

He shook his head. "He said he'd give me a report. I need to get a cup of coffee and then go back to my office and make a few dozen calls to tell everyone that we might have been given a reprieve. I'll see you in the morning." He headed toward the elevator.

Kendra glanced at Jessie. "Jessie?"

"I'd rather go down to the AV lab." She shook her head emphatically. "If I caught sight of Noah in my present mood, I might cut his throat. I don't want excuses about why he did that to Dee. I thought he was her friend. I even convinced Kelland he should let Noah pay that ransom. I didn't have any idea that his enormous bankroll means more to him than he brags. Or that he believed he was smart enough to get that sneaky move past those goons. He took a chance and I'm not about to forgive him." She started toward the elevator. "See if you can't persuade Lynch to give it up and go to my place for the night. I know you've been worried about him."

"I've been worried about everyone."

"Yeah, me, too." She tried to smile. "But maybe I'll get good news from those audio guys. Kelland says they're amazing."

"From what I've learned about current AV advances, I don't doubt it," Kendra said gently. "I'd like copies of those audio files. I want to listen to them myself."

"I figured you would," Jessie said. "I'll make sure you get

them." She turned away. "I'll call you when I'm through here."

Good news, Kendra thought as she went toward the conference room. Amazing. She could use a little herself right now.

But Lynch didn't look as if he had any of that commodity available when she walked into the conference room. She was surprised to see he was the only one there. He was sitting with a cup of coffee and looked as tense and alert as when she'd left him earlier in the day. His gaze instantly flew to her face. "Dee?"

"We just heard. They'll accept the new delivery. Noah has to furnish another five million. Instructions tomorrow." She added bitterly, "They said they won't give us another proof of life until then, too. Jessie thinks they're trying to punish us."

"And they could be. Five million?" he said thoughtfully. "They could have asked for more. If they're angry, why didn't they do it?"

"Maybe they're getting as tired of these negotiations as we are and want them over." She dropped down in the chair next to him. "I hope that's why. Where's Noah? Are we going to have any trouble getting that extra five million from him?"

He shook his head. "He's too busy insisting how innocent he is and trying to pin the blame on one of his executives. Right now he's zeroed in on Ed Carruthers, the most likely candidate, and he's in the other office grilling him." His lips twisted cynically. "I expect him to come out in a few minutes with a full confession from the man that will prove Noah is clean as the driven snow."

"You don't believe that."

"No, the greedy bastard's probably used bribery or intimidation to save his neck and reputation. But I'll accept it for the time being, because we need that five million to move very fast and Noah will make sure it does if I don't cause waves." He shrugged. "But he already knows that I'll be watching him. He just doesn't know what a long memory I have."

But Kendra did, and she realized that Noah would as well before this was over. She'd seldom seen Lynch this angry. "I still can't believe he'd do this to Dee."

"Believe it. Some people only see what they want to see. Noah was probably starting to make excuses for himself the minute he gave the order to hedge his bet to protect that twenty million." He added coolly, "But I'll make certain that he knows exactly what he did after we have Dee back safe and sound."

"It was Carruthers!" Noah strode out of the other office. "Just as I thought, Lynch. He confessed and I'm turning him over to my personal security force. I'll make certain that he's prosecuted to the full extent of the law." He caught sight of Kendra. "Hello, Kendra, you're just in time. Isn't she, Lynch?"

"Yes, just in time. I was telling her how helpful you were being." The words breathed irony. "I'll call and let Kelland know we've solved that puzzle. But it appears you're going to have to fork out another five million, so you'd better call those financial wizards of yours and get them working on it. That won't be a problem, will it?"

"Of course not," Noah said quickly. Then he smiled with

relief. "That must mean what Carruthers did caused no real harm. Delilah will still be released. I knew it!"

"Did you?" Lynch asked softly. "I didn't." He took a step toward him. "You must have a sixth sense about—"

"Come on, Lynch," Kendra interrupted as she grabbed his arm. He seemed to have entirely forgotten about not making waves. "I need to get you somewhere we can tend to that wound. You've left it too long." She was leading him toward the door. "Get on the phone now, Noah. We'll expect that cash here by early tomorrow. I'll call Kelland and tell him how cooperative you're being."

"Yes, do that," Noah said eagerly. "Make certain he knows that even though this wasn't my fault, I'll work hard to make sure the next time will be different." He frowned. "And tell him to keep Matt Dalborne from smearing me. That scumbag politician has called me twice today and yelled at me. I know he's going to try to use this to gather enough press coverage to ride it straight to the White House."

"I think we all realize there's no question there won't be a repeat of this disaster." She slammed the door behind them.

"You didn't have to rescue him from me. I probably wouldn't have done anything too lethal," Lynch murmured. "Though I admit he was annoying me."

"Obviously. I didn't trust you." She shook her head wearily. "I didn't trust myself. You're not the only one who wanted to sock him. Too many bad things are happening, and I'm not reacting well. I need to take back my control. So after I give Jessie a call, the first thing I'm doing is driving you to the ER and getting you a CAT scan. Then if they tell me your head

191

isn't going to blow up, we'll go to Jessie's place and you can get some rest."

"I promise my head's not going to blow up, Kendra."

"That would be nice, but like I said, I don't trust you. I want to make sure of something, anything."

"Okay." He took her hand and held it tightly. "Then we'll make sure my head's going to remain in one piece."

"That sounded patronizing."

"It's your imagination. I wouldn't dare. Now let's get out of here..."

---

Dimness, curved walls, long, narrow room...

Same place as before, Dee thought dazedly as she opened her eyes. For the first time, she was aware of a white panel in the back with a large silver door. It looked new, unlike the worn walls, ceiling, and floor everywhere else.

She had been drifting in and out of sleep for the last few hours, but she hadn't let that witch, Charlotte, know she'd regained consciousness after being yanked roughly wide awake to answer that damn ransom question the woman had hurled at her. She would have told her to go to hell if she hadn't realized that very personal question must have come from Jessie. Besides, the one thing Dee had learned during those last encounters with Charlotte was that all she'd get from her was threats and ugliness.

She'd decided she'd do better to just try to get her bearings, think about all the things Jessie had taught her over the years, move forward, and hope that someone else would show up who would be more accommodating. And this time when she drifted back to awareness, she realized that she might have gotten lucky. Because whoever Charlotte was speaking to now was receiving the same scathing venom she'd been handing out to Dee earlier.

And it was also definitely the same bitter voice. "It's ridiculous." Charlotte was standing just out of Dee's field of vision, but her voice was even more angry than it had been the moment Dee faded into unconsciousness. "You're all fools, Dorset. You were given a simple job to do and you couldn't even bring home that money. It's a wonder that you weren't caught. I was the only one who did everything right. If it had been me in charge, I would have found a way to make you pay for that carelessness. Didn't anyone tell you we have mafia contacts at our disposal? How would you like to deal with them?"

"Do you think I'm not paying?" It was a man's voice and it was just as bitter. "He cut my share in half for the next go-round, and he sent me here to help you guard that bitch. He got tired of you complaining. I think he was afraid you'd kill her and leave us with nothing."

"And I would, if I could talk sense into him. She's not worth the bother." She was silent. "But he recognizes my value and knows that I deserve something better than being a watchdog to that cash cow you're all so eager to keep penned up here." She added, "So I'll take your help, Dorset. You'll do what I say or I'll cut her throat and tell him you did it."

"He wouldn't believe you."

"But you're not sure, are you?" She added in a whisper, "You've never been sure about me. Now get out of here. I thought I heard her stirring. I'll call you when I need you."

Dee heard a curse, and then a slashing bolt of light lit the dimness—that must have been the silver door opening.

"You *are* awake." Charlotte's face was suddenly above her. "Listening to us? Not that it did you any good. All it proved was that you're surrounded by people who care nothing about you. They couldn't even get the instructions about the ransom right. They tried to pull a fast one and trap us. Now they're probably shivering in their boots afraid that we'll send them your head in a box."

"And are you going to do that?"

"I haven't decided."

She shook her head. "It's not up to you. I heard that much." She paused. "Who does make the decision, Charlotte?"

"If I told you, then I'd have to kill you." She chuckled. "Maybe that's what I should do. The perfect excuse. I'll have to think about it."

And she might decide to make use of that or any other excuse, Dee thought. "You would have done it before if you'd had the option. And I must be worthwhile to someone or they wouldn't have sent that man to keep you under control and make sure it wouldn't happen. I think I might be safer than you'd like me to believe."

"Are you? Think what you want." Her smile was ugly. "But not if you rely on Dorset. He was sent because I was more important than him and always will be. Which means you can't be sure when I'll get my way." She said softly, "But you can bet it won't be your way, Delilah." She was unfastening the IV. "Sit up. There's only one thing good about Dorset showing up and that's that I can make him take care of you until this is over. I got sick of getting calls with questions about whether you were still alive and if I was getting that drug right. From now on Dorset can do it."

"He can't be worse than you are." Dee's gaze was once more raking her surroundings. Curved walls...that bolt of brilliant daylight. Even in this dimness she was able to recognize where she was. "This is an airplane. A big one. Maybe even a jumbo jet. There aren't any seats, but I can see where they used to be. We must be on the ground because there's no noise from the engines. What am I doing in an airplane?"

"Being a pain in the ass," Charlotte said sourly. "Why not? If you give us too much trouble, we'll just take off and drop you in the Pacific Ocean. Maybe we'll do it anyway."

And that bolt of brilliant light had been Dorset opening the door and leaving the aircraft. The reason it was so dim in here now was that all the windows were covered. But the only way she might determine where they were located would be listening to what was going on beyond that door. "You're actually going to let me sit up? Oh, that's right, you're not to be trusted to keep me under those drugs indefinitely."

"That's all you know. None of those clowns are more trusted than I am. They're all disposable. You'll be handcuffed in that metal chair over there. It will be easier if we have to take a photo of you for proof of life."

"You might have more proof of life than you think if you

don't let me go to the bathroom," she said dryly. "How long did you have me under?"

"Long enough," Charlotte said. "But if you think I'm going to take you to pee, you're crazy. I've done enough holding your hand since you were thrown at me."

"Then what will be, will be."

Charlotte scowled and then strode over to the door. "Dorset," she called as she threw open the door. "Your first job. Take the bitch to the bathroom." She stepped aside to let him come back in. "After that you can tie her up and fix her something to eat."

Dee blinked as Dorset came into view. His features appeared almost boyish, maybe those of a nineteen- or twenty-year-old. She hadn't expected that from the rough tone of his voice. "You could do all that," he growled. "I'm just supposed to guard her."

"That's what you're doing. You can stay and babysit her while I go take a walk and get some air." She was going past him and down the steps. "If you think you can keep her from getting away. That bathroom is tiny, but so is your brain. Though you might be able to do it. Ask me if I give a damn." She slammed the door behind her.

Dorset was cursing as he stalked across the plane toward Dee. "Bitch. Bitch. Bitch."

She knew he wasn't talking about her. "I agree," Dee said. "Look, all I asked was to go to the bathroom."

"Then let's go do it and get it over with." Dorset jerked her to her feet. "And if you think that you're going to get away from me, think again. That dragon bitch would like nothing

196

better than to report I'm doing something wrong. I'm already in trouble enough." He was pushing her down the aisle. "And now I'm supposed to deal with you? It's all nuts. Everyone told me they'd be so eager after waiting to get the ransom note that they'd be begging to give it to us. Why didn't they just turn over the money?"

"I have no idea. It must have been a slipup. I'm worth too much to too many people for them to deliberately do something that would get me killed." If she'd had any hopes that Dorset was going to be any easier to deal with than Charlotte, they were fading fast. He was surly and bad-tempered, and her best bet was just to pretend meekness. "But I'll tell you what I told her. It would be very bad press for them to let you kill me. They'll cooperate if they can. Just give them a chance."

"We did. Those bills weren't supposed to have been marked. We'd have probably been caught if we'd taken that payment." He was shaking his head. "This whole deal has been screwy since the beginning. The money was always good, but I've never worked with people like this before. I can't figure them out." They had reached the bathroom, and he opened the door to reveal the usual tiny aircraft lavatory. "I'll give you ten minutes."

She held out her cuffed hands. "If you want me to be quick, unlock these. You can't expect me to be able to do anything trussed up like this."

He hesitated. Then he unlocked the manacles. "Don't lock the door. Give me any problems and I'll break both your wrists."

"I'm not going to cause you problems. I gave Charlotte her

damn proof of life, didn't I? If you run into any trouble from anyone else, I'll help you deal with them. I don't give a damn about the money. I want to *live*."

She closed the door and drew a deep breath.

*Okay, Jessie. Here I am. What do I do next?*

Take care of business first. She eliminated quickly and then looked down at her wrists. She had to find a way to slip her hands out of those manacles. Jessie had shown her how to do it when she was making that film about that CIA agent. But playing games was different from the real thing. She couldn't expect to have it come together in one ten-minute session. Concentrate. She would get it. Just remember everything Jessie had told her...

—◆—

Jessie still wasn't home when Kendra drove Lynch to her house a couple hours later. She called her after she let Lynch into the house. "You're still at the audio lab?"

"Kelland was right. They're amazing. I think there's a chance that we might learn something, though it's not going as fast as I hoped. Kelland dropped in and checked the results and told me to go home. So I'll stick around for a little while longer and then leave here. How is Lynch?"

"Not bad. Minor concussion. Though the doctor said he should rest. He's disgustingly self-satisfied and aching to say 'I told you so.'"

"In other words, typical Lynch." She paused. "But I'm glad you know for sure. You'll feel better now."

"Maybe. I'll see you when you get home. Don't stay too long." She hesitated. "Kelland didn't have any other news?"

"No news. We're still hanging. See you later." She cut the connection.

Kendra turned back to Lynch. "Jessie is glad that you checked out okay."

"I heard you," he said dryly. "Not kind. I thought that I was behaving with extreme self-restraint. Any other news?"

She shook her head. "Only that she's enthusiastic about the chances of an audio trace. She keeps saying it's remarkable technology."

"Yes, it is. I recently ran across a completely new and innovative method developed by the Swiss that impressed me." He frowned thoughtfully. "I wonder what method Kelland's techs are using."

"You can ask him tomorrow. But I've sometimes found that innovation can get in the way and cause you to ignore the basics." She grimaced. "Though I hope we're going to be too busy tomorrow dealing with that damn ransom to worry about the audios."

"Nice place." Lynch was glancing casually around Jessie's living room. "It looks like her. Sleek, tough, but full of grace."

"I guess it does. When I first saw it, I was fascinated by the things it told me about her that I'd never known before. Jessie's very warm, but she's always been a bit of a mystery."

"I can see that." He was looking at the assortment of objects mounted on Jessie's living room wall. "This is a mystery I'd like to solve."

"Getting some decorating ideas?"

He turned away from the display. "Uh, no. Not my style."

"They're mementos of Jessie's cases."

"Then that does make me want to ask about a few of these. What significance does the tennis ball have? Or the red bow tie?"

"No idea. I just know I wouldn't want anything in my home reminding me of my investigations. Bad dreams do that enough."

Lynch was suddenly behind her, his hands massaging the small of her back. "You've helped a lot of people. Saved a lot of lives. That's what you've got to remember."

"I try." She arched as she felt her tense spinal muscles begin to relax. "Sometimes all I can remember are the ones I wasn't able to help."

"You're going to help Delilah Winter."

"I hope so. But that's another mystery, isn't it? Like Jessie."

"Most interesting people don't let you see everything they are at one time. You have to earn it." He smiled. "Heaven knows that applies to you. How long have I been struggling to see beyond what you show the world?"

"I'm not that complex."

He made a rude sound. "No more than Einstein."

"Bullshit." She gestured to the hall. "Go get some rest. Two guest rooms. I'm occupying the first one. I'll see you first thing in the morning."

His brows rose. "Don't you want to share and keep an eye on me? I know that doctor said my head is safe from imminent explosion, but you can never tell if I'll have a relapse."

"I'll take the chance. You haven't been worried since the moment those bastards shot you. Why should I bother?"

"Because you will, because you whisked me to the ER because you couldn't help yourself. Because you'll probably check on me during the night just to make sure that I'm doing okay. I'd do the same with you." He paused. "And because though you try to fight it, there will always be something that keeps us coming back to each other. You don't want it. It disturbs you, but it's there. Why not just call a truce for right now and accept it? I'm not going to push you or try to persuade you while you're going through this hell about Dee. You know me better than that."

Yes, she did, but that very fact also filled her with bewilderment. She wasn't sure what to answer.

"Or maybe you don't," he said wearily. "I've done everything I can. You'll have to make up your own mind." He turned and strode down the hall toward that second guest room.

# CHAPTER
## 9

It wasn't more than twenty minutes before she followed him down the hall and threw open his door. "Are you awake? I need to talk to you."

"I am now." He rolled over in bed and raised himself on one elbow to look at her framed in the doorway against the light in the hallway. "You've changed your mind about me getting that rest? Come in and tell me about it."

She was already walking toward him. "No, I haven't changed my mind." She sat down on the bed. "Move over, damn you. I won't be long; I just have to get this out. It's been building all day and then you gave me that speech and marched off. Which will probably make certain I get no sleep until I get this straightened out."

Lynch didn't move. "I know this isn't a seduction. Is it an apology?"

"No. Maybe. It could be an explanation."

"Then by all means, go for it."

"Everything you said was true. But that only makes it more confusing for me." Her hand was clenching the sheet. "I went through hell while you were down in those gutters today. I knew you were going to die and there was nothing I could do about it. Then a miracle happened, and you lived through it. But when I saw you lying there unconscious with your head covered in blood, I thought it was only a matter of time."

"I told you that it wasn't serious."

"And I was supposed to believe you?" She reached out and yanked down the sheet to bare his naked abdomen. "When I've seen every one of those scars you received over the years from all those terrorists and murderers who targeted you. You've even joked about some of them."

"It's either that or plastic surgery. Scalpels terrify me."

"See? Shut up. I have to get this out. And then you ignored what had happened to you and I had to do that, too."

"We had no choice."

"Do you think I don't know that?" she asked fiercely. "You were great today, magnificent, no one could have done it better. Anyone else would have been dead. That's why they keep sending for you when no one else can do the job. That's why they'll always send for you. You're unique, Lynch."

"How nice to be appreciated."

"I didn't want you to think that I wasn't grateful and didn't realize that we're lucky to have you." She was trying to smile. "But perhaps I'm not as unique as you are because I'm having trouble adjusting to all the blood and having to chase after you to get you to go to a hospital. Which leads me to the thought that I'm probably not suited to a relationship with you." She shook her head ruefully. "You knew this was coming. We're really nothing alike. And I don't know why you'd want a relationship with me, either."

"Sex, amusement, respect, admiration, mental stimulation." He reached out and touched her lips with his index finger. "And several other facets of character and philosophy that are gradually leading us both to deeper and more mysterious places to explore. I could name a few dozen others if you like." He added softly, "But not now. Truce, Kendra. Let everything else go. I promise we'll settle everything later when we're not walking an emotional tightrope."

She nodded jerkily. "I didn't come in here to back you into a corner on any level. After risking your life in that hideous fiasco today, I thought you deserved honesty and everything to be clear between us." She got to her feet. "That's all I've got to say. Go to sleep." She bent down and brushed her lips over the cut on his temple. "But you're right, I probably will come and check on you sometime during the night. I wouldn't want to waste the effort I put in dragging you to that ER."

"You notice I let you do it." He cupped her face in his two hands and pulled her down and kissed her, long and hard. "That's called compromise and might be the beginning of something truly exceptional." He pushed her away. "Now go get some sleep yourself unless you've changed your mind about the seduction. I can always be persuaded..."

"I know you can." She smiled as she headed for the door. "Good night."

"It's going to be a good day, Kendra," he called after her. "Today was pure hell but things are going to start to go right. Dee is out there, still alive. We're going to find a way to get to her, and it's going to start when we hit the ground running."

She looked back at him over her shoulder. He had absolutely nothing on which to base what he was saying after the defeats they'd suffered lately. But as she gazed at him, in that moment he appeared everything that was strong, powerful, with an iron-hard determination. They were both intelligent and innovative. Why shouldn't it be true? They could *do* this. She smiled at him. "I believe you."

---

A few hours later, Lynch woke to hear the front door slam and then low conversation. It must be Jessie coming home, he thought drowsily because silence followed almost immediately.

Almost.

Because there were other sounds coming from the direction of the living room. Who? Why? He wasn't going to sleep until he found out.

He got out of bed and slipped on his pants and padded barefoot down the hall. He stood in the doorway of the living room to find Kendra connecting her laptop's audio output to Jessie's stereo system.

"What the hell are you doing?"

"You're not supposed to be awake." Kendra looked guiltily over her shoulder. "Go back to bed."

"I've had enough sleep. You know I don't require much. And I was curious when I heard you rattling around in here."

"I don't rattle. I thought I was being quiet."

He shook his head. "No way."

"Well, not everyone is black-ops-trained to notice if someone isn't absolutely silent." He was looking at her, waiting, and she shrugged resignedly. "Okay, I couldn't sleep. Jessie came in exhausted and discouraged because the lab techs hadn't gotten anywhere on the audio of our phone call with the kidnapper. After she went to bed, I decided I'd work on the audio and see what I could come up with. I have a little experience in that area."

"The FBI has an entire lab for this kind of thing. If you wanted to work on it, why didn't you join Jessie and the audio techs there?"

"Jessie was so hopeful that they'd come up with something wonderful. I was hoping, too. But it hasn't happened yet and I'm getting impatient."

He gazed at her speculatively. "And that's the only reason?"

She hesitated and then shrugged. "This is all so bad for Jessie. Dee is special to her in so many ways. She needed something to keep her busy, occupy her mind, and give her that hope."

"And I bet you didn't mention that you knew a 'little' in the area of audio?"

"I'm not an expert like those techs." She made a face. "But

you know I tend to step in and take over when I get involved. I was trying not to be pushy." She smiled. "But someone recently told me this was going to be a good day. I thought I'd help it along a little. I'm more comfortable working with my own gear. And there's a limit to what they can do with their forensic tools. I figure it can't hurt to take another approach." She turned back to her laptop and loaded the audio file into her laptop's Pro Tools audio program. "I need to listen to this conversation again. I have a gnawing feeling about something…"

"About what?"

"I'm almost positive Dee is being held by a woman."

Lynch stared at her for a moment. *"Really?"*

She nodded. "I think we were talking to a woman yesterday morning. And she's most likely wherever Dee is, since she was very quick to come back with the answer to Jessie's question."

"How could you tell? The voice was electronically altered."

"You're right, it was. But not enough to mask some very specific speech patterns. Women's pitch often rises at the ends of sentences, almost like when we ask questions. Men's voices go lower, like when we make definitive statements."

"I never realized that," Lynch said.

"Well, you should. You do it more than just about any man I know."

"Great. Now I'll be self-conscious about every sentence that comes out of my mouth."

"You'll get over it. Supremely confident men always do."

"You're not making me feel any better."

"Women also tend to use more intensifiers in their speech, adding *very* and *so* more than men do."

"That is so very interesting."

"Funny. Women also tend to be more linguistically precise than men. They're less likely to drop *g*'s at the end of their words. And they're far more likely to use *whom* correctly in a sentence than a man."

"Your years in the dark told you all this?"

"Maybe subconsciously. When you're blind, how people speak becomes much more important in how you size them up."

"I can imagine."

"I'm also sensitive to it because of my music therapy work. Some autistic patients respond better to certain vocal patterns than others, just like they respond differently to various types of music."

She placed her hand over the laptop keyboard. "Listen to the telephone conversation and see if what I just told you doesn't line up with what you hear."

Kendra played the recording, which began just a few seconds after she'd picked up the call to her cell phone.

Lynch nodded and smiled as almost every one of the gender indicators was ticked off in the caller's heavily altered speech.

Kendra paused the recording. "See what I mean?"

"Yes. Right on target."

"In most cases it's impossible to reconstruct an electronically altered voice because too much information is discarded. But knowing it's a woman, we can raise the pitch and maybe try out a few options."

Kendra's hands flew over her keyboard and moved a few of the on-screen sliders. She restarted the recording, and this time the voice clearly sounded like a woman.

"That's amazing," Lynch said.

"We have no way of knowing if it's really her pitch, but it's a start." Kendra pushed more sliders and tried again. The voice was still recognizably feminine, but now slightly lower in tone.

"Nice. Does this tell you anything helpful about her?"

"Hard to say. Electronic filters strip away so much of the voice's character. Even if I happened to get the pitch right, we're still missing a lot of what might make her voice and dialect unique. Hopefully they'll have better luck with that at the AV lab." She listened for another moment. "Wait a minute. There was something else there. Something mechanical . . ."

"I didn't hear it."

"Sure you did. You just weren't paying attention."

She moved some sliders on the on-screen equalizer to filter out the vocals. She raised the volume, and they both listened to a low droning sound.

"It's an engine of some kind," Lynch said.

"But *what* kind?"

She moved the cursor back and created a seven-second loop of the sound so that it played continuously. She placed her ear close to the speaker. "It isn't a car. And I don't think it's a truck."

"Forklift?"

"Maybe. It's still being affected by the voice-changing

tech, but the pitch may now be closer to the real thing. It sounds familiar, but I can't quite put my finger on it." She listened for another moment before picking up her phone. "I'll call Kelland. Maybe the AV lab has some thoughts."

———◆———

"We're on it," Kelland said after Kendra brought him up to speed on her audio discoveries. "Our sound guy thinks it may be a tractor."

"I disagree."

"He's pretty good, Kendra."

"I'm sure he is, but I don't believe it's a tractor."

"What do *you* think it is?"

"I don't know." She listened as the audio loop continued to play on her laptop. "But most tractors have an edgier, harsher sound. Tell your sound guy what I told you about the voice being a woman's. Tell him to raise the pitch and give it another listen."

"Sure. But in the meantime, we're sending agents to every farm in a hundred-mile radius."

She sighed. "You may be wasting your resources."

For the first time, she heard him speak in an annoyed tone. "Until I get something more concrete from you, this is how we're playing it, Kendra."

"Understood. Did your techs get anything else off that recording?"

"Not really." His tone softened, as if he'd suddenly become

aware of his harshness. "They didn't even pick up on it being a woman, so thanks for that. We sent a copy off to Washington, so they may have something for us."

"Good. Thanks, Kelland. I'll see you in the morning." She turned back to Lynch. "He's very stubborn."

"Amazing. Know anyone else like that?"

"Shut up." She was frowning. "And you should go back to bed. You may not usually need to sleep, but you know that doctor said you should get extra rest."

"Are you going to bed?"

"Not yet. I'm going to see if I can come up with anything else."

"Then I'll hang out and keep you company." He dropped down on the easy chair and draped his legs over the arm. "When you decide to give it up, I'll go back to bed."

And he probably thought that would be sooner rather than later since she'd practically ordered him to go back to bed. His eyes were twinkling with mischief. He was naked to below the waist and his feet were also bare as he idly swung one back and forth over the chair arm. He was everything that was teasing and arrogant and sexual at this moment.

But he was not going to get what he wanted this time. "Do what you like." She started to play the audio again. "If you go to sleep, I'll cover you with that throw from the couch..."

8:05 A.M.

"Lynch and I are out of here, Jessie." Kendra came into her bedroom. "We're on our way back down to the FBI headquarters."

"You heard from Kelland?" Jessie sat up straight in bed. "Why didn't you wake me?"

"No, we didn't hear from Kelland." She grimaced. "Well, not about the ransom drop. I did talk to him about some work on the audio I did after you came home last night. We agreed that maybe I'd made a little progress on it. Nothing earth shaking. I'll call after we're on the road and tell you about it. But Lynch is impatient to get back and make sure nothing goes wrong with the ransom setup this time. He wants to make sure Noah is toeing the line." She shook her head. "I'll be doing well if I can keep him from volunteering to do the delivery again. I told him that would be a disaster. He's the last person those goons want to see again."

Jessie jumped out of bed. "I'll be right with you."

Kendra shook her head. "You only got to sleep a few hours ago. Come a little later. I'll call and let you know if we hear anything. We spent hours yesterday just waiting around for them to contact us." She turned to go. "It's going to be okay to slow down and just think, Jessie, and not let them dangle us like puppets. That's why I decided to do a little work myself on those audio recordings. I knew it would make me feel as if I had a little control of the situation. I *needed* that feeling. Lynch has me convinced that today is going to be a good day."

"Now he's just got to convince me," Jessie said wryly.

But Kendra had already left the room.

And there was no way that Jessie could go back to sleep. She waited fifteen minutes and then called Kendra to find out what on earth she'd been talking about regarding the audio work she'd done last night. When she hung up, it was with mixed feelings of admiration and depression. What Kendra had accomplished might not have been world shaking, but it was clever, and she'd gotten farther along than anyone else had with those audio recordings. Give her a little more time and there was no telling what she would put together. Jessie slowly headed for the shower. She was tempted to ignore Kendra's advice and just follow them to the FBI office; she felt almost compelled to be there, like the puppets Kendra had called them. The only break had been when Jessie had been in the AV lab watching them trying to put together the calls. That had felt different, as if she was close to accomplishing something. Still, she'd really only been an observer while Kendra had changed the dynamic and actually reached out and started to bring the process under control. Now it was clear Jessie wasn't needed and Kelland, the techs, and Kendra would be able to move forward quite well without her. Which meant sitting around and waiting again. More puppet work.

To hell with that, she told herself impatiently as she jumped out of the shower. As Kendra had said, taking control of the situation was everything. So go down another road and make it her own.

She was reaching for her phone and punching in Colin

Parks's number while she finished drying off. The call went to voicemail, so she dialed again. "Answer me, Parks. I need you, dammit."

He picked up. "You always knew how to push my buttons, Jessie." He was clearly smothering a yawn. "How could I resist a message like that? In all these years I don't remember you ever telling anyone you needed them."

"Then you should have answered me the first time. Meet me at Dee's house and bring the video and audio surveillance recordings that you had your guy copy from there."

Silence. "Copy? I turned over the originals to Kelland the minute the FBI was called into the case."

"I don't doubt it. But not before you had them copied so that you could study them yourself. You wouldn't interfere with the case, but you lost two men that night plus your client. I know you too well. The first thing you'd do would be to go on the hunt yourself."

"Just as you would." He paused. "I wouldn't withhold evidence. I went over those tapes with a fine-tooth comb and there wasn't anything on the copies that Kelland doesn't have."

"Different people sometimes see different things. All I want is to examine the tapes at the sites where they were taken and see if I can notice..." She broke off and then started again, "Look, you want me to say I need your help again? I'll do it. You have to know after yesterday that things aren't going well for us."

"Understatement. I actually felt sorry for Kelland." He added gloomily, "What am I saying? He'll at least be able

215

to get a job. I'm not sure I will. My other clients are abandoning me like a sinking ship. They don't believe I can protect them." He hesitated and then said gruffly, "Okay. I'll meet you at Dee's, but you're not going to find anything that I didn't."

"Thanks, Parks. Twenty minutes." She cut the connection.

---

LIBRARY

DEE'S MANSION

"I told you that you weren't going to find anything." Parks turned off the last video. "Just Dee being Dee. Kidding all the staff. Cracking jokes. Rushing from one appointment to another. None of those videos caught any strangers or anything that wasn't normal to the household." He made a face. "If your household comprised a bunch of teenagers and twenty-something fans whom Dee treated like family instead of employees. Between the blaring music and the arguing about what was best for Dee, it always surprised me that they managed to get any work done."

Jessie knew what he meant. Dee had a large staff: house-keepers, gardeners, drivers, hair and makeup artists, chef, maintenance workers. Probably more than that since Jessie had been here. She shrugged. "You know how estranged she was from her own family. Was it any wonder she wanted to gather a new family around her to push away the loneliness? Besides, they all loved Dee. Most of them were smart and savvy, and if anyone stepped out of line, the other members of the staff found a way to discipline them for it." Her gaze was suddenly narrowed on his face. "At least, that's the way I always found it. Did you run across any employees who caused Dee any problems?"

He shook his head. "It was just a weird conglomeration of people, and Dee was the least temperamental of any of them. I don't know how she even kept track of them."

She grinned. "That was the housekeeper's job. Actually Laura Blair was an accountant before she decided she'd rather work for Dee."

"I didn't know that. I'm surprised you'd remember." His lips twisted sardonically. "You fit right into this menagerie, didn't you? Much better than I did. It's no wonder you blamed me when I lost Dee. I've been thinking maybe I deserved it."

"I was upset. You did a good job taking care of her, Parks. These people who snatched her have funds and people and they've spent some time planning it. I haven't done such a good job myself of getting her back." She grimaced. "And I'm the one who picked you for this job, so I've no right to blame you."

"That's very generous of you. How much of it do you believe?"

She smiled. "Maybe forty percent."

He chuckled. "I can always trust you to be bluntly honest with me. But it's one of the things that made me run like hell whenever I was tempted to try to get you in bed."

"Nah, it wasn't. You could have taken the honesty, but I

think I intimidated you. I affect some people that way. You should have bitten the bullet and just gone for it. I adore sex. We could have had a hell of a time."

He tilted his head. "Is it too late?"

"I don't know. We'll have to see." She got to her feet. "Will you make me a copy of these tapes and leave it on the desk? I'm getting edgy about not hearing from Kendra about the drop yet. I should get back to FBI headquarters, but I want to say hello to some of the staff before I go."

He nodded ruefully. "I'll do anything to prove you don't intimidate me."

She smiled. "Thanks, Colin."

She left the library and started up the grand staircase in search of Laura, the housekeeper. Her gaze raked the beautiful beige- and cream-colored tiles and wonderful stained-glass windows that constituted the foyer. Everything about this mansion was gleaming and rich and as sunny as Dee had wanted it to be. But none of it was really Dee. This was all window dressing for her career and the parties that were part of her image.

"What are you doing here?" Laura was hurrying down the staircase toward her. "Did you hear something about Dee?"

"No." Jessie gave her a quick hug. "Maybe later today. I just wanted to say hello and ask if there was anything you think I should know about what was going on here during those last days."

Laura shook her head. "It was the usual chaos. Well, maybe not quite. Dee was composing more than she usually did. Some really good stuff, Jessie. It was like John Williams meets Andrew Lloyd Webber."

"That's quite a combination. And definitely not at all her usual style."

"But maybe it was heading in that direction?" She shook her head. "I don't know. It was just touching and beautiful and...different. *She* was different."

"I noticed that, too," she said gently. "I was blaming it on growing pains. But I was really asking about staff or any of her friends who might have dropped in to see her lately."

"Like I said, she was doing a lot of composing. She was mostly in the garden or at the beach. I can't remember her inviting anyone here to the house."

"I know the detectives must have questioned you all after the kidnapping. You didn't notice anyone strange on the grounds?"

"We're all pretty strange ourselves, Jessie. They'd blend right in," she said dryly. "But you know how careful I am about accepting new hires or contractors on the property. I didn't do it this time, either. And none of our guys saw anyone suspicious on the grounds during that period."

Jessie nodded. "I had to check." She gave Laura's hand a squeeze and started past her up the staircase. "I'm going to go and look around Dee's bedroom. I won't be long."

"Those detectives and FBI guys were in there for hours," she said sourly. "And I stayed right there with them to make sure they didn't bother any of her stuff. Cops or not, she was such a big celebrity they might have wanted trophies." Her eyes suddenly misted. "I said 'was,' past tense. You make sure that doesn't come true. There's nothing past tense about Dee."

"No there isn't," Jessie said. "And Kendra was just saying before I came here that this was going to be a good day."

"Right." She continued down the stairs. "Let me know before you leave if there's anything else you need. Everything's just the way she left it."

And when Jessie opened the bedroom door a minute later, she could see that Laura had been telling the truth. Just the way she left it. It wasn't like any of the other rich, sunny, spectacular rooms in the house. There was only a double bed with a simple, colorful patchwork bedspread and several pillows tossed against the oak headboard. Across the room, there was a carved desk that Jessie remembered picking up for Dee on the first tour after she'd come to work for her. Set against the wall, near the bed, was the guitar that she treasured. That Gibson Firebird instrument was the only expensive item in the room. Other than that it could have still been the room of that teenage girl in the cramped apartment who had sung her songs only for herself before the world had discovered the great Delilah Winter and turned her into a commodity.

She went to the nightstand and picked up a framed picture of Dee and her on a day when Jessie had taken her to the set of one of Jessie's stunt movies. There was a second photo that had a shot of the two of them in Paris. Still another of them sitting cross-legged together on the corner of the stage while they listened to a John Williams rehearsal at the Hollywood Bowl. No photos at all of Dee's mother. Jessie could feel the tears sting her eyes as she put the photo she'd picked up back down on the nightstand.

She turned and went over to the desk, looking down at several sheets of music scores tossed hurriedly, carelessly, over the carved surface as if Dee had just pushed away from the desk and left them. There was another pile of scores set neatly in a box on the corner. Which were the rejects?

She picked up one of the sheets on the desk. Scrawled at the top was a title. "Sun Song."

She spent a lot of time in the garden.

Jessie smiled as she put down the sheet. Music written with boldness and passion as if Dee couldn't wait to put down the words and music. Not that neat pile she'd stacked to consider at a later date.

"Sun Song."

She suddenly stiffened as she gazed down at the title.

She spent a lot of time in the garden . . .

Then she was running out of the room and down the staircase. "Laura!"

She found her on the patio. "Laura, I was just thinking about something you said. Or maybe it was the *way* you said it. Anyway, it struck me and I had to ask you."

"What are talking about?" She frowned. "Was it something you found in Dee's room?"

"Yes. Not really. It was that new music. 'Sun Song.' You were talking about Dee spending time in the garden. I was asking you about strangers and you told me how careful you were about accepting new hires or construction." Laura was nodding, and Jessie held up her hand. "But then you said something else and it didn't occur to me it sounded odd until just now. You said, 'And I didn't do it this time, either.' Why did

221

you say it like that? Did someone ask you to accept a new hire or a different construction company during that period?"

Her eyes widened. "Not during that time, maybe a week or so before. Miguel Santiago, the gardener. He said he had a friend from the orphanage where he grew up who needed a job. I told him what I tell everyone—that I was sorry, but they'd have to go through the same checks and references as any other applicant. No exceptions. Miguel dropped it immediately." She frowned. "You know he's a good guy, Jessie. That was why I didn't even think of mentioning it. It was a nonissue."

"Maybe. I need to talk to him. Where can I find him?"

"The rose garden. Do you want me to go with you?"

"No, thanks, Laura." She was already out the French doors and striding down the paths toward the roses. She could see Santiago working in the garden near the fountain. He was a young man in his early twenties.

He looked up with a wary expression. "Hello, Jessie. Have you heard anything about Dee?"

She shook her head. "I just came to ask you about the man you asked Laura to consider hiring a few weeks ago. What do you know about him?"

"Not much." He moistened his lips. "I didn't remember him from the home, but that's not unusual. There were so many of us there. He seemed like a nice guy. Some of the other guys at the orphanage had told him about my cushy job here with Dee and he thought he'd try his luck. He told me that if I helped him get the job, I wouldn't regret it. He even offered to pay me half of his first week's salary."

222

"How generous. What was his name?"

"Jack Caseman."

She wrote it down in her notebook. "How long was he here with you?"

"About half a day. He helped me with the weeding. We worked and joked and shot the breeze about the teachers and people we knew at the home. I told him I wasn't sure I could manage to get him the job, but he helped me anyway. Like I said, he was a nice guy."

And while he was obligingly helping with the weeding, he could look around and find out about the staff and schedule. "And he left immediately after you checked with Laura and was told that he wasn't going to be hired?"

He nodded. "He was disappointed, but he thanked me, shook my hand, and left." He paused. "This isn't about Dee, is it? He never asked anything about her. He only said it would be nice to work with someone famous. That's what everyone says."

"It might be about Dee. If you can think of anything else about this Jack Caseman, I'd like you to call me."

He hesitated. "Did I do something wrong?"

"Only trusted someone you shouldn't, but we all do that sometimes. Don't worry. We'll work this out. Since the kidnapping didn't actually take place here, evidently Caseman's visit was purely exploratory. You might have actually been a help, Miguel."

She hoped she was telling the truth. She'd only know after she went over those tapes again.

She turned and ran down the path toward the library.

Twenty minutes later she shoved the tapes aside. Not as promising as she'd hoped, but then she hadn't really expected them to be. She spent another thirty minutes on the phone checking out Jack Caseman's credentials at the orphanage. Nonexistent. Still, that didn't mean she'd necessarily come up with zeros; she just had to dig deeper.

But she had neither the time nor the authority to bring that search to a speedy conclusion. So find someone who did. Kelland? She didn't want to take anyone away from the active job involved in bringing Dee home. She hesitated and then quickly punched in a number. "Metcalf? Jessie Mercado. I was told you were loaned to the L.A. FBI for the duration of the investigation. I bet it's driving you crazy drifting around like a lost puppy."

"You might say that," Metcalf said warily. "Though I offered to go."

"I think I've run across a lead that might turn into something important. But I can't follow up and I need someone good, efficient, and very fast to get out here to Dee's house and help me. Are you interested?"

"Definitely." Metcalf gave a deep, profound sigh of relief. "Thank you."

◆

LOS ANGELES REGIONAL FBI OFFICE

"We'll be there." Kendra ended the call she'd just received from Jessie and turned to Lynch. "Jessie just pulled into the parking lot and wants us to meet her at the AV lab."

"Why?"

"A lead." She was already pushing her way through the crowd of agents in the hall outside Kelland's office. "Something she ran across at Dee's house. What difference does it make? We're not getting anywhere standing here waiting for those bastards to contact us. It's almost noon and they're still playing their games."

"Easy." He took her elbow and nudged her toward the elevator. "I know you're scared, but this stall doesn't mean they're not going to go through with it. It's much more likely that you and Jessie were right about them being pissed off and trying to punish us for not obeying orders."

"That sounded much more reasonable before we had to sit here all morning and wait to hear if Dee is alive or dead." She made an impatient gesture. "Forget I said that. My optimism is sagging a bit right now. I'll try to look on the bright side. Noah came through with the additional five million. We're ready to deliver the ransom. Now Jessie has come up with something positive. That should prove it's going to be a good day."

"Exactly." As they got on the elevator, he punched the button for the AV lab. "And Jessie would never lead us down a wrong path."

———◆———

"I don't know if it's going to do us any good or not," Jessie said when she met them at the door of the lab. She quickly went over the details of her talk with Miguel. "But there's a chance and we haven't been able to identify any other members of the

225

gang. The man who showed up at Dee's house looking for a job was definitely bogus. I called the orphanage and there was never a Jack Caseman registered there. But he knew the names of some of the teachers, even some of the students Miguel knew before he left there. Caseman had done his research and was well prepared when he came to see Miguel." She nodded at the techs. "They're having trouble with the trace or ID on the phone calls because of static interference. But I just gave them a copy of the audiotape taken the day Caseman was schmoozing Miguel in the garden. It might not be the same person, but it could be. Anyway, it was much more clear than the phone calls."

"Just the audio?" Kendra asked. "You couldn't get the video of him?"

"No video. I told you he was prepared and very careful not to be seen. He did a masterful job of hiding his face from the cameras. But he could hardly spend half a day with Miguel without talking to him and I guess he considered it safe."

"Not if he has a record," Lynch said. "And I'd bet it's one that will pop up no matter how nice a guy Miguel thought him. The minute we get it, we'll put it through facial recognition and get a list of known associates." He took a step toward the techs and demanded, "How soon?"

"Leave them alone," Jessie said. "They said not long. And we're not desperate yet. I called Metcalf before I left Dee's place and set him to trying to locate anyone besides Miguel on the property who could find us a video. Otherwise, we'll just have to have Miguel go to the sketch artist. At any rate, I don't want you intimidating these guys, Lynch."

"Moi?" He tapped his chest. "I'm a pussycat."

"With tiger instincts."

"It takes one to know one."

Jessie nodded wryly. "Yeah, I know about intimidation. I had a talk with Colin about it earlier today. But this is my lead, so you'll do what I say, Lynch."

He shrugged and dropped down into a chair beside the door. "Just trying to add a little encouragement."

"After lecturing me on being patient," Kendra said.

"That was different." He grinned. "That was a case of hurry up and wait. This is something I can get my teeth into."

"And we're back to the tiger instinct again," Kendra said. "Do you think I don't know how pissed off you were to get so close to those bastards and then have the chance yanked away from you?"

His smile faded. "You can't say I tried to hide it. And there's no way in hell Kelland is going to let me deliver the ransom this time. I was a little too efficient and probably left a bad taste in their mouths. They might even set up another method of delivery. Which leaves me twiddling my thumbs unless I can figure another way to take them down." His gaze shifted to Jessie. "So I'll follow your lead, if that's the only way I can do it. Give me your marching orders."

Jessie blinked. "Now, that's an offer I'll probably never receive again."

"Yep. No promises." His gaze went back to the techs. "So are you sure you don't want a little help right now?"

"I'm sure. I can wait until they—" The ringtone on her phone was sounding, and she looked down at the ID. She tensed. "Kelland. Why the hell is he calling me? Unless they told him—" Her hand was shaking as she pressed the microphone. "Jessie Mercado. Have you heard about the proof of life on Dee, Kelland?"

"Yes. No. Maybe," Kelland said curtly. "I've just received a call and they say they're ready to deal. But they won't talk to me or Lynch. They want to give proof of life info only to you, Jessie."

"What?" She stiffened in shock. "Why?"

"How the hell do I know? Maybe because you were the one who was furnishing Dee with the question to answer before."

"Or it could be that she's already dead and they just want to twist the knife." Her teeth bit into her lower lip. "The bastards would realize the shock value would be that much more terrible if they told one of her best friends that they'd killed her."

Kelland was silent. "I won't deny that's a possibility. But you're not going to refuse to come up here to my office and listen to what they have to say."

"No, I can't do that," she said hoarsely. "You know I have to hear it. I'll be right there." She cut the connection. "You heard him," she said to Lynch and Kendra as she turned toward the door. "I seem to be in demand. I'll let you know as soon as I find out why."

"I'm going with you." Kendra was following her. "I won't let you face this alone."

"I wasn't going to argue," Jessie said. "I'm feeling a bit shaky at the moment." She glanced at Lynch. "You're getting your marching orders a bit sooner than you thought. Stay here and get those results for me on Caseman. I might want them very badly after I'm finished with this call."

"You'll have them," Lynch said grimly. "But I'm betting that they weren't stupid enough to kill Dee. Now get out of here and get that proof of life."

# CHAPTER

# 10

The hall outside Kelland's office was just as crowded as when Kendra had left it a short time ago, but Jessie ignored them. She held open the door and whisked Kendra inside the room.

"I'm here, Kelland." She slammed the door and came toward his desk. "I brought Kendra because I didn't know whether or not you'd invited me to a private party. Have you?"

"No." He gestured to a chair. "Sit down, Kendra. Glad to have you here. I don't know what to expect from these jokers. They keep changing the rule book."

Kendra nodded. "This is the first time they haven't contacted us through my cell phone."

"Who am I supposed to talk to?" Jessie asked. "Some message on the mausoleum wall or a real person?"

"It's not the mausoleum." He pulled her down in the chair in front of his computer. "And since the audio bears a strong resemblance to the one we had to suffer through at the drop site, I don't know how real he is." He grimaced. "Or *she* is. I don't think we'd better indicate we believe her to be a woman. The less they know about the investigation, the better. We'll refer to her as masculine."

"Whatever." Jessie looked at Kendra. "Audio strikes again?"

"Not entirely," Kelland said. "The goon who called me appears to be the same guy, but when I went back on the line after contacting you to tell him you'd be here to talk to him, he said you wouldn't be talking to him." He met her eyes. "He said you'd be talking to Delilah Winter."

"Thank God." Jessie closed her eyes for an instant. "Not a trick? That would be so cruel."

"Yes, it would. But you'll be able to tell for yourself in the next couple minutes. I don't know what they're doing. They refused us flat when we asked to talk to her before and now, they're practically pushing Dee at us on Skype."

"Then talk to her." Kendra leaned forward and took Jessie's hand. "It's *Dee*. Stop this idiotic questioning. You can see if she's well and maybe she can tell us something."

"I seem to have my orders." Jessie turned to Kelland. "Turn on the Skype."

He flicked on the monitor. "Special Agent Kelland. I have Jessie Mercado. You wished to speak to her regarding the new arrangements for the ransom?"

"I have my instructions." The voice was sour. "I obey instructions, unlike some other people. You want proof of life? I'll show you Delilah. She has her instructions, too. Don't make us kill her because you want to trick us again."

"I'd never do that. Just let me see her."

The screen suddenly blacked out and then came back on.

Dee!

The lights in the room were dim, and the walls and the chair on which Dee was sitting were equally blurred and indistinct. For a moment Jessie couldn't be certain it was really her. Then there was a sudden close-up and Jessie could see that she was manacled to a chair.

Dee's red hair was tousled, and she was a little pale, but no one could mistake those delicate features or blazing eyes. Particularly when she looked directly at the camera and made a face. "Jessie? They said I was going to talk to you. But the lighting values here aren't what I'm accustomed to. If you're going to ransom me, you should really insist that I be given my due."

"I'll take that under consideration." Jessie was trying to keep her voice steady. "How are you? Did they hurt you?"

"No, though that sedative they kept giving me was no fun. Of course, neither were the people here." Her voice lowered to a mock whisper. "Which I can't discuss on pain of dire consequences. They have no sense of humor."

"I can imagine. And sometimes your humor is a bit off the wall, so could I ask you not to demonstrate any practical jokes that might offend them?"

"I suppose I could hold my tongue. I hear they screwed up my ransom. They want me to tell you not to do that again." She looked directly at the camera. "I *miss* you. They're not the nicest kidnappers. If I'd had my choice, I wouldn't have picked them." Then suddenly she lifted her chin and was smiling.

233

"You can tell I don't like this place. They need lessons on how to treat a star. Remember when you took me on that picnic to show me where you did those stunt jumps? You gave me caviar and champagne and I got a little drunk."

Jessie tensed. What the hell? Then she smiled back at Dee. "More than a little. You were just a teenager. I almost lost my job."

"Yeah. But I would have saved it."

"I know you would. But now we have to concentrate on saving you. I promise we won't screw up that ransom again."

"Hey, I know I can count on you. And I always remember everything you taught me." A pause. "They're telling me I have to go now. Goodbye, Jessie. Be very careful." She cut the connection.

The next moment the first voice came back on the line. "So touching." The words dripped sarcasm. "You can see she's healthy as a horse and we've been treating her better than she deserves. I'll contact you tomorrow with complete instructions, and this time there won't be any slipups. No media coverage, no leaks, and you'll be ready to move the minute we give you the word."

"Which one of my men do you want to handle the drop?"

"Men? I thought I'd made that clear. Jessie Mercado is handling the drop. She's a private investigator and capable of doing what needs to be done. Besides, all that touching bullshit shouldn't be wasted. She obviously cares about our Delilah and would never risk getting her killed."

"I don't think that—" Kelland stopped. "He hung up. I guess you're the chosen one, Jessie. Sorry."

"I'm not." She drew a deep breath. "I'm not sorry about any of it. It went terrifically." She turned to Kendra. "She looked a little pale but otherwise okay. Don't you think?"

Kendra nodded. "And the same Dee. Lord, it was good to see her." She gazed quizzically at her. "But I can't believe you let Dee get drunk when she was under your care. She was only sixteen when you were first hired to protect her."

"You know I wouldn't let her drink even if Dee had tried to get me to do it. Which she'd never do in a million years. Dee doesn't drink at all. She saw her mother stagger home too many times after she'd dragged Dee to publicity parties when she was just a kid. She doesn't make a big thing of it, but it's always something nonalcoholic in those glasses."

Kendra nodded. "I thought I remembered you telling me that." Her eyes narrowed on Jessie's face. "So what was going on between the two of you?"

"Just what you thought would go on when you told me to quit being scared and dive in." She was smiling. "I found out she was alive and well..." She paused. "And maybe a few other things that were even more interesting."

"What?" Kelland asked. "You two might know what's going on, but I don't."

"Jessie?" Kendra asked. "Caviar and champagne?"

"Dee was trying to tell me something. She coded it with those two gourmet foods she knew I'd recognize as a signal. Then she went on to mention that picnic I took her on right after I started to work for her. I still had a last commitment to fulfill to do a stunt in a film about World War One, and

I took her along as a treat." She was frowning thoughtfully. "That had to be the purpose of the message."

"What message?" Kelland asked.

"I'm thinking about it." She was going over the words in her mind, trying to isolate and clarify. "It was a picnic? It has something to do with me being a stuntwoman. Champagne...celebration?" Then it all came together. "The photo. I only took her to watch me do a stunt the one time. She insisted on taking a photo of it. She loved that photo. She had it framed and kept it on her nightstand. I saw it when I was at her place today. For some reason she wanted me to look at that photo."

Kelland got to his feet. "Then let's go get it."

"I don't have to go anywhere," Jessie said. "That day meant something to me, too. Do you think I wouldn't keep a copy of it for myself?" She reached in her pocket and pulled out her wallet. "Mine is much smaller than the one she had framed, but all the detail is there." She pulled out the photo and threw it on the desk. "It's a kind of silly picture but it was a happy day and Dee kept giggling and saying she was going to use it to blackmail me with the rest of the team." She made a face. "I admit it would have destroyed my reputation if they ever saw me in that World War One pilot's getup. The movie was all about aerial combat, and I had a couple parachute jumps." The photo was of Dee and Jessie leaning against the propeller of an ancient single-seater plane. Both were convulsed in laughter. Jessie felt her throat tighten as she gazed at Dee's luminous expression. "Yeah, it was a great day."

"And what she was trying to tell you?" Kelland asked. "Where was it taken?"

"At a farm near Bakersfield. The movie company rented the entire farm so we could get low enough on the aerial battle scenes." She wrinkled her nose. "And of course my wonderful parachute jump, which was as melodramatic as it was ridiculously grandiose. I won't tell you how many times they made me do it over. No wonder Dee was practically in hysterics." She tapped the photo with her index finger. "You're thinking she might have been trying to tell me she's somewhere near Bakersfield or this movie set?" She shook her head. "The Ventura wildfires destroyed the farm and surrounding acreage two years ago. I remember because Dee went down and gave a benefit for the survivors that summer."

"Then what was it?" Kendra murmured. "Dee's smart. She wouldn't have wasted her time if she hadn't believed she could help us."

Jessie shrugged. "It's just the two of us...laughing and having a great time. The only thing that stands out is how utterly ridiculous I look in that leather jacket, huge goggles, and jodhpur pants."

"Then let's look at it," Kendra said. "You were supposed to be a World War One pilot standing next to that vintage plane?"

Jessie nodded. "That's right."

"Then it has to be the plane," Kendra said slowly. "She's trying to tell us that where she's being held has something to do with a plane, or perhaps an airport."

"Shit. That's a bit vague, Kendra," Jessie said. "How many

airports are there in the California, Arizona, Nevada area? As for planes, that goes up into the stratosphere."

"I'm just the interpreter here. I'm sure Dee did the best she could to give us a clue we could use. It might not even be a plane. I only thought it was the most logical." She paused. "And I believe we shouldn't publicize any deductions we make from anything Dee told you today. Where there's this much media coverage, there's bound to be leaks. Leaks could be very dangerous for Dee. You were warned about that, Kelland."

"Since there's no evidence on which to base this pure guesswork, I'm not about to hand out any leaks to the media," he said sarcastically. "If I can find something more concrete, then we'll discuss it." His gaze shifted to Jessie. "You're still determined to go along with the ransom delivery?"

She nodded. "I couldn't do anything else. That asshole was right about me. Another thing that I learned from that conversation with Dee is that she knows what she's facing and it's scaring her. But she also said that she remembered everything I've taught her." She took a deep breath. "I'm an overachiever and I taught her a lot. I know she's going to try to use it. That's her nature." She moistened her lips. "It could get her killed. You're damn right I'll be there for her."

———◆———

Charlotte received a telephone call at 1·40 P.M. that lasted only a few minutes. "Of course I understand. Do you think I'm a fool?" She listened for a moment more. "No, I'll have no problem taking care of the girl. I did just fine without him.

You're the one who sent him." She pressed to disconnect and turned to Dee. "It appears I'm going to be stuck with you again. Won't that be fun?"

"Delightful."

"I thought you'd feel that way." She got to her feet and went to throw open the exterior door. "Dorset!"

"You don't have to bellow," Dorset growled. "What does she need now?"

"Nothing that I can't get for her. You were just a convenience. Go get your stuff and get out of here. You're supposed to meet someone called Paul at the warehouse. They want to make sure to have enough men when this drop goes down."

"*Yes*," Dorset said eagerly. "I thought they'd be calling me back. I was too valuable to be pushed out of the deal like that. They were only waiting until they decided what move to make."

"Yeah, that's it." Charlotte's tone was ironic. "After the last mess you all made, more likely he thought you could hardly do any worse."

"I'm done listening to you." He turned to Dee. "I'd feel sorry for you having to put up with this ugly dragon bitch, but you've had it so good all your life that it's your turn to have it rough. Hell, who knows, you can never tell what's going to happen. You might even get out of this alive." He grabbed his duffel. "But don't count on it." He slammed the door behind him.

"At least we agree on one thing." Charlotte shrugged as she turned away. "By all means, pay no attention to anything that fool tells you." Her voice was mockingly caustic. "From now on I'm the one in control, the only one of importance in your life. He doesn't matter at all any longer..."

———◆———

Kendra got the call Jessie had told her to expect from Metcalf late on the afternoon of that same day. She checked the ID. "It's him," she told Lynch as she punched the access. "Where the hell have you been, Metcalf?"

"Missed me?"

"Okay, let's not get carried away."

"Of course not. I just wanted to give you an update on the lead Jessie gave me. Is she around?"

"I think she's somewhere in the building, picking out her protective gear for the money drop. After what happened to Lynch, we've got to hope she'll have head-to-toe body armor."

Silence. "Money drop? Shit. Jessie didn't mention anything about her doing the money drop when I talked to her."

"She probably didn't know it at the time. Things have been moving very fast since yesterday. We've been told we'll be getting exact instructions any time now. But you can give the update to me. In case you haven't heard, there's a rumor going around that we're on the same team. I could use some awesome news right now."

"Awesome is my middle name, Kendra."

"You're getting carried away again."

"No, I'm not. I followed up on the lead Jessie gave me about that guy who briefly worked in Delilah's house. I talked to her employees and came up with zilch. Then I started canvassing her neighbors on the same street and got security camera footage from most of them."

She gave a low whistle. "Great idea."

"You bet. I got footage from two neighbors' cameras of the guy when he left that afternoon. He parked two blocks away, but I have a shot of him climbing into his pickup truck."

"Tell me we have a license plate."

"We have his license plate. Razor-sharp, too."

Kendra sighed with relief. "Awesome is truly your middle name."

"We also have a name and address from the auto registration. Has the name James Dorset come up in the investigation yet?"

She glanced at Lynch and then shook her head. "No, I think we'd have been told if it had."

"I didn't think so. I called around, and Dee's friends and household staff didn't know the name, either."

"You've been busy. Should we pay him a visit?"

"Funny you should say that. I'm at his address now. It's an apartment in Burbank. It's empty. The handyman says he cleared out three weeks ago. No forwarding address."

"Damn. What do we know about him?"

"He's twenty-eight years old, but he looks younger on the photo in his driver's license I got from the DMV. He grew up in Gilroy and has a bit of a record. Petty theft, assault and battery, nothing major. No known associates."

"Is that all?" Kendra asked. "Anything else?"

"You don't want much," Metcalf said. "Jessie asked me to do my best to find this son of a bitch and I not only found him, I wrapped him up and put a bow on him."

"But you haven't found him," she said absently. "Not yet. Still, you've come very close. You've done great. Jessie will be over the moon as soon as I tell her. I just wanted to make certain that I had the details right."

"As right as I can get them. I have to call Kelland now and report into him." He added dryly, "Which I should have done before this. I just wanted to get the word to you first. But now I can turn Kelland's agents loose on Dorset and see what they can come up with. No young guy like Dorset lives in a vacuum. We'll find the others." He paused. "I did good?"

"Terrific. Now call Kelland and make certain he knows how terrific you are so that he won't send you back to San Diego. We need you here."

"That won't happen. Once I officially turn over this lead, I'll be golden. Bye, Kendra." He cut the connection.

She jumped to her feet and was halfway to the door. "I've got to talk to Jessie."

"Phone her," Lynch suggested.

"I tried before. I probably still won't be able to get in touch with her. Kelland has her closeted with those same Kevlar wardrobe guys he tried to saddle you with. Since she won't have specially tailored body armor like you did, she'll probably end up going with the standard issue." She added grimly, "But I'm going to make damn sure she wears a helmet."

Then she was gone.

It took her a few minutes to locate the room where Jessie was being outfitted. Judging by the seven or eight guys surrounding her, it was going to take another couple minutes to overcome arguments and resistance to actually get to talk to her. It would be easier just to let Jessie handle it. "Tell them to get out," she called across the room. "Metcalf called and you're going to like the news."

Jessie went tense. "Dee?"

"No. But we're closer."

In seconds Jessie had all the agents in the room whisked out into the hall with lightning efficiency that bordered on brutality. Then she whirled on Kendra. "Talk."

When Kendra had finished giving her Metcalf's report, she said with a grin, "Stop frowning, Jessie. You're the one who pulled Metcalf into this and he did a great job. It's not his fault we want the universe and he could only give us the world. We're going to get Kelland to fill in the rest of what we need."

"But it might not be in time." Jessie glanced around the dressing room with all the body armor scattered on chairs and tables. "I was hoping not to have to use all this crap. I was thinking maybe a quick ambush that would let us whisk Dee away from the bad guys before we had to run any risk to her." She shrugged. "Though after listening to her on that Skype call, I'd really like to go after that bitch holding her. She sounded afraid, and Dee's not easy to scare."

"Maybe it was only a pretense," Kendra said. "She was trying to fool them throughout the entire conversation. Maybe that was only another trick."

"Are you trying to make me feel better?"

"Yes, of course I am. But it still might be true. You know as well as I do how brave she is and how hard she'd fight to save herself..." She hesitated. "And to save you, Jessie. You're a team, a partnership, and she loves you." She shook her head. "But you know all that stuff."

"Yeah, I know all that stuff." Her voice was husky. "Just as I know we're a pretty good team ourselves, Kendra." She cleared her throat. "That's why I'm going to ask you to do me a favor. Sometimes things can go south. I don't know what to expect from those freaks." She hesitated. "If anything happens to me, I want you to make sure Dee still comes home."

Kendra gazed at her, stricken. It only lasted for an instant before it turned to outrage. "You *idiot*. That sounds like something Lynch might say. Nothing is going to happen to you. How many times have you saved my ass when I thought I was dead? How often did you get medals for saving your buddies in Afghanistan? How much more of a reason do you have for saving Dee? There's no way you'd let her die." Her voice was starting to shake. "Any more than I'd let you die. So just stop talking bullshit." She took three steps toward her before enveloping her in a fierce embrace. Then she turned on her heel and headed for the door. She stopped and gave a last glance at the body armor scattered over the room. "In fact, you're so tough you'd hardly need all this junk, but I suppose you'd better wear it."

"You think?" Jessie's lips were twitching. "I appreciate the vote of confidence, but I'll definitely wear it."

"Except for the headgear, I told Lynch I was going to make

sure they'd fit for you. Don't you dare wear it." Her hands clenched into fists at her sides. "You go home and get your motorcycle helmet and wear that instead. It will remind you of who you are."

Her smile ebbed and then vanished. "The invincible Jessie Mercado?"

"You've got it. Just don't you forget it."

"I'd have trouble doing that after today, Kendra." Her voice was uneven. "But if I need reinforcement, may I come back and let you remind me?"

"Nah, that wouldn't be you." She opened the door. "You don't need anyone. Except maybe a friend. Then you come to me."

After she'd closed the door, she had to wait a minute to gather strength to control her emotions. She'd purposely not let herself think of the danger Jessie would be confronting until that moment when she'd shocked her with that unexpected request. Now she was having trouble thinking of anything else. It wasn't that Jessie was a woman and more vulnerable than Lynch. Jessie would not accept vulnerability. It was probably just that Kendra identified with her as another woman. Or maybe in that moment when she'd mentioned how afraid Dee must be, Kendra had realized no matter how strong Jessie seemed, she was also terribly human...

Screw it. Try to cover all the bases. She quickly punched in a call to Lynch. "I don't think it's enough."

"What are you talking about? Jessie wasn't happy with Metcalf's report?"

"Happy enough. But she said something about how afraid

245

Dee must be of that bitch who's holding her captive. It reminded me that maybe we should have been concentrating more on her. Who is she? How much of a danger is she to Dee? She acts as if she has a certain importance. Will you ask the techs to see if they can nail anything more down about her?" She had another thought. "And contact those Swiss AV experts you mentioned and see if they can pull a rabbit out of the hat that Kelland's guys are missing."

"You *are* worried." He paused. "I'd tell you I'd get right on it, but I have to confess I already gave them a call after you went to bed last night."

"Without discussing it with me?"

"You were doing great. I didn't want to disturb your flow. But more is always better, and the head of that Swiss lab owed me a favor."

"Someone always owes you a favor."

"Yeah, ain't it grand?"

"This time I won't argue with you. Did he give you any time frame?"

"Soon. Very soon." He paused. "You're not coming back down here?"

"No, I think I'll stick with Kelland and his agents until Jessie's ready to leave. Though she'll probably be so busy that she won't even know I'm around."

"Oh, I imagine she'll know you're there for her. I always do." He was silent. "Not a bad idea," he said gently. "I'll see you there."

Kendra gazed out the window as a rare evening rain shower fell over Westwood. She was part of a large group packed into a twelfth-floor FBI conference room. At the front of the room, the lectern had been shoved aside in favor of a small table that now held a leather bag filled with the twenty-five-million-dollar ransom. Calderon's armored car security officers stood next to it, though their authority was somewhat neutered by the empty holsters at their sides. They'd been forced to surrender their firearms before entering the building.

"Hope they don't call the ransom drop on account of rain," Metcalf cracked.

"Not funny, Metcalf." Kendra turned from the window. Metcalf was standing next to Lynch, Jessie, and Kelland. Half a dozen other agents were hovering anxiously nearby. Noah Calderon was in the corner of the room typing furiously on his phone. Kendra also knew that, in the large parking lot in front of the building, at least forty more FBI agents and police officers waited in their fleet of cars and tactical vans.

Lynch motioned toward the bag. "They have twenty-five million reasons not to cancel. We'll hear from them one way or another. The only question is how."

"We know they know how to reach me and Kelland," Kendra said.

Lynch called out to Noah, "No trackers this time, right?"

Noah pocketed his phone. "No trackers. But don't take my word for it."

Kelland nodded. "We didn't. The guys downstairs spent an hour sweeping it. It's totally clean."

"It's almost as if you didn't trust me." Noah actually looked hurt. "I've done everything I could to make sure that stupid betrayal wouldn't happen again."

Jessie rolled her eyes. "Don't even start." She was dressed in a black Kevlar suit, much like those worn by FBI tactical teams. She flexed her arms to ease the stiffness.

"Is the jacket okay?" Lynch said.

"Fine. Maybe not up to the standards of your Abu Dhabi armor specialist, but it'll work. It's very lightweight. I wore something similar in Afghanistan." She turned to Kelland. "Still no leaks to the press?"

"Not as far as we know. This won't be like last time. The only people following you should be us." He stepped closer to Jessie. "You know...you don't have to do this."

Her lips tightened. "They asked for me."

"I know. And the more I think of that, the less I like it. We don't have to accept their every term. We can negotiate. We have a roomful of agents here, and any one of them will do it."

"No, it should be me. I have to do this."

"Okay, it's your—"

She held up her hand to cut him off. "Don't say it's my funeral."

He smiled. "I was going to say it's your decision. But if that's where your head is at, maybe another reason to reconsider." He checked his watch and called out to a young assistant. "You're sure my phone has been patched through to ring in here?"

"We won't need your phone," Jessie said.

"What makes you say that?"

She raised her iPhone for everyone to see. The screen was illuminated with the caller ID: DELILAH SAYS HI.

"Just like mine the other day," Kendra murmured.

The room quieted as Jessie pressed the button to put the call on speaker. "This is Jessie Mercado."

"Hello, Jessie." It was the same electronically altered voice they'd heard from the earlier call—the one Kendra had identified as a woman.

Kendra exchanged a quick glance with Lynch. He nodded.

"So, are we gonna do this?" Kendra could see Jessie struggling to rein in her anger and impatience.

"Yes, we are. I'm sure you're surrounded by a small army of L.A.'s best and brightest. Hello, everyone. I'm going to ask you fine people to exercise some restraint this evening. I'll be asking Jessie to start our adventure downtown, at the Art District Dog Park. She must be alone. I don't want to see any of you within two blocks of her. And I don't want to see any helicopters in the area."

Kelland stepped closer to the phone. "I can guarantee the first, but we don't control all of the flight traffic over downtown L.A."

"You will tonight. You have sixty minutes to make it happen. Jessie, I'll call you at the Art District Dog Park in one hour. It's at Fourth and Molino. You'll be alone, and you'll have the money with you. Are my instructions clear?"

"Yes." Jessie paused. "And once you have the money, you'll release Delilah?"

"You'll see her tonight. You have my word."

Jessie looked hopefully at Kendra. "Good. I'll be there with the money in an hour."

The caller cut the connection.

Kelland sprang for his phone. "I'll get tactical teams in place."

"None closer than two blocks," Kendra said.

Kelland punched the extension number. "Not our first rodeo, Kendra. My guys know what they're doing."

Lynch joined several other agents at a wall-size map of Los Angeles at the end of the room. They'd already identified the rendezvous point and were marking possible surveillance positions on the erasable board.

Jessie turned toward Kendra. "It's happening."

"I wish I was going with you."

Jessie smiled as she tightened her flak jacket cuffs. "In case you haven't noticed, I'm pretty good at taking care of myself."

"Oh, I've noticed."

Kelland put down the phone. "Okay, Jessie, I'm riding with you and the money in the armored car."

Noah stepped quickly forward. "Where my money goes, I go."

Kelland shook his head. "Nope. You can ride in the van with Kendra, Lynch, and Metcalf. It's parked just off the foyer downstairs. We'll set up our mobile command center in Little Tokyo." He twirled his index finger in the air. "Let's move!"

---

An hour later, Jessie climbed out of the armored car and the back door slammed shut behind her. The vehicle sped away, leaving her alone on the quiet street holding the brown satchel of cash.

Jessie looked at the tall buildings lining the industrial area. Kelland's agents had done a good job discreetly staking out their positions in and on top of those structures, especially on such short notice. Not that their presence would do her a lot of good if things suddenly went south.

She was on her own.

The rain fell harder as she entered the small dog park, which consisted of a few dozen square yards of turf, a water fountain, and a waste can with attached plastic poop bag dispenser.

Her phone rang. Once again, the caller ID read DELILAH SAYS HI. She answered it.

"I'm here with your money. FYI, you may want to bring an umbrella."

"That won't be necessary," the electronically altered voice said. "Go to the trash can and lift out the plastic liner."

"Something tells me I'm about to be up to my elbows in dog shit."

"Just do it."

Jessie lifted the trash can's metal rim and pulled out the plastic bag. "Got it. What now?"

"Toss the bag aside. It doesn't concern us."

Jessie dropped the bag onto the soggy ground. "Done."

"Look into the can."

Jessie peered into the receptacle. At first it appeared to be empty, but after her eyes adjusted to the darkness, she spotted a black plastic garbage bag. "I see something. Another bag."

"Take it out and open it. No dog feces, I assure you."

"Thank goodness for small favors."

Jessie pulled it out. It was a heavy black contractor's garbage bag. She reached in and found a phone and earpiece, black rain jacket, and a waterproof nylon gym bag, like those she'd seen provided to Lynch.

"Put your money bag inside the gym bag. Insert the Bluetooth earpiece into your ear, then put on the jacket and zip it up tight."

She looked up at the falling rain and slid on the jacket. "Considerate of you, but somehow I don't think you care if I catch a cold or not." She inserted the money satchel into the large gym bag and zipped it. She placed the earpiece into her right ear.

The phone rang and she answered it. The voice was now in her ear. "Hang up your own phone and drop it into the trash can. You won't be taking it with you."

Jessie did as she was told. "Done."

"Good. We're finished here. Turn around, exit the dog park, and turn right on Fourth Street."

Jessie walked out of the park and took the right turn. She walked up Fourth Street, past a row of what appeared to be factory buildings. After another two blocks, she stopped in front of a tall chain-link fence blocking the street.

"Okay, I'm at a fence. I can't go any farther."

"Yes, you can. Several of the chain links have been cut for you. You can slide through on the right side."

She found the opening and slid through. "Why is the street closed?"

"It isn't just a street, Jessie."

"Then what is it?"

"You'll know soon. Keep walking."

Jessie realized that the closed roadway was actually a bridge anchored by two tall white art deco spires on each side, decorated by several smaller lighted spires. She crossed over a series of railroad tracks, then found herself over a large concrete channel, perhaps a hundred yards across, filled with rushing water.

"Stop."

Jessie stopped. Standing over the channel was akin to being caught in a wind tunnel, with strong gusts hitting her along with the pounding rain. "What now?"

"Reach into the right pocket of your jacket. There's something there you'll need."

Jessie jammed her hand into the pocket and felt something cold and metallic. She pulled it out. "Handcuffs."

"Yes."

"What are these for?"

"You're about to find out, Jessie." The voice sounded malicious. "This is going to be fun."

———◆———

"I don't like this." Kendra was watching Jessie through a pair of high-powered binoculars from the rooftop of a medical supply three blocks from the bridge. She, Lynch, Kelland, and Metcalf wore FBI rain parkas that provided only scant protection from the pounding rain. "What is this place?"

"It's the Fourth Street Viaduct," Kelland said. "The bridge

has been closed for the past few years. It's marked for renovation. It crosses the Los Angeles River."

She tried to get a better look with her binoculars. "That's an actual river?"

"That's what it's called, but it's really a fifty-mile concrete drainage channel. It's dry three hundred and fifty days a year. But after we've had a good rain like this week, it can be pretty ferocious. This is the stretch where John Travolta raced his car at the end of *Grease*. Remember that?"

Kendra shook her head. "I listened to that movie a hundred times when I was a teenager. I haven't gotten around to actually seeing it since I've had my sight." She turned to face Noah, who had strapped a large, odd-looking pair of goggles to his face. "What on earth are you *wearing*?"

He pulled off the goggles and showed them to her. "Something I've been developing with my company. High-powered night-vision binoculars and virtual-reality goggles, all in one. We think the military will be a big market for them."

Trust Noah to come up with something this bizarre, Kendra thought. She pointed to a deep octagonal crease across Noah's cheeks and forehead left by the goggles. "Not if they're that painful to wear. Those things sure leave their mark."

Noah looked offended as he put the goggles back on. "Just a matter of padding. We'll work out the kinks. I'll send you a pair. You'll have one of maybe half a dozen in the world."

"I can hardly wait."

Lynch was still watching Jessie on the bridge intently. "She's talking. She has something in her hands. Can any of you make out what it is?"

No one said anything for a long moment, but Metcalf finally spoke up. "Handcuffs."

Kendra cursed. "You're right. We have to get down there." She put down her binoculars and ran toward the stairwell door.

Lynch caught up and grabbed her arm. "Get down there and do what, exactly?"

"Help her."

"You heard the call. The kidnappers want a two-block perimeter."

Kendra tried to break free. "We can't just stand here and watch!"

"That's exactly what we're going to do. Jessie wouldn't have it any other way. If we botch this by rushing toward her before the drop is complete, do you know how pissed she's going to be?"

Kendra cursed again. Lynch was right. After the last debacle when they'd believed they'd lost Dee, Jessie would never forgive her.

"My people are ready to engage when I give the order," Kelland said. "They'll be all over that bridge faster than you or I could ever be, Kendra."

Lynch was still gripping her arm. "And Jessie can take care of herself."

"I know. It's just that...she'd do anything for Dee. She would put her life on the line for her. The kidnappers know that, and they might use it against her."

Lynch finally loosened his grip. "That's why we're here. Right?"

Kendra pulled away and turned back toward the bridge. "What if it isn't enough?"

"It will be," he said quietly.

For some reason his words brought her immediate comfort. Maybe it was the supreme confidence in his tone; maybe it was because she wanted it to be true.

She raised the binoculars back to her eyes. "Okay," she said unsteadily. "But we just need to be ready for anything."

———◆———

Jessie held up the heavy police-issue handcuffs. "What the hell am I supposed to do with these things?"

"Snap one cuff around the handle of that gym bag."

She fed it through the handle and pushed the ratchet teeth into the locking mechanism. "Okay."

"Now put the other cuff around your left wrist."

"Trust me, I'm not letting go of this bag."

"Humor me."

She closed the other cuff around her wrist. "Okay, now what?"

"Jump."

Jessie didn't respond at first. The silence was filled by the rushing water below her. "You want me to . . ."

"Jump. Jump into the water."

"You're insane."

"Quite the opposite."

"This water is deep right now. And moving fast."

"You can handle it, Jessie."

"What makes you think *that*?"

256

"Your performance on *American Ninja* all those years ago.
You scored higher on the water challenge than anyone in the
show's history. We studied it on YouTube. Very impressive."

"It was a stupid game. On TV."

"It was no game the way you jumped into the reservoir on
the night we took Delilah. That's what gave us the idea."

Jessie stared into the dark churning water. There were no
lights, nothing to guide her. "People die in this thing every
year, in water a lot calmer and shallower than this."

"Those people aren't you, Jessie."

"What am I supposed to do once I drop into the water?"

"Stay alive."

"That's it?"

"That's it. Let the current take you."

"Take me where? The Pacific Ocean?"

"We'll take care of it. You're wasting time. If you want to
see Delilah alive again, jump into the water. It's as simple as
that. You have to the count of five."

Jessie climbed onto the white railing and stared into the void.

"One..."

She looked back, wondering what Kelland and his agents
were thinking right now.

"Two..."

Of course. They were thinking she was out of her freakin'
mind.

"Three..."

Which she probably was.

"Four..."

She jumped into the water.

———◆———

"No!" Kendra's scream could be heard all over the perimeter. Kelland was already on his walkie-talkie, issuing orders to the team.

Lynch stepped forward. "We need lights on that channel. *Now.*"

Kelland put down the walkie-talkie. "Helicopters are four minutes out. They have searchlights."

"They said no copters," Metcalf said.

"I don't give a shit," Kendra said. "We didn't bargain for this." She threw off her poncho and ran for the stairwell. "Let's go."

———◆———

Jessie felt herself being twisted by the cold, roiling water as it carried her into the darkness. At first she wasn't even aware of her direction, but after a few moments she got her bearings.

She hadn't even touched bottom when she jumped from the bridge. Was it fifteen feet deep? Eighteen?

THWAPP! Something struck her head and shoulders, then disappeared. Was that an old bicycle?

She felt the gym bag tugging at her wrist, and she pulled it close. She spun crazily for another few seconds before righting herself.

What in the hell was the plan?

Stay alive, they'd said. Right...

She hurtled toward the pillars of another bridge. She

extended her legs and kicked off from a concrete pillar, tumbling almost head over heels through the water.

The current was moving faster here. Shit.

She lifted her chin to keep her nose and mouth above the churning water. She was helped, she realized, by a thin buoyancy vest sewn into the lining of the jacket.

Again, small favors.

She dove to avoid a spinning fiberglass car bumper but surfaced just in time to be struck in the left eye by something else. A boot, she realized. What was next, a tire? An old lawn mower?

She was getting the hell beat out of her.

The second bridge had already receded into darkness behind her. She figured she'd already traveled a mile, maybe more.

After a few more painful collisions and a potentially fatal near-miss with another bridge pillar, she was suddenly aware that her jacket was glowing a vibrant purple hue.

Just above the waterline to her right, an ultraviolet light was aimed in her direction.

"There she is!" a voice called out.

She suddenly stopped cold, as if someone had just pulled the emergency brake.

What in the hell?

She'd slammed into an expanse of netting pulled across the channel's right side.

Another man's voice. "We've got her!"

Not an accident.

Not a rescue.

Part of the plan.

Her neck twisted as the net curled around her and pulled her toward the slanted concrete embankment.

A man in a ski mask leaned over her. "She's alive."

"Barely, you son of a bitch," she muttered.

She felt a twinge in her arm. Suddenly she couldn't move. Had to be a sedative...

Another man in a ski mask extricated her from the netting while the first unlocked the handcuffs and picked up the gym bag.

Dee... You've got what you want, she tried to tell them. Give us Dee.

But she couldn't form the words.

Her eyes closed.

Darkness.

———◆———

Kendra and Lynch joined the scores of cops and FBI agents running down the cement upper banks of the Los Angeles River. Everyone aimed their flashlights downward, but murky water swallowed the beams whole.

"I can't see her. Where in the hell is she?" Kendra yelled to Lynch.

"The water's moving fast," Lynch said. "Faster than we are. She went into the river over fifteen minutes ago, so she could be in Compton by now."

Kendra pointed to two shafts of light up ahead. "Helicopters."

Lynch nodded. "One of them is stopped. I think they've spotted something."

Kendra put on an extra burst of speed. "Hurry!"

In less than five minutes they reached the place where the helicopter was lighting up the channel. Kelland was already there.

"Oh, my God," Kendra said under her breath.

She'd just seen the large, tangled netting at the water's edge, now being inspected by Kelland and two of his agents.

"They used that to catch her here," Lynch yelled over the helicopter's rotor, which was almost deafening as it echoed in the concrete channel. "They planned this all out. Just like they've planned everything else."

"Okay, so they grabbed the ransom. But where is Jessie?"

Lynch shook his head. "I don't know, Kendra."

Kendra nodded as she absorbed the awful realization. "Then either she drowned." She swallowed. "Or they took her."

"That's what it looks like."

"Jessie swims like a fish. I won't believe she drowned. But I can't see why in hell they'd have any reason to take her, either."

Kelland had heard her. He looked up from the netting and shook his head. Then he pointed to the concrete embankment next to him.

There, just inches from the water, was Jessie's motorcycle helmet.

# CHAPTER

# 11

James Dorset leaned impatiently back behind the wheel of his pickup truck, trying to ignore the awful smell coming off his skin and hair. He hadn't been able to shower since pulling Jessie Mercado out of the Los Angeles River the night before, and the smell was only getting worse.

He took another look around at his surroundings. This was a lousy place for him to have to cool his heels while he waited. He was parked behind the large main building of what was once the Shelby Machine and Tool Company, which obviously hadn't seen any action in years, maybe decades. The buildings sat in the middle of a thousand-acre parking lot riddled with potholes and desert weeds protruding from every crack in the asphalt. Winds howled across the desolate landscape.

Dorset wasn't even aware of the place's existence until a few days before, when he and Paul Fantinelli had stowed a motorcycle there after their highway run-in with Jessie Mercado and Kendra Michaels. His hand instinctively went to his injured right leg, which still might require surgery.

Bitches.

No matter. In spite of everything that had gone wrong last night, he had made himself a very rich man. Now if only Fantinelli would get his ass back here so that he could—

Fantinelli's van sped around the far end of the building. Finally. As the van approached, Dorset climbed out of his pickup.

Fantinelli parked, opened his door, and joined Dorset in the shadow of the building's rusty awning. He was a tall man with a thick red beard. "How's the leg?"

"Hurts like hell," he said sourly. "I still think you should have let me punch Mercado's face a few times on the way out of town."

"Huh. I ask you, what kind of man wants to beat up an unconscious woman?"

"My kind. Especially if she's why I may have to walk with a limp for the rest of my life."

"I see your point." Fantinelli smiled. "But Kendra Michaels is the one you should be mad at. She's the one who sent you sailing over your handlebars."

"Trust me, I haven't forgotten about her." Dorset gestured toward the dilapidated building. "I might pay her a visit one day soon. Are you sure no one's around?"

"Nah, it's been deserted since the 'nineties. Half my family used to work here. It went belly-up when the aerospace industry collapsed. Don't get nervous. We're safe out here."

Dorset nodded. "Okay, if it's so safe, maybe you can tell me why the boss wanted me to hang out here and not go with you and the other guys when you took Mercado and the money back with you?"

Fantinelli looked uneasy. "I need to talk to you about that."

Dorset stiffened. "This doesn't sound good."

"It isn't."

Dorset's face flushed with anger. "What the hell? Is he trying to screw me?"

"No. Calm down. It's not that at all."

"Then what is it?"

Fantinelli hesitated for a long moment. "It may just be smarter for you not to be seen. They may be onto you."

"What?"

"The FBI's been sniffing around. An agent even went to your old apartment building in Burbank."

"Oh, shit."

"Is there any other reason the Feds might be interested in you right now?"

Dorset shook his head. "No. How in the hell did this happen?"

"I don't know. Maybe they typed your DNA from blood off your wrecked motorcycle."

"I told you, my DNA isn't in any database."

"It is now, Dorset, even if your name isn't attached to it. And if they catch you, you're one blood test away from being placed on that highway where we offed Adrian."

"Shit."

"And as long as you have this kind of heat on you, you

can't be anywhere near Delilah Winter. Or any of us. You'll have to lay low."

"Here in this rat trap of a factory?" Dorset tried to quell the panic and anger he heard in his own voice. "How long am I supposed to stay here? What the hell am I supposed to do?"

Fantinelli took a deep breath as he looked out at the barren landscape. Then he said soothingly, "Not long. I wouldn't leave you in the lurch. Don't worry, Dorset. We have a plan."

---

"Listen, you have to open your eyes, Jessie. I can't take this."

Dee... It was Dee's voice.

"Wake up!" Dee's voice was fierce. "I know she lied. She just wanted to hurt me. You're going to be fine. I won't let her do that to us. But you have to open your eyes and prove it to her." She sounded so upset that Jessie forced her lids to open. Dee was looking down at her, tears pouring down her cheeks. "See. I told you. It wasn't poison; it was just more of that damn sedative she gave me." She wiped the tears away with the back of her manacled hands and lifted her chin. "Now, don't you dare go back to sleep."

"I have no intention of doing that." Jessie shook her head to clear it. "Are you okay?" She looked around and recognized the interior of an aircraft of some sort. Plane. They'd been right about what Dee had been trying to tell them... "This has to be where you've been kept since you were kidnapped?" Her gaze flew to Dee's face. "What was that about poison?"

"Listen to you." Dee's voice was shaking. "You're always

worried about me. I'm fine. This isn't about me. I'm not the one those nutcases tried to drown. They almost *killed* you. I told you to be careful."

"This is still very much about you," Jessie said. "And I don't like it that they didn't release you. They got the ransom?"

"So Charlotte told me."

"Charlotte?"

"Dorset called her the dragon bitch." She gestured around the plane. "She kind of runs things around here."

"Where is everybody?" Her gaze was wandering over the plane's interior. "We're alone here?"

"For the time being. She's outside talking to Fantinelli, one of the men who brought you here. There were three of them, Muntz, Blackman, and Fantinelli. I think Fantinelli was the one in charge of the others, but he left after they'd finished sedating and handcuffing you. He only just came back, and Charlotte said she had to talk to him."

"You mentioned...Dorset. He was here with you?"

"For a little while. I think he was supposed to protect me from Charlotte. I appear to be her least favorite person." Her eyes suddenly lit with eagerness. "What do you know about Dorset?"

"Not enough. But we were on our way to locating him before I took my spectacular dive tonight." She sat up and reached out for Dee's hand before she realized she was still wearing manacles. "And Kendra and Lynch and the others will keep on working to find you. They won't give up. But we can't give up, either." She added grimly, "Because it appears we're at ground zero." She glanced at the door leading to the back of the plane. "And I've got to learn as much as I can as quick as I can before your dragon bitch comes back. So I'm going to fire questions at you. Okay?"

Dee nodded. "I don't know what Charlotte's real name is if that's one of the questions. And I have no idea who is responsible for taking me. I've heard her on the phone talking to someone occasionally, but it was brief, and I didn't get a hint of who it might be. I don't know much about her except that she has enough power to argue about how I'm being treated with whoever is in charge." She made a face. "And she believes it's far too good. She disapproves not only of me, but of everyone and everything connected to the kidnapping."

"Why?" Jessie asked. "And why would anyone who had staged such an elaborate crime pay any attention to her? Twenty-five million dollars is a lure that must be irresistible. How would she dare to argue with him?"

Dee shrugged. "All I know is that Dorset was nervous about crossing her and she was always super confident."

"Why?" Jessie asked again. "Blackmail?"

Dee shook her head. "I've told you all I know." She added, "Except that I believe she could be very dangerous. At first, I thought she was almost like a cartoon character, but the longer I was with her the more viciousness I noticed. She might not be the one in control, but I can see her striking out like a rattlesnake."

"Which brings me back to that remark you made about poison. Did she try to poison you?"

"No. She told me she'd poisoned *you*." Her lips tightened bitterly. "It was one of her sweet tricks to try to make me

268

bleed a little more. You were delivered here by three guys who had been part of grabbing the money drop. She was pissed off that you'd been brought here for her to care for and she exploded. She was yelling that you were sopping wet and stinking like a drowned rat and ordered them to toss you in the shower and get the smell off you." She swallowed. "You were still unconscious. I thought they were really going to drown you then. They wouldn't let me help, Jessie."

"Well, it appears I survived it." She looked down and realized for the first time she was wearing jeans and a black cotton shirt. "Where did I get the dry clothes?"

Dee shook her head. "They brought them with them in a canvas bag." She grimaced. "And they changed your clothes. Like I said, they wouldn't let me help."

"I'm sure I didn't care at the time." She was gazing down at the jeans. "They fit. They were prepared. Your Charlotte might have caused a fuss about my arrival, but I'd bet someone was expecting me." She added slowly, "Which brings another layer to be explored. One more question. Are you ready to blow this joint?"

Dee smiled. "You bet I am. Willing and very ready."

"I thought you would be." She was looking around the aircraft, checking out the plaques beneath the windows.

"And we might just get lucky. This is an old Airbus A300 that Frontier Airlines evidently discarded. We had Airbus cargo planes when I was in Afghanistan, and there may be some similarities."

"I assume you're not going to try to fly us out of here?"

269

"Not practical. Instead, I believe we'll have to see how much you remembered about what I taught you—"

"I see you're awake," Charlotte said as she opened the silver door and swept into the compartment. "Pity. I was hoping to put our Delilah through a little more stress before she realized that her old friend Jessie would be around a bit longer. Spoiled brats like her need every lesson we can give them."

"I've never found her spoiled," Jessie said coldly. "She's incredibly disciplined considering what her lifestyle demands. And you didn't fool her for long, Charlotte...if that's really your name. She's smart enough to realize what's real and what's just plain ugly."

"You're fooled by her like everyone else." Charlotte's lips curled. "That pretty face and her bouncing around on that stage singing and making her seem like she's something special. She's nothing but a troublemaker."

"Then why didn't you let her go after you got the money?" Jessie asked. "Then all your trouble would have been over."

"No, it wouldn't. I told you, she can fool anyone."

"Second question. Why am I here? That doesn't make sense, either. You didn't need me once you had that ransom."

"You're here because we obey orders. And you have no right to question me. He thought he needed you, so you're here." She scowled. "It's just more foolishness, but that's the way it has to be. Now be quiet or I'll have you gagged."

"You broke the agreement with the FBI. You didn't release the hostage. They're going to assume you've killed her and go after you with guns blazing." Jessie's voice lowered to a hiss. "You may think Dee's not important, but she's enormously popular with her fans. The sheer public pressure to catch you will make certain they'll have you in jail on death row within a few months. The only way to save yourself is to let her go."

"You don't know anything. No one is going to put me in jail. He's smarter than all of you. He got what he wanted, and this will all be over soon." Her hands clenched into fists at her sides. "One way or the other." She took a step closer to Jessie. "So you keep your mouth shut and you might live through this. Though I doubt it. I've told those three men outside on guard that they won't receive any part of those millions if they let you escape. I'm going to have them handcuff both of you to those chairs over there and check you every hour." She added with a sneer, "Those fools told me you were supposed to be so tough while they were scrubbing you down. But here you are handcuffed and helpless and so that must have been lies." She turned away. "Just like all those lies about your bitch friend Delilah."

"Where are you going?" Jessie's eyes were suddenly narrowed on Charlotte's face. "That sounds like you're leaving us. I was told you ran things around here."

"Of course I do. But that doesn't mean I have to stay here and wipe your asses. I'm going for a drive. We're coming down to the end and I have a few arrangements to make. I don't want those goons listening to my calls. They brought a case of champagne with them and that might make them so stinko, they might not care what I'm saying. I have to be sure, though." She shrugged. "Those idiots will do exactly what I tell them whether I'm here or not." She added sarcastically

271

as she headed for the silver door, "Do be good for them, Jessie. Otherwise I'll tell them they have permission to rape Delilah. You might have been the one who was brought here to exert pressure, but I'd much rather see it happen to her. And it would be amusing to give those assholes their last chance at screwing the great Delilah." She was smiling maliciously. "Oh, yes, definitely their last chance. I guarantee they'd be willing. They won't see why they shouldn't have their fun now that they already have the money. That's even funnier." She was laughing as the heavy door slammed behind her.

"I told you." Dee drew a deep breath. "I'm her least favorite person."

"Definitely," Jessie said grimly. "There's real antagonism. Another question mark."

"She's trying to use us against each other," Dee said. "You can't let her do that. You shouldn't have even come after me. I'm not that kid who you thought you had to take care of. I can do that myself these days." Her lips twisted. "Though I might have let you think that because it kept you close to me. Not very nice, right? So you let me take my share of the hard knocks from now on. Do you hear me?"

"I hear you," she said gently. "We'll discuss the distribution of the hard knocks later." She frowned. "I was more interested that Charlotte got careless enough to perhaps let us know why I was brought here. I'll have to think about it." She shook her head impatiently. "But I don't want to worry about it right now. That was a hollow threat she made. She's not going to turn the beasts on you now. As she said, they're too near their payday, but no matter what she boasts, she's not the one in control." The door was opening again, and she whispered quickly, "Don't argue, don't fight them. Just notice everything about them and what they do that might help us. All we want is to let them chain us up and then get the hell out of here so that we can get busy…"

———◆———

Kendra glanced at the caller ID as she jumped on the phone to answer it. At last! "Metcalf, tell me you have some good news from checking those traffic cams."

"Sorry, but there's nothing so far. They probably switched vehicles and jumped onto the 10 Freeway. We're checking every garage and storage unit in the area, but nothing's turned up yet."

"Damn."

"But there is something else… we got a hit on our Be On the Look Out for James Dorset."

Her hand clenched on the phone. "You found him?"

"Not exactly. But his pickup truck has turned up."

"Where?"

"North L.A. County, up in Lancaster. It's parked behind an old factory there. A sheriff's department helicopter spotted it. It must have looked out of place to them, so they ran his plate and picked up the BOLO."

"No sign of Dorset?"

"He's not in the building or anywhere in the surrounding

grounds. The truck is clean, so it was probably abandoned recently."

"I want to see it."

"I had no doubt. A tow truck is en route to bring it to the FBI garage in West L.A. You can examine it there tonight."

"I want to see it right where it is. Lynch and I are heading up to Lancaster right now."

Lynch wrinkled his brow and mouthed, *We are?*

"Kendra, our tow truck is already—"

"If they get there before we do, have them wait. Don't let them touch anything. Do you understand?"

"Of course I understand," Metcalf said. "But remember this operation is being run out of the L.A. regional office. They're not used to taking orders from you here."

"Come on, I never *order*. I politely request."

"Ha. Keep telling yourself that, Kendra. Get yourself up there as quickly as you can. Don't worry, I'll buy you some time before they haul the car away."

"You're the best. Text me the address?"

"Already done."

"Thanks, Metcalf."

---

Kendra and Lynch were halfway to the factory when Lynch received a call from the Swiss AV lab. His conversation was in French, and Kendra could only understand a few words before he hung up. She watched as he took a few notes. "Good?"

"Probably better than good. They've identified the software

used to alter the voice, and they reverse-engineered the recording to give us an accurate facsimile of the caller. Karl said he's going to finish the last bit and transmit it to us within the hour."

"You're right: better than good." She was nibbling nervously at her lower lip. "How accurate?"

"Every detail. You wouldn't be able to tell the difference if you were listening to the actual caller's speaking voice and accents."

"Shit. I want to hear it *now*."

"I know you do." He chuckled. "That was a given. But you'll have to wait until he transmits it. Be patient. At least you have something to keep you busy until you can get your hands on it." He glanced at his watch. "We should be at the factory very soon."

Kendra and Lynch reached the abandoned factory in slightly less than twenty minutes. They pulled into the lot and circled around until they saw the large pickup truck and an L.A. County Sheriff's police cruiser parked behind the main building. Kendra stopped, and she and Lynch climbed out of her car.

Two sheriff's deputies were getting out of the cruiser to greet them. The larger of the two men spoke. "Kendra Michaels?"

"Yes."

He nodded. "I'm Deputy Locker, this is Merritt. We were told to extend every courtesy to you."

Lynch smiled. "Anyone mention the name Adam Lynch to you?"

"Sorry."

"No worries. It's healthy to be occasionally put in my place."

Kendra walked around the pickup truck, examining it with the intensity of a laser scanner. It was a white Dodge Ram 3500, jacked up to an almost ridiculous degree and equipped with a locked hard-plastic bed cover. "I'm surprised you guys found this out here."

Merritt stepped toward her. "It was our helicopter patrol. I guess the pickup looked suspicious, like maybe there was a drug deal going down. Then they found out you were looking for it."

"We're really looking for its owner. James Dorset."

"No sign of him, I'm afraid." He pointed to the chained-and-padlocked main door of the factory. "The building is locked up tight as a drum. No one's been in there for years."

"Wrong. Someone's been in there in the last week." Kendra ignored the deputies' surprised looks and crouched next to the right front quarter panel. "Well, maybe his car can help us find him."

Lynch squatted beside her. "What's it telling you?'"

"That this car has been in Santa Monica recently. Several times. It's been parked near the coast pretty much every night since he left his apartment in Burbank."

"That's obvious," Lynch said solemnly, though his eyes were twinkling. "Only to you, of course."

Still in a crouched position, she moved back a few feet. "But he's been driving up here almost every day." She cocked her head. "Actually, no. Not here. Maybe thirty miles north of here."

"It's a long commute," Lynch said. "He must have had a good reason to make that run every day."

Locker stared at her as if she were from another planet. "What the hell's going on here?"

Kendra stood. "Just doing what I came here to do."

"Are you . . . psychic?"

"I don't think I believe in psychics." She crossed around to the other side of the car. "Do you?"

"Not until about thirty seconds ago."

"I'm not seeing anything you guys didn't see. I just don't take things I see for granted."

Lynch clicked his tongue. "Put them out of their misery, Kendra."

"Only them?"

"Okay, me too."

"Look at the tires on the driver's side."

Lynch and the deputies walked around and leaned over.

"See those obnoxious chalk marks?"

"Yes," Lynch said, "Bright yellow, lime green, hot pink . . ."

"Meter maid marks," Deputy Locker identified eagerly.

"Very good," Kendra said. "Although your law-enforcement brethren may object to the nomenclature. Santa Monica parking enforcement uses these at night for cars parked in busy areas like Third Street Promenade, so they can see if they've overstayed the posted limits."

"Almost every place does that," Deputy Merritt said. "We do it here."

"But Santa Monica is the only place I know of that uses this bright, almost-fluorescent chalk. It makes it easier to see at night, but it doesn't fade as quickly. It's been annoying the hell out of people." She glanced at Lynch. "I got one on my car when I visited Jessie's office last month."

"How do you know this car's been driving up north of here?" Merritt said.

"Look at the grille. Lots of dead bugs, including yucca moths. They pollinate yucca flowers up in the Mojave Desert. And I see lots of dragonflies, which are also common up there. The bugs are in various states of decay, meaning this car has recently made repeated trips."

Merritt nodded. "Huh."

"But there's something else here . . . " Kendra pointed to the right headlight. "There's sand lodged here around the plastic headlight casing. It's true on the other side, and in back. I know sand can blow across the roads up there, but this looks like this vehicle has been going off road."

"They could be keeping Delilah somewhere up there," Lynch said.

"And now maybe Jessie." Kendra crossed around to the back of the vehicle. "We need to—" She froze. "Oh, God."

Lynch rushed to her side. "What is it?"

She backed away and pointed to the covered compartment. "There's a dead body here."

"You can smell it?" Lynch said.

She nodded jerkily.

"Because I've been around more than my share of corpses,"

Lynch said. "I know what death smells like, and I'm not picking anything up."

Kendra backed farther away, trying to get away from that awful odor. "So do I. This is fresh, only hours old."

"In my experience, it takes at least a day for a body to begin giving off—"

"Not true," she said. "Ask any hospice nurse."

Lynch turned to the deputies. "Open this compartment. Now."

Merritt grabbed a pry bar from his squad car. He ran back and started working on the locked cover.

Kendra couldn't take her eyes away. What—or who—was she going to see in there? Logically it was clear it wasn't going to be a good outcome. A brutal kidnapping. A ransom delivered and yet the victims not returned.

The victims . . . Dee? Jessie? Please, no . . .

"Easy." Lynch pulled her closer.

Merritt popped the trunk, and then stepped back. "Oh, God. You're right. We gotta call this in."

Kendra could see the figure curled in the trunk. She stepped nearer to get a better view.

It wasn't Jessie.

It wasn't Dee.

Oh, thank you, God.

It was a man.

She forced herself to examine his features, which she had seen before on the photo on his car license.

Dorset, she realized. "James Dorset."

"They knew we were on to him," Lynch said. "He was a loose end they needed to clip off."

Kendra pulled a pair of evidence gloves from her pocket and slid them on. She checked the dead man's pockets. Empty.

"His hair smells like that spot of the Los Angeles River we were on last night. But there's nothing here," she said. "No wallet, nothing."

"You were expecting a hand-drawn map to the kidnappers' secret prison?" Lynch pulled out his phone and snapped photos of the corpse.

"Would have been nice." She thought for a minute. "We think Dee was trying to tell us something... having to do with an airplane. Are there any airports in the desert up there?"

"Edwards Air Force Base."

She shook her head. "Military. Doesn't seem too likely."

"I agree..." Lynch suddenly whirled toward her. "But wait a minute... What if it isn't an airport at all?"

"What are you talking about?"

His gaze was narrowed, his expression intense. "The Boneyard."

"I still don't follow."

"It's an outdoor storage site for civilian aircraft. It's in the desert and it goes on for miles. Over a thousand commercial airliners are stored out there, almost in the middle of nowhere. What better place to hide Dee? You could lose an army in that—"

"Of course, you could." Kendra was already running back toward her car. "Let's go. I'll call Kelland on the way."

Kendra had already pulled onto State Route 14 by the time she'd called Kelland and explained what she and Lynch had seen and put together.

"Let's check it out," he said instantly. "I'll put together a team and rendezvous with you and Lynch at the Mojave Air and Space Port. We can be there inside of two hours."

"We're not waiting around," Kendra said. "We're less than twenty-five minutes out."

"Kendra, listen to me..."

"*You* listen. They have their money, and they still haven't released Dee. And now they have Jessie. There's no telling what they'll do. They have to be on edge. They've just killed one of their own men in the last couple hours. We can't waste time."

"I'm in charge of this investigation. I'm ordering you to wait for us, Kendra."

"Sorry, Kelland. Call me when you get there." She cut the connection and glanced at Lynch. "We're on the same page, right?"

"Of course. It was my idea, and I'm far too arrogant not to believe it's a good one," Lynch said. "But Kelland may have a point. Who knows what we may find out there?"

"We may find nothing." Her hands clenched on the steering wheel. "But I can't just sit around for hours when Dee and Jessie might need us."

"And I agree. But we don't know who and how many people we may find ourselves up against. I wasn't exaggerating when I told you there might be over a thousand commercial planes to search through. We need to be careful."

She gazed at him in disbelief. "Now I've heard everything. What is the world coming to when Adam Lynch wants to be cautious? It's almost as if—" She broke off as Lynch's phone rang.

"Do you suppose you can stop harassing me so that I can take this call from Karl?" Lynch said dryly.

"Karl? I almost forgot about that transmission."

"You had something else to think about." He pressed the button. "But I think that you have time to analyze it now, don't you? Lean back and listen."

He didn't have to tell her twice. All of her attention was focused on that voice. It was incredibly clear in every detail. "Keep playing it." She closed her eyes. "Over and over. There's something…there."

Lynch didn't answer, he just put the message on repeat and remained silent. The voice was surrounding her, becoming part of her, the roughness, the sarcasm, the intonations…She inhaled sharply and then paused for a long moment. Her lids flew open. "Holy shit."

"What is it? Is it a voice you recognize?"

She shook her head. "I've never heard it before in my life."

"Then what—"

"Wait, don't talk to me for a minute." She rode in silence for a few moments, letting the thought percolate. It was possible and yet it was difficult to believe that it could be true. She didn't want it to be true because it increased the deadliness that Dee and Jessie were facing. Yet could she be right?

Lynch leaned toward her. "Kendra?"

"Okay. Okay. But you're probably not going to believe what I'm about to tell you."

"What?"

She looked straight ahead and then just went for it. "I think I know who did this."

———◆———

"For God's sake, I told you to play it cool," Jessie said impatiently as she gazed at Dee's bleeding lip. "What part of that didn't you understand?"

"The part where that ape was groping you when he was supposedly checking your manacles." She scowled. "And I was pretty cool. I only bit his arm to distract him. It did the job. He left, didn't he? You said Charlotte wouldn't turn them loose on me. You didn't mention that you might still be on their menu." She met her eyes. "But you probably knew it might happen, didn't you?"

"Of course I did," she said curtly. "They probably guessed I was fair game or would be soon. Plus they were bored and eager to get their share of the money. Sexual dominance was bound to be the next move now that your dragon bitch was temporarily out of the picture. And it might not have gone any farther if I'd just let him feel me up and have a taste of fun."

"And what if it had? Was I supposed to watch him rape you?" Dee emphatically shook her head. "No way. I got pretty tired of seeing them toss you around and half drown you after they got you here. I'm not going to let it go on. I'll find a way to stop it."

Jessie should have known that Dee would have that response, but it was too dangerous to ignore. She had to convince her that restraint was the way to handle this nightmare. No, that wasn't all, she also had to give her a weapon to fight it if everything went to hell. "Look, bad things sometimes happen. It's not only assholes like those guys. I've seen it in Afghanistan, in the slums of New Orleans..." She hesitated. "And it can seem terrible at the time. But no matter what they do, it doesn't mean that they've beaten me. I just close out whatever bad has happened to me and go on. Because, in the end, that's the only way to win."

"That's very inspiring. Are you finished?"

"Not unless you understand what I'm trying to tell you. I've often found situations don't escalate if no overt action is taken. Will you trust me on this?"

"I always trust you." Dee was smiling. "And I'm very touched that you're trying to gently let me into the dark side of your world that you've struggled so hard to keep from me. But it's not as if I didn't know it was there. From the moment you came into my life, you were the most important person in it. You were the one who would always tell me the truth, the one who believed in me when I wasn't sure I believed in myself. Did you think that I wouldn't make sure I knew what was below the surface?"

Jessie stared at her for a long moment. Dee was smiling, but beneath it her expression held a kind of serenity. "What are you trying to tell me?"

"I'm trying to tell you that I hope you'll be my friend forever, but I won't keep you chained by pretending to be what I'm not." She added quietly, "I don't *need* you, Jessie. I can survive almost anything that comes my way these days and come out stronger. So don't tell me not to help you when and if I choose."

Jessie found her lips quirking. "I'll try to keep my advice to myself."

Dee frowned. "I didn't mean to be rude."

"You can't shout out a declaration of emancipation like that and then apologize. It doesn't work that way. It was a great declaration and you should keep it intact."

"You're being bossy. But you're right, it was pretty awesome."

"If I can offer a suggestion, would you wipe that blood on your lip on your shirtsleeve? It hurts me to see it."

Dee immediately wiped away the blood. "You're very manipulative."

"Just to show you that need comes in many shapes and nuances."

"I knew that." Her voice was suddenly husky. "I just didn't want you to feel that particular nuance was an obligation."

"Exception noted." She paused. "But if that situation occurs again, I want you to remember what I said." She shrugged and then said slowly, "Though it might not occur. Perhaps the play is already in motion. I was just thinking of what Charlotte said before she left. It was half threat, but there was something...very ugly when she was talking about those assholes who delivered me here."

"Ugly?" Dee was frowning as she mentally went over that conversation. "She said it would be amusing to give those assholes their last chance at screwing me."

Jessie nodded. "And then she repeated something about it definitely would be their last chance. She thought it was funny."

"I must have missed the humor." Then Dee slowly nodded as she realized where Jessie was going. "It wasn't entirely aimed at me. You believe there's no way those bastards are going to get their share of the ransom."

"They're not needed any longer," Jessie said simply. "It just depends what time and method is going to be chosen to get rid of them. I'd judge that Charlotte's sudden exit and craving for privacy have something to do with that decision."

She shuddered. "What did I say about a rattlesnake?"

"You always did have a way with imagery. That's why your lyrics come out so well." Her gaze shifted to the door. "The rattlesnake or the ape? Now all we have to do is wait and see which one comes through that door in the next hour. I'm betting on the reptile..."

# CHAPTER

# 12

It was Charlotte who eventually threw open the door. "Here I am. Did you miss me?"

"Not really," Jessie said. She could see that color was flushing Charlotte's cheeks and her attitude was breathing defiance. She wondered what had occurred to cause that change. "We were only discussing what a liar you are. You said that those assholes were going to check on us every hour. Not that we missed them, but it just goes to show that you're far from being as efficient as you bragged."

"Shut up. I won't put up with that nonsense right now." She was striding toward them. "For your information, your guards were indisposed."

"Drunk?"

"I didn't mean that. I should have said permanently indisposed. Muntz, Fantinelli, Blackman... They were all fools."

Her glance shifted to Dee and she stiffened. "What happened to your mouth? It's cut."

"She had an encounter with one of your apes. I believe it was Muntz," Jessie said. "But it doesn't really matter which one. Since you're in charge, you're responsible." She tilted her head. "You should have come back sooner."

"I couldn't come back sooner. I had to give them time to finish that bottle of champagne." Her eyes were blazing. "And I'm not to blame for this. Nothing happened to her all the time I had the bitch here. I didn't choose those men. It's his fault."

"Whose fault?" Dee asked softly. "And why were you so careful about those guys guzzling down that champagne? Jessie thinks that you were planning on ridding yourself of them." She paused. "If that's true, I have to ask myself: What weapon? If you were going to do it, the answer would be poison. Everyone knows poison is the prime weapon used by women." Her lips twisted. "And it would suit your twisted humor to put the poison in the champagne that was meant to celebrate their newfound wealth."

"It was just convenient." She lifted her chin. "I could have used any weapon."

"But you didn't?"

"No, I didn't. The idea did amuse me." She added, "So maybe you could be smarter than I thought. But it won't do you any good. In the end, he always comes back to me." She turned and strode toward the bathroom. "I don't have time to talk to you any longer. He'll be here soon. I'll get a washcloth and clean up that cut, and he'll just be happy that he had me to keep them from hurting you even more..."

"Rattlesnake, indeed," Jessie murmured, gazing after her. "And you were firing on all cylinders while you were probing her just now."

"Because I suddenly put everything together about the reason why she had to be involved in this," Dee said. "Though it's bizarre and I can't—"

"He's here." Charlotte was hurrying out of the bathroom. "I know the sound of that monster car." She carelessly wiped Dee's mouth with the wet cloth. "Now don't give me any trouble or you'll be sorry."

"I'll do my best," Dee said. "I wouldn't want you to be upset with me when we've grown so close. You might—"

The door was thrown wide open. "Hello, Delilah!"

Dee and Jessie turned and stared in disbelief at the man standing in the doorway.

It was Noah Calderon.

"Are you all right?" He hurried forward. "I can't tell you how worried I've been about you. You have to understand why this happened. Why it had to be like this."

"Understand?" Dee was still staring at him in bewilderment. "Unless you're here to rescue me, then I don't think that's a possibility. *You* did this, Noah?"

"Son of a bitch," Jessie murmured.

"Shut up," Noah said savagely. "This is partly your fault. She was always talking about you when we were together, and I could see that she wanted to be like you. You were only a glorified bodyguard. She couldn't understand that she was so much more than you'd ever be." His lips twisted bitterly. "And that the two of us together could rule the world if we chose. We were the perfect couple."

"Except Dee didn't agree with you," Jessie said sarcastically. "And I don't even remember commenting on you to her while she was dating you. She must have had the good sense to make up her own mind what a loser you were."

"I wouldn't insult me if I were you," Noah said with soft venom. "I have a possible use for you, but that can change in a heartbeat. Why do you think I chose you to deliver that ransom? A threat or pain to you and Delilah would do anything I wanted. But I'm beginning to believe it might be time to totally eliminate your influence with her."

"What are you talking about?" Dee asked through set teeth. "I've been listening to all this bullshit you've been muttering but I can't believe it. You have to say the words. Did you actually have the insanity to do this to me?"

"Of course I did," Noah said calmly. "There was nothing insane about it. You wouldn't pay any attention to me when I tried to talk you out of breaking up with me. You even laughed when I tried to tell you we should stay together, that the two of us were perfect for each other." His lower lip curled. "No one laughs at me. I was brilliant, everyone admired me, look at all I had accomplished. And yet whenever you were with me, you were like a shooting star that made me shine even brighter. You were wrong to try to destroy that. So I had to keep it from happening."

"I liked you, Noah. I thought you were fun. I didn't mean to hurt your feelings. I only wondered if you were getting too serious when I had a career to think about." She was still shaking her head. "And what you did *was* insane. How could you even think it wasn't?"

"People have told me before that they thought I was crazy, but it was only because they were jealous of what I'd become. All you have to do is understand that we were meant to be together and obey me." He frowned. "Though it's going to be much more difficult now. I had to do a lot of shifting and adjusting. I'll have to take you away and see if we can come to some kind of agreement that will please me."

"Take me away?" Dee's voice was suddenly hoarse with anger. "You *took* me away, you son of a bitch. And you killed people to do it. Is that what you call shifting and adjusting?"

"You don't know what I've gone through for you." He bent toward her. "Do you realize I risked twenty-five million to make this work?"

Dee shook her head. "What are you talking about?"

"He paid the ransom to himself," Jessie said. "It drew away suspicion and brought him access to the investigation. He was right there with us."

Noah smiled. "Exactly." Then he added quickly, "But that didn't mean I wasn't forced to put that money at risk. I had to trust some men who had proven to me they would do almost anything for cash. I had no assurance that they wouldn't take off with that ransom payment, so I placed tracking chips in the money bands. I gave them a signal sweeper that shouldn't have detected those chips, but one of the men, in a moment of rare initiative, brought another one of his own that was more powerful." He grimaced. "The cash tracking chips were detected, and the whole thing almost blew up in our faces."

"But then you had your chance to do it again and sent me into the Los Angeles River," Jessie said sardonically.

Noah clapped his hands together. "Yes, well done, by the way. It kept me in the investigation's inner circle, and brought you to us. Necessity really is the mother of invention, isn't it?"

"And you sound so proud of yourself." Dee was gazing at him incredulously. "Don't you realize what a monster you've been? You've killed people, you've kidnapped me and brought me to this hellhole, and you've made me put up with that vicious bitch." She held out her manacled wrists. "Dammit, now take these off me!"

"I can't do that yet," he said. "You'll have to earn your rewards, Delilah. I'm still very angry with you. Perhaps when we're out of here and you can convince me that you're sorry for the way you've treated me."

"Out of here? Where the hell are we supposed to be going?"

"I have a lovely private island set up in the South Pacific where we can get to know each other all over again. It's very well guarded, and you'll stay there until you learn your proper place in my life." He checked his watch. "My pilot will be landing in about an hour to pick us up. However, Charlotte and I have a few things to attend to before he gets here, so you'll forgive me if I leave you for a while." His lips suddenly tightened. "But before I do, I want you to apologize to Charlotte for calling her a bitch. I realize she can be difficult, but she's been very helpful to me in this situation. From now on the two of you will have to get along or you'll both hear from me."

"And you think that would make a difference?" Dee asked in amazement.

"Yes, because I'll let her punish you whenever she wishes from now on." He leaned forward, his gaze holding her own. "I can't tell you how hard it was to keep her in check. But now I'm not even sure that all this was worth the effort. You didn't appreciate me." He glanced at Charlotte. "And my Charlotte has always appreciated me. Haven't you, my dear?"

"Always," Charlotte said gruffly. "From the time they put you in my care, you were my little boy. I was the one who kept you safe. I kept you safe this time, too. But this foolishness has to end, Noah. I know you were angry with her, but you can get a woman anywhere."

"I wanted this one."

"And I went along with it, didn't I? But she wasn't like that model in Paris that you made disappear two years ago. All it took was a fat check to have one of your mafia friends remove her when you were bored with her. But I knew people would notice this time." Her voice roughened. "You were obsessed with her, and look where we are now."

"I was careful. I was smart. There was no reason why I couldn't have her." His voice was pettish. "You were just jealous. You thought I liked her too much."

"This is all very interesting," Jessie said. "But would you like to explain to us just who Charlotte is?"

"Charlotte Palker," Noah said. "My parents hired her to take care of me when I was five. Then they promptly forgot I existed unless I did something extraordinary. Of course, I did that frequently." He smiled at Charlotte. "I was never a good boy. But bad or good, she was always there for me. She lives at my house in London now... except when I get in trouble and need her."

"I won't go to that island," she said sourly. "Get rid of her. Get rid of both of them."

"We'll talk about it." His voice was soothing. "I admit it might save trouble." He turned and headed for the door. "But now I need you to help me. You've only done half the job. We've got to get those stupid bastards stuffed away in one of those other planes before that jet gets here."

"We'll manage," Charlotte said brusquely. "There are only three, and I've set up carts to transport them." She smiled. "But don't expect me not to try to convince you to do things my way. It's much easier to have everyone think that the kidnappers eliminated her and just drop her into the ocean once we leave here. Then you'll be free of any suspicion." Her voice was butter-soft. "Do what I ask. Let me help you as I always have before, Noah."

He hesitated as he looked over his shoulder. "Perhaps... We'll talk about it after we finish." He glanced mockingly back at Jessie. "You might not be needed after all. How sad for you." Then the door slammed behind them.

Dee drew a deep breath. "What an incredibly loathsome twosome. Being in the same room with them made me feel dirty. Charlotte Palker is a cross between Madame Defarge knitting at the guillotine and that hag-housekeeper who ruled the mansion in that movie *Rebecca*."

"And Noah is no better," Jessie said quietly. "He was very defensive but there's no doubt that he's a psychopath. And you weren't his first victim, Dee. There's no telling how many others there have been. That Paris model you told me he was dating must not have healed his ego enough for him to keep her around."

Dee shivered. "And he has a mafia Good Fella on the payroll? No wonder he thought he could have anything he wanted."

"Apparently." Jessie grimaced. "I believe Charlotte might genuinely care about him, but he probably uses her just as he uses everyone else. Either way, they're both sickos who deserve each other. Agreed?"

"Absolutely." Dee began to work quickly at her manacles. "And I don't know how much time we're going to have to get away from here while they're burying corpses. So we'd better get a move on while we have the chance..."

Jessie tested her wrist restraints as she looked around the aircraft interior. "We need to get out of here. Noah said his plane will touch down in under an hour."

"I've already tried," Dee said. "I couldn't even crack these windows."

"They're built to withstand thousands of pounds of pressure. There's no way you could have—" Jessie looked at her. "Wait a minute. How could you get to those windows? Your restraints don't give you that much room."

Dee smiled. "No, they don't."

"So how in the hell—?"

"I listened to you," she said simply. "What you taught

me. The only chance I had was when Dorset took me to the bathroom, and he must have thought I had one hell of a bladder infection to have to go so often. But every time I went to the bathroom, I did push-ups and got pumped up as much as I could. And when Dorset put the straps back on, I tensed up and swelled up my muscles a little more. Most times it got me to an extra hole on the strap buckle. After a while, when my arms shrank back to normal, I was able to work my way out. Didn't you tell me Houdini used that trick?"

"Wow. You always looked bored during my safety tutorials. I was never sure you were really listening."

"I always listened to you, Jessie. You were the only one I did pay attention to. But it hasn't done me any good here. I couldn't even slip out of these cuffs to help you. I was afraid I'd blow any chances for us to escape." She shook her head. "And there's no way out. The silver door they've been using is locked, and those forward aircraft doors don't work."

Jessie tugged at her restraints. "I was unconscious when they put me in these straps, dammit. I wasn't able to do the Houdini trick. Do you think you could get out now?"

"Possibly." Dee grinned as she waved with her free right hand.

"Hallelujah! Get me out of these things!"

Dee unbuckled the strap from her other arm, then released Jessie from her restraints. Jessie jumped to her feet and went to the front left aircraft boarding door. She moved the large lever from left to right.

The door didn't move.

"See?" Dee said. "I think it needs power."

"No. These doors use compressed gases. A bottle of nitrogen makes it work."

Dee looked at her curiously. "How do you know so much about this?"

Jessie knelt and examined the floor panels. "I told you, they used Airbus equipment in Afghanistan. For a while, I worked at the base machine shop when I was serving there." She pried loose a floor panel in front of the door. "This one isn't bolted down. The crew probably just left it that way after they mothballed this plane."

Jessie frowned as she looked down into the floor compartment.

"What do you see?" Dee asked.

"Not much that makes any sense to me . . . But I do see two loose hose ends. And some other loose parts rolling around in there. It looks like this plane was at least partially stripped. It's a mess. Nothing but—" She inhaled sharply. "Wait!"

"What is it?"

Jessie pulled out a steel canister with a yellow tab on top. She rested it on the floor. "This may be the nitrogen." She pulled out the hose ends. One of them had a yellow valve screw; one was red. Jessie attached the yellow hose to the canister screw top.

A mild hissing sound came from the door for a few seconds, then silence.

They both stared at the canister for a moment.

"That's it?" Dee asked blankly.

"No idea. I didn't say I was an actual mechanic. I just saw other people working on these things." Jessie stood. "Okay, back up. I'm going to arm this door and pull the lever."

"What will that do?"

"Assuming this works, the door will open by itself. If there's still a slide in here, it may deploy. If there isn't, we may have to jump, tuck, and roll. Got it?"

"That's a lot of ifs."

"It's all we've got. It's going to make some noise, so we'll have to get out the second we can."

Jessie opened a cover and pulled down the switch to arm the door. She turned back to Dee. "Ready?"

"Do it."

Jessie pulled down the door lever, and then . . .

Nothing.

"Shit," Jessie muttered.

A moment later, the hissing sound returned.

"What's happening?" Dee asked.

The door slid open!

With a deafening whoosh, the escape slide instantly inflated and shot into the darkness.

"Now!"

Dee jumped onto the slide and crossed her arms in front of her. Jessie was a second behind.

They tumbled down the slide and landed in a heap on the desert floor!

KENDRA'S TOYOTA

"Noah Calderon?" Lynch gave a low whistle of disbelief. "Are you sure?"

Kendra nodded. "Pretty damn sure. It became clear when I heard the audio reconstruction your Swiss technical group did. Not even then until I went over and over it and finally I realized what I was hearing."

"You recognized her voice?"

"No, I'm sure I've never heard it before. But I recognized the pattern of her voice, the suppressed consonants, the slightly elongated vowels, trace of a singsong lilt at the beginning of the sentences...It's the pattern of someone from the northeast United States who has also spent several years in extreme northern England."

"As opposed to moderately northern England?"

"Totally different sound."

"You're not joking."

"No, it's a sound I recognized in another voice lately. Someone who was born in Connecticut but spent several years attending a private school in Newcastle upon Tyne in northern England."

"Noah Calderon."

She nodded. "It's really too close to be a coincidence." She paused. "And there were other things...Remember how Jessie said that Noah had been taken care of by servants all his life wherever he was sent?"

"So?"

"If he was in partnership with this woman, they must

have been very close, and they would have had to establish a relationship." She paused. "And I know where they established that relationship. It was all on that call we listened to just now. Noah and his parents are American. So is this woman. Noah has traveled on the Continent; so has this woman. Possibly with him." She went on. "But one place I'm certain she was with him was near his school in England. He attended that private school for a few years as a youngster, and I can tell by intonations in her dialect that she spent at least that amount of time there, too. I doubt if she was a teacher, though she sounds well educated. So that leaves a guardian of some sort who was paid to watch over wild Noah and keep an eye on him while he was at school." She was frowning as she tried to put it together. "Of course, it's all guesswork. She might be a relative, but I believe she was a servant."

"You're certain of all this?"

"I can't be certain. Not yet. How could I be? But I'd bet it was him. Their nuances, intonations, phrasing, are like mirrors. They can probably finish each other's sentences. They've been together a long time." She paused before adding grimly, "Besides, there's something else that cinches it."

"What?"

"Pull up the pictures of Dorset's body on your phone."

Lynch pulled up the photos and swiped his finger across the screen. "Any one in particular?"

"A good shot of his face."

After a few more swipes, Lynch held up his phone. "Got it."

"Look at his upper cheeks. See a faint bruising there?"

He increased the image size. "Very faint."

"It's the same mark left by the lower edge of Noah's stupid night-vision goggles last night. I just realized it when I started to think of all this in terms of him. He said there's only a few of those in existence. He must have loaned them to his men who were charged with finding and plucking Jessie from the water." She glanced quickly at his face. "If I'd had any doubts before about his involvement, it ended when I thought about that bruise. Maybe I'd accept the possibility of one coincidence linking him to the crime, but not two."

Lynch sat in silence for a moment. "It all makes sense. When you make the jump to Calderon, there's even a reason for his demand for that twenty-five-million-dollar ransom."

She nodded. "Access. It immediately made him part of our team. He was there for most of the key moments of our investigation. Both money drops, but also the planning and coordination that went into them. It gave him an inside line on what we were doing and thinking."

He was frowning. "The tracking chips on the money bands..."

"I don't care about that right now," she said impatiently. "We can figure it out later. Who knows what a paranoid nutcase like Noah would be thinking? All that matters is that we know he's the one who took Dee and Jessie and that we have to go after him."

He shook his head. "That's not quite all that matters. I know you want to rush forward and take Noah down. I'm not arguing. But it still leaves us with one major question."

"Why in the hell would he kidnap her?"

"Yes. Noah Calderon is literally a man who has everything."

"Sometimes the man who has everything wants the one thing he *can't* have. In the years since they dated, he's watched Dee become one of the most famous and desired women in the world. And he wouldn't be the first man to abuse his ex." She reached out and grasped his arm. "He did this, Lynch. I *know* it. Don't put roadblocks in my way."

His hand covered her own on his arm. "I wouldn't think of it. Right or wrong, it makes too much sense not to go with your instinct." Lynch picked up his phone and was swiping through the contacts. "But we need to loop Kelland in on this."

Lynch put his phone on speaker, and Kelland answered on the first ring. "Lynch, I hope this means you were able to talk Kendra out of barging into the Boneyard."

"You really don't know her very well, do you, Kelland?"

"I'm starting to. Give us a chance. We just got on the road."

Kendra spoke in the direction of Lynch's phone. "Kelland, do you know where Noah Calderon is right now?"

"No, he hasn't been around today. Why?"

"We need to find him. *Now.* Can you get some people on that?"

"Maybe after you tell me why."

Kendra quickly filled him in. After she finished, there was only silence from Kelland's side of the call.

"Kelland? Are you there?"

"Yes," he finally responded. "I get what you're saying, Kendra. It seems to make sense. But if you're wrong about this, the shit's going to come down hard. Noah Calderon maintains multimillion-dollar PACs for half the members of Congress.

That's what's kept them from breaking up his company years ago. They could make life miserable for all of us."

"Man up, Kelland," she said curtly. "Two women's lives are on the line."

"I know that. I'm just trying to talk reason to you."

"Then while you're at it, maybe you can reach out to the FAA. See if he or his company owns a plane in storage up in Mojave."

"Metcalf is here in the van with me. He's already on it."

"Good. We're less than ten minutes away. We'll keep you posted." She watched as Lynch pressed to disconnect. "Nothing like a little pressure," she muttered.

"Woman up," he said. "You believe you're right. We're going to go with it. Screw Kelland and Noah's super PACs."

# CHAPTER

# 13

I t's eerie," Kendra said as she gazed at the dozens of old commercial airliners silhouetted by the setting desert sun. The planes were arranged in neat rows, on thousands of acres adjacent to a remote airstrip. Most of them still wore airline logos and markings, and some were sealed by plastic covers.

Lynch nodded in response to her observation. "*Eerie* is the perfect word for it. Eerie and a little sad."

They had pulled off State Route 14 into the parking lot of a roadside restaurant and an establishment that billed it-self a "medical marijuana collective." The Boneyard's eastern perimeter was less than half a mile away.

"It's massive," Kendra said. "Where do we even start?"

"Kelland and the FBI tactical team will have infrared scanners with them. When they get here, we can sweep the planes one by one and see if anyone's inside."

"I don't want to wait. You and I should go take a look first, but we'll have to be stealthy about it. If the kidnappers get wind we're here, it won't go well for Dee and Jessie." Kendra cocked her head. "Oh, my God."

"What is it?"

"Listen."

Above the sound of the howling desert winds, a rumbling engine became increasingly audible.

Lynch turned to Kendra. "The sound on the phone call recording?"

Kendra nodded. "The FBI thought it might be a tractor." She pointed down to the hangar. "Close, but no cigar. It's an aircraft tow rig."

Lynch looked at the white four-wheeled tug, similar to those used to tow planes to their gates at most large airports. The uniformed operator parked the tug at the hangar, exited the glass-enclosed driver's compartment, and went into a wire-enclosed employee parking lot that was almost vacant. He climbed into a Ford sedan and started his car, only stopping to lock the gate before he drove away.

"That's our cue," Lynch said. "The place appears to be pretty much deserted with only a token staff. We'll probably have the place to ourselves, and we can look around without creating a disturbance. It'll be dark by the time we get down there."

Kendra glanced down at the khaki trousers and white tunic shirt she was wearing. "And I'll show up in that dark like a summer Popsicle. Not exactly the right apparel for hunt and chase. Let me grab my windbreaker out of the trunk." The next moment she was opening the trunk of her car and picking up the navy-blue windbreaker. She stiffened and then smiled as something else caught her eye tucked in the corner of the trunk.

"What is it?" Lynch was gazing at her expression.

Kendra hesitated. *Why the hell not?* she thought recklessly. She slipped the object into the windbreaker's large inside pocket. "Nothing. Let's go."

She slammed the trunk lid closed.

———◆———

"Come on!" Jessie jerked Dee to her feet and pulled her away from the airliner that had been their prison. "Noah had to have heard that loud blowout. We have to get out of here."

Dee looked at the rows of planes extending seemingly into infinity as she ran after her. "What kind of place is this?"

"Airplane graveyard." Jessie pulled Dee behind the landing gear of a weather-beaten Eastern Air Lines jet. "I've heard about this place. I thought that was probably where we were when I saw that Frontier Airline plaque on that Airbus. It's like a maze. We have to find our way out."

"Delilah!"

Noah's voice thundering somewhere behind them.

Jessie and Dee ducked behind the wheel.

"Delilah . . . I know you're close. I know you can hear me."

Jessie glanced over her shoulder. Noah's voice was definitely coming from behind them, maybe thirty yards away.

"I don't want to hurt you, Delilah! I realize that's what you might have thought. I swear that's not what this is about."

Calderon was coming closer. Shit.

Jessie pointed to the next row of parked aircraft, and Dee nodded. They sprinted into the shadows and found refuge behind a set of rusty jet stairs. They crouched and waited. After a few moments, Noah appeared and walked past the spot where they had just been.

He was holding a semiautomatic rifle.

"Delilah, I only did this because I love you. I know I went about it the wrong way."

"You think?" Dee whispered grimly.

Jessie shushed her with a finger to her lips.

"We just need some time together. Some time alone. I've built a beautiful place for you, Delilah. An island far from everything and everybody that pulled us apart."

Jessie lifted her head as she heard something. A plane, she realized. She turned and saw the twinkling red lights of a jet approaching from the east.

"That's *Unicorn One*," Noah shouted. "You always loved that plane. It's here to take us to our new home. We'll have everything there. It's what you need, Delilah. It's what we both need."

The plane's engine grew louder. Jessie gestured for Dee to follow her.

They ducked low and crossed over to the next row of planes.

———◆———

Kendra and Lynch pressed themselves against a 1970s-era People Express airliner as the small private jet circled overhead and landed on the airstrip. It taxied past the hangar.

"That plane's too nice to be stored here," Kendra said.

Lynch nodded. "You got that right. It's a Bombardier BD-700. One of the most expensive private jets in the world."

"One guess who it belongs to."

"Unless Oprah's out for an evening jaunt, I'd say it's the property of Noah Calderon."

The plane taxied to a stop, then the front-loading door opened and slowly flipped down to reveal a short set of stairs.

The plane sat on the landing strip for a long moment.

"I'd like to storm that jet and throttle him," Lynch said. "Want to cover me?"

"Hell no. I want to be right there with you." Kendra watched the plane for another long moment. "But what if he isn't on it?"

"You think he's already here?"

"Could be."

A man descended from the stairs. He was holding a walkie-talkie in one hand, an assault rifle in the other. His spoke into the walkie-talkie and placed it against his ear. He repeated the motion twice more before finally clipping the radio to his belt.

BLAMM!

BLAMM!

Gunshots. From somewhere in the Boneyard.

BLAMM!

Kendra spun around, trying to get a better fix on the shots' location.

The gunman obviously heard them, too. He took off running between a row of parked planes.

BLAMM!

"Oh, God," Kendra said. "You don't think—?"

"This way." Lynch drew his gun and sped away.

---

Noah fired another round into the air.

BLAMM!

"Our plane is on the ground and waiting, Delilah." Calderon's pleading tone had crossed into annoyance. "I'm getting impatient. I don't want to hurt you, but you're coming with me."

"We're boxed in," Jessie whispered. She pointed to a row of identical small commuter planes. "Hide over there and lie flat on your stomach."

"What are you going to do?"

"What I do best. Go."

Dee ran for the planes and rolled underneath.

"Don't make me hunt you down!" Calderon was on the move, stepping closer with each word. "I've put it all on the line. No one's ever done more for you than I have."

Jessie ran from one landing gear to the next, trying to get a fix on Noah's voice.

"We understand each other. We always have."

Jessie peered over a stack of tires. There he was, holding that assault rifle and wearing a vest padded with ammo magazines. He'd look ridiculous under any other circumstances.

But here, one lucky trigger squeeze could take her head off.

She crept back a row, planning her attack.

"I think I'm going to have to hurt you. You know I can't let you leave. I'm sorry. One day you'll understand this is all for the best."

Jessie prepared to leap from her hiding place. She couldn't wait to shut this psycho up.

Three...Two...

CLICK-CLACK!

Jessie knew that sound. It was the slide being racked on an automatic handgun.

Inches from her head.

"Stay where you are, Jessie."

Dammit. Jessie slowly raised her hands. She recognized Charlotte's cool, impassive voice.

"Stand up. Slowly."

Jessie stood. Charlotte had moved a few feet back with her gun.

"Step out into the open, where Noah can see you."

Jessie stepped forward.

"Noah!" Charlotte yelled. "Back here!"

Noah turned and walked toward them. "You shouldn't have tried to run, Jessie. You've only made things harder for you and Delilah."

Jessie smiled. "Dee is long gone. She's probably at the highway already. The first person she sees will call the police. It's over."

Charlotte stiffened, definitely disturbed, but Noah clearly wasn't buying it. He stepped closer to Jessie with his assault rifle. "Nice try, but you forget that I know you, Jessie. You wouldn't let Delilah out of your sight." He hefted his gun. "Particularly not with me waving this around."

"That's why I stayed behind," Jessie said. "To keep an eye on you. Ask your scary friend here. Dee isn't with me."

"I didn't see her," Charlotte told him.

"Oh, she's nearby." Noah turned in a circle and shouted in every direction. "Delilah, now you *have* to come out. Don't be afraid. Come on, honey."

No response.

"See?" Jessie said. "She's sitting in the cab of a big rig talking on the phone to the local police. And you're gonna have some serious 'splainin' to do."

Noah turned and rammed the barrel of his assault rifle against Jessie's throat. "Delilah, show yourself in the next ten seconds or I'll kill your friend. You've always told me that you've never had anyone you trusted as you do Jessie. Is that something you want to live with?"

"She isn't here." Jessie hoped she was speaking loud enough for Dee to hear. "You're wasting your time."

"Five seconds!" Noah yelled. "I'll have no problem pulling this trigger. You know I never liked Jessie."

Jessie half smiled. "I'm finding this out now?"

"Stop!" Dee ran from her hiding place and stood in the clearing. "Noah, put down the gun. I'm here."

He smiled. "Of course you are."

Jessie's shoulders slumped. Damn.

Noah lowered the gun barrel from Jessie's throat. "Come closer. Delilah."

Dee stepped from the shadows and stopped about ten

feet away. "Noah...I didn't understand. I've been think-ing about it ever since we ran away and wondering if I hadn't made a mistake. I didn't know you felt this way about me."

"Of course I do. I never stopped loving you, Dee."

Her voice softened with wonder. "You actually fought the entire world for me? The FBI and everyone else? I feel like Helen of Troy or Cleopatra or some other vamp. And you really built a place for me where no one could ever bother us?"

"Yes. And it's beautiful, Dee. You'll love it."

She smiled. "No one's ever done anything like that for me before. I know you know how people have always used me. My mother...the record companies..."

"I'll always take care of you from now on." He took an impulsive step forward. "Think about what I've done for you already."

"I can see that now. I don't know any other man who would do what you've done to prove how much you care about me. It's incredible."

Noah stared at Dee for a long moment, as if trying to size her up. "You should realize by now I don't do anything halfway."

Dee laughed and flipped back her red hair. Her gray-green eyes were glittering, and she stood there in the moonlight vibrantly alive and totally desirable. "That's for sure. It made me remember all the good times we had when we were together."

Jessie looked between the two. Noah appeared totally

bemused; he might actually be buying Dee's abrupt change of heart. Maybe.

Dee took another step toward him. "That's why I'm willing to give it a chance, Noah," she said softly. "I'm willing to give *us* a chance."

"Really?" He actually sounded as if he was getting a little choked up.

"Don't believe her," Charlotte said. "The girl is lying. She's trying to make a fool of you."

"Shut up!" Noah shouted. He stared at Dee for a moment longer. "She's right, you know. How do I know I can trust you?"

"Let me prove it."

"How?"

She stepped closer to him. "I'll go with you, Noah. Will-ingly. No force. Tonight. Right now."

"You'll do that?"

She nodded. "Yes. I just wish I'd known before what you felt for me."

"I tried to tell you," he said, frustrated. "I knew we were meant to be together. You wouldn't listen to me."

"My life just got crazy, Noah. I couldn't focus on the things that really mattered. You know how that is, don't you? Like you said, we're the same type of people."

"Yes. I do."

Charlotte clicked her tongue. "Don't be an idiot, Noah."

Noah turned. "I told you to be quiet. I *want* this. You never understood. I know what I'm doing." He turned back to Dee. "I'd like to believe you." He paused. "But I don't.

I'm not a fool, Delilah. This is too fast, and what I did you'd instinctively find horrible. You'd have trouble forgiving me." He smiled wryly. "Yet I stand here looking at you and I know that someday you will. Because I won't accept anything else."

"You're wrong," Dee said quickly. "Let me show you."

He shook his head. "Tempting. But I know that the next thing you're going to demand is that I let Jessie go. That's not possible. She'll tell. She'll ruin everything."

"She won't if I ask her to keep quiet. It would spoil how I feel about you now if you hurt her." Her voice was soft, pleading. "You've convinced me we have a chance for something wonderful. Let her go. Jessie always does what I tell her to do. Isn't that right, Jessie?"

"Whatever you want. It wouldn't be the first secret I've kept for you." Jessie wasn't sure if she was quite as convincing as Dee. Any more than she was sure that no matter what Noah said, he'd actually give Dee what she asked. Dee had never been more beguiling, and Noah wanted to believe her. Not only was he convinced he was always right, but the bastard had already proved to be a psychopath. His attitude could change in a heartbeat.

"See?" Dee stepped closer to him and looked up at him. "And do you really need that gun?"

"I'm afraid so. Be for real, Delilah. At least until we get into the air."

Dee moistened her lips. "I understand. But you'll let Jessie go?"

"I'm thinking about it." He was silent a moment. "It's a big risk. But it might be a way that I can give you final proof that I really do care about you. That's important to me."

"And proof that you don't if you kill her," Dee said.

"Then I'd better make the grand gesture, hadn't I?"

Noah turned back to Charlotte. "Let Jessie go after Delilah and I are on the plane. We'll wait for you there."

Charlotte hesitated. "You're sure this is what you want?"

"I said it, didn't I?" Noah motioned for Dee to walk in front of him. "The plane is this way."

Dee hesitated after glancing at Jessie and then hurried ahead of him. "Thank you, Noah."

Jessie watched Dee and Calderon disappear into the darkness and turn to the right, in the direction of his still-idling private jet. After a few moments, Jessie turned to Charlotte. "You're not going to let me go, are you?"

Charlotte smiled. "Why on earth would I do that? Since we're being honest with each other. There's no way you would keep quiet about all this. You and I both know that, even if Noah doesn't."

"I think he knows. And he also knows you'll clean up his mess. He never would have taken that chance if he didn't."

"I've been cleaning up his messes since he was a boy. This is a particularly nasty one. But once he's over this temporary insanity, he'll stop believing the bullshit she's handing him. Then he'll let me step in and take care of her, too. I almost had him persuaded before we left you before." Charlotte raised the gun. "Just another minute or two. It wouldn't do for me to ruin his play if I let his beloved Delilah hear a gunshot right now, would it?"

"Depends."

Charlotte's eyes narrowed on her. "Depends on what?"

"If you really believe Dee was fooled by either one of you. Personally, I think that up to the last minute she was working at getting him away to the plane to give me my chance."

Charlotte's smile was a sneer. "Your chance to do what?"

Jessie's left hand flew to a lightning underchop of Charlotte's wrist! Her right hand caught the barrel of the gun and twisted it.

BLAMM! BLAMM!

Charlotte squeezed off two more shots as they fought over the gun. Jessie elbowed her in the face three times, brutally breaking her nose. Blood spurted from her nostrils.

Jessie finally wrestled the gun from Charlotte's grip and struck her head with it repeatedly.

Charlotte collapsed onto the ground, blood from her nose and head oozing onto the desert floor.

Jessie cocked her head. Someone was coming. One of Noah's men?

She gripped the gun and whirled toward the sound, preparing to fire.

"Jessie!"

It was Kendra and Lynch.

Then Kendra was next to her, giving her a quick hug. "Are you all right?"

"Fine." She was already whirling away from them and running toward the jet. "But Noah is taking Dee to his plane. We'll have to hurry."

"Right." Kendra started at a run back toward the row of

planes from which she and Lynch had just come. "We saw it land. This way."

The moon had now risen full in the night sky, casting the entire Boneyard in a bluish glow. Noah's idling jet still roared in the distance, echoing through and around the rows of old airliners.

"Noah's totally lost it," Jessie said jerkily. "Dee's trying to use his feelings for her, but he's not buying it. She's playing a dangerous game."

Lynch nodded grimly. "There's no way we can let that plane take off with her."

They rounded a corner and were met with a volley of gun-fire! Kendra and Jessie dove behind a row of barrels and Lynch hit the ground just beside them.

The gunman was twenty yards ahead, crouched beside a small TWA jet.

"That's the guy we saw leaving Noah's plane," Lynch whispered.

Kendra peered around the edge of the barrel. "He's giving cover to Noah. He and Dee are just a few feet away."

"I don't see them," Lynch said.

"Their shadows are just over the gunman's left shoulder."

"Got it." Lynch shimmied back a few feet. "I'm going to try and get between them and the plane. Keep them here for as long as you can." He stood up and sped away.

Kendra shouted, "Let Dee go, Noah. You're making a mistake. The FBI knows all about you. As long as you have Dee, they'll never stop looking for you."

"You're lying. I have contacts. I can handle anything you

throw at me," Noah yelled. They still could only see his shadow. "Where's Charlotte?"

"No use you calling out for her expecting her to save you," Jessie answered. "I made sure that she won't be helping you ever again."

Noah cursed. "You bitch. Do you know how valuable she was to me? I may make you pay for that one day when you least expect it."

"Let Dee go," Kendra said. "Let her go and we won't stop you from getting on that plane. You'll be the FBI's problem, not ours."

"You've got to be kidding, Kendra. We've all come too far for me to just give up now. Delilah is what this is all about. It's not as if I can't still win. With all the money I've got, I can still find a way to have anything I want. All I have to do is—"

The gunman cut loose with another barrage from his assault weapon!

Kendra and Jessie ducked. When they looked up again, the gunman was gone and there was no sign of the shadow that had been Noah.

Kendra jumped to her feet. "They're on the move. Come on."

———◆———

Noah pushed Dee ahead of him as they neared his jet. "I remodeled my plane's interior, Dee. I even hired that Italian designer you like so much. Storaro?"

She just stared at him in disbelief.

"Nice man, even though he doesn't speak a word of

English. He appreciated the honor I did him. And it was all for you."

"Stop this," she hissed. "You were right not to have believed those lies I told you. I never wanted this, Noah."

"Sometimes we don't know what we want. Or what we need. I'm sorry the past few days have been so uncomfortable for you. We needed to be in position to hop aboard my jet as soon as my arrangements were finalized. But when you see the place I built for you, I think you'll agree the wait was worth it." He spoke to his pilot, who was leading them down the row of planes. "You've fueled the jet for the trip, Chester?"

They'd finally reached the airstrip where his plane was positioned and warming for takeoff. Chester gestured toward it. "Yes, only one more refuel in Maui."

She wasn't getting through to Noah. He seemed to have lost touch with reality. "Didn't you hear what they said, Noah? You've lost. It's over."

"I never lose. Though it may be more difficult now that they've taken my Charlotte away." His lips tightened bitterly. "The first thing I'll do when we get in the air is contact my friend Nick Parillo in Las Vegas and arrange a contract on both of them."

Dee stopped short and whirled to face him. "Leave them alone! I'm the one who took her away, you idiot. I knew all I needed to do was give Jessie the opportunity to make her move. I knew that bitch was going to kill her, and there was no way I'd let that happen."

He flinched. "You shouldn't have told me that. I really preferred to ignore the possibility. I'm afraid I'll have to punish you, too. I really owe it to Charlotte. But not before I've enjoyed you in all the ways there are. I'm afraid some of them will hurt very much, Delilah."

"Go to hell, Noah. So much for—"

"Hush." Noah stiffened and then turned back toward the rows of old planes behind them. "Do you hear that?"

Chester nodded and raised his assault rifle. "They're right behind us, sir."

"Not for long." Noah whirled toward Dee and jerked his thumb toward his jet's open loading stairs. "Get inside and move toward the back of the plane. Stay away from the door and all windows."

"No." Her hands clenched into fists. "It ends here. I'm not going anywhere."

His hand lashed out and connected with her face with full force.

Pain.

Dizziness.

She fell to the ground and was only vaguely aware of him standing above her. His eyes were blazing down at her and he was pointing his gun at her. "It could be that you're right," he said hoarsely. "Maybe it does end here. Maybe Charlotte was right about you."

She shook her head to clear it. "What a cowardly son of a bitch you are. What do you think you're going to do?"

"I'm finishing it." He aimed his gun at her. "Go."

Dee hesitated; she had no doubt in this moment that he'd press that trigger. She had no weapon but perhaps she could find one on the plane and use it to go after him. He wouldn't expect an attack from behind. At any rate, she'd have to make certain that Noah found a surprise if he made it back here to the plane alive.

"Whatever you say." She struggled to her feet and gave him one more defiant look as she started up the steps toward the plane. "By all means finish it, Noah. I'll be waiting for you."

———◆———

With the sound of Noah's idling jet engines as their guide, Kendra and Jessie made their way through the maze of old airliners.

"We're almost there," Kendra said. "Just one more turn, and—"

She and Jessie froze.

Noah stood on the path in front of them, his assault rifle leveled at their heads. "Throw your guns down. Both of you."

"Let Dee go, Noah," Kendra said. "Do that and we won't try to stop you. You won't get a better deal all day."

"Throw down your guns," he repeated. "You won't need them. Dee is already on the plane. If I get so much as a scratch out here, my pilot has been ordered to kill her immediately."

"Nice. Does she know that?" Jessie said.

"It doesn't matter. She's a great prize but self-preservation is everything. If you really care about Dee, get rid of your guns. Throw them as far away as you can."

Kendra and Jessie looked at each other, then tossed their handguns.

Noah cautiously looked around. "Where's Lynch?"

"We don't know," Kendra said.

He gave her a suspicious glance.

"I'm telling the truth. I have no idea."

"Let's just hope he doesn't do something foolish. It wouldn't be good for you or Delilah." He motioned with the barrel of his gun. "Step out onto the airstrip."

As Kendra and Jessie walked onto the airstrip, they saw Noah's waiting plane. His hired gun, Chester, stood guard next to the plane's open stairs.

Noah stepped close to Kendra and placed his gun barrel under her chin. "You've caused me so much trouble," he murmured. "I gave you a chance to just go away. You should have taken it."

"Why?" She looked him straight in the eye. "Your life is over, Noah."

"Funny. I was just about to say the same thing to you."

Before she could respond, they both heard the plane's engines suddenly roaring, kicking up sand from the desert floor!

They whirled to hear Chester screaming as his feet left the ground and he was sucked into plane's left engine.

Blood sprayed onto the jet's tail, and the engine sputtered in a shower of sparks.

Noah, Kendra, and Jessie stared in horror at the smoking engine. Then their gaze was drawn to the cockpit window.

Lynch was in the pilot's seat.

"Nooo!" Noah screamed and raised his gun to point toward the cockpit. But only halfway, because in the next second Kendra lunged toward him with an object she'd taken from her windbreaker's right pocket.

She stabbed him once, then again, deep in the chest.

Noah froze for a long moment, then dropped his gun. He took one step, then another, then looked in puzzlement at the ornate object protruding from his chest. He dropped to his knees, then finally fell unconscious onto the airstrip. Dead.

"What in the hell is that?" Jessie asked, gazing at the weapon in Noah's chest.

Kendra kicked Noah's gun away. "A gift from Lynch. A Lhasa Tibetan phurba. It's for fighting demons."

Jessie slowly nodded. "I think it works."

They heard the pounding of footsteps from the jet's stairs. Dee ran across the airstrip and threw her arms around Jessie. "I was so afraid for you."

"You were the one being dragged off," Jessie said. "I knew you were going to raise hell with him."

"I didn't have a weapon. So I had to go on the plane and look for one." She turned around and smiled at Lynch, who was now coming down the steps behind her. Her hand made a little flourish in his direction. "And I found one!"

Kendra turned toward him. "How in the hell did you pull that off?"

"I got here a minute or so before Noah did. The pilot was obviously better with a flight stick than he was with a handgun."

"No, not that." Kendra grimaced as she pointed to the bloody jet engine. "I mean *that.*"

Lynch gently turned her away from the plane. "Just a matter of turning the throttle from minimum idle to full thrust. I noticed that Calderon's thug was in flagrant violation of FAA safety rules. So I took advantage of the situation."

Headlights were suddenly piercing the darkness. They looked over to see a small convoy of FBI vehicles entering the Boneyard and roaring down the landing strip.

Lynch smiled. "Just in time to do clean up."

"Kelland isn't going to be happy about that job description," Kendra said dryly.

"You take what you can get," Lynch said as he started toward Kelland's vehicle. His attitude was brimming with pure triumph and a hint of malicious mischief as he stepped out into the beams of Kelland's headlights. "We got the bad guys, so he has to settle for what's left over." He lifted his head and called out to Kelland: "Welcome. I was just telling Kendra you're right on time. Let me tell you about it..."

# EPILOGUE

C ome on, Dee!" Jessie threw open the door of the FBI van Kelland had assigned to Dee while his agents took her statement. "The invasion has started. I'm getting you out of here."

"What are you talking about?" Dee jumped to her feet and ran toward the door. "What invasion? What's happened?" Then as she pushed past Jessie and looked outside, she stopped short. "Oh, shit."

Driving toward the plane graveyard was a virtual armada of vehicles of all descriptions, but principally jeeps and cars emblazoned with network news insignias and a cavalcade of television and cable trucks. Dee wrinkled her nose. "Invasion, indeed. I thought I'd have a little more time."

"And you will," Jessie said grimly as she grabbed Dee's arm. "Come on. I'll get you out of here. I've borrowed a car from one of Kelland's guys and parked it on the runway. You've had enough to contend with, and I'm not going to let the paparazzi tear you apart."

"They're not all paparazzi," Dee said quietly. "There are probably quite a few first-rate journalists in that horde who are only trying to do their jobs. I'm a big story." She pulled away from Jessie's hold. "And the quickest way to get rid of them is to give it to them."

"Then let me do it."

She shook her head. "You opted out years ago and it's taken me a long time to let you go." She smiled teasingly. "And look at you, still being all protective. It's no wonder that a kid like me could get confused." She looked back at the reporters, who had almost reached the planes. "This is my life and I'll figure it out. It may take a while and I'll make mistakes. But I'll stand tall and I'll never be a victim again." She gestured to the journalists now pouring out of their vehicles and running toward them. "So step away so that they can get some good shots of me that will please them. I'll handle this, Jessie."

Jessie hesitated. "I would have let you do it. I just thought you needed a break."

"After all the sedatives that witch pumped down me? Be for real. If I were more relaxed, I'd be comatose." She held up her hand as she was suddenly deluged by the crowd. "Hi, everyone." Her smile was brilliant. "I'm so glad to see you. Now give me a minute to get my breath and I'll try to give you something to tell those nice people who have been so concerned about me. First, I want to thank everyone in the media who was so helpful during the kidnap negotiations." Her smile faded. "And I want to express my sadness at the

328

loss of those who died because Noah Calderon was a monster. You'll hear more about him and his ego and selfishness later, but that's how I'll always think of him. You'll all receive a copy of the statement I gave the FBI regarding what occurred that night and here today, and it will be the entire truth. But after you receive that statement, I'll never speak of what happened at that concert ever again." A smile lit her face. "So accept that in another month I'll be old news and let me go back to doing what I love and what I hope my audiences love. I actually think I'm going to surprise you down the road someday. Isn't working to turn out something beautiful so much better than clinging to darkness?"

But the questions and clamor from the journalists were becoming overwhelming and Dee instinctively took a step back. "Sure it is. Think about it. But I can see my friend Jessie here is getting nervous, so I believe I'll have to leave you now. I'll see that you get those statements by tomorrow at the latest. Trust me."

"Out!" Jessie was pulling Dee away from the crowd and ducking underneath the body of the plane to drag her toward the FBI vehicle she'd parked on the runway. She glanced over her shoulder but saw that only a few journalists had as yet managed to follow them. "Get in the damn car. I want to get you out of here."

Dee was already in the passenger seat as Jessie pressed the accelerator. She laughed as the car jumped forward. "This reminds me of when we bolted out of the gates of Kendra's school and had all those paparazzi trailing behind us. Did I tell you how totally awesome you were that day?"

"Well, don't think I'm going to do a repeat." She glanced behind her and saw that the reporters were once more in hot pursuit. "I made a few advance arrangements to ensure I'd get you away from here with absolutely no problem."

"Really? How are you going—" Then Dee started to laugh as she saw the string of FBI vehicles and police cars ahead of them blocking the storage facility entrance. "Now, that's totally worthy of you." She waved at Kelland as he motioned for two FBI vehicles to pull aside so that Jessie could get beyond the barrier and then close it tightly again. The media vehicles screeched to a halt as they saw Kelland walk casually toward them. "The FBI may be getting some very bad press," she murmured.

"Nonsense. You saw how charming and professional Kelland can be, and he's totally within his rights. This is a crime scene and they have no right to disturb it. And by the time they get a helicopter out here, I'll have you safely stashed away somewhere."

"And I'll let you do it." Dee smiled. "For the next four days. I figure it will take that long for me to complete my plans and set up my own exit strategy."

"Exit strategy?" she repeated warily.

"You weren't listening to my wonderful press conference. I told them what I was going to do. I just didn't tell them how I was going to do it. I'm not sure of all the details yet myself, but when I was sitting in that van waiting for you, I realized it was going to have to contain an exit strategy."

"And are you going to tell me about it?"

"Of course I am. But not right now. I'm going to enjoy

these next four days with my good friend because I'm already feeling a little sad..." She leaned back in the seat. "But don't worry, it will all come together..."

◆

PALM DESERT AIRFIELD
SOUTHERN CALIFORNIA
FIVE DAYS LATER

"Will you please tell me why the hell I'm here?" Kendra asked as she saw Lynch walking across the tarmac toward her. "I was supposed to stay late at the school today." She glanced around the almost-deserted airport. "For that matter, I should ask where I am. My GPS wouldn't even acknowledge this airport. If you hadn't given me directions, I never would have found it."

"I would have tracked you down."

"Really? Until I got that text from you, I hadn't seen or heard from you for the last week."

"You told me you were going to be busy catching up. I aim to please."

"I was busy. I'm still busy. I'm here, but I don't know why. I should be working."

"No, you shouldn't." He smiled. "I spent a lot of time pulling strings and making arrangements and I won't have you spoiling them." He glanced up at the sky as a C-130E cargo plane that had been on the approach landed and was now taxiing down the runway. "And it looks as if that pilot under-stands it, too. He's right on time. Dee will be pleased."

"Dee?" Kendra's eyes narrowed as she gazed at the plane with renewed interest. "What does she have to do with that old beat-up cargo plane?"

"Hey, it's a little old but it's not beat-up. Jessie would never have let her negotiate with me to get her anything but top-quality merchandise."

"Negotiate? What are you talking about?"

"Ask her yourself." He jerked his head at Jessie's car, which was driving through the airport gates. "I'm just putty in their hands."

"Yeah, sure."

But then Jessie had pulled up beside them and Dee was jumping out of the passenger seat. "It's wonderful." She dove into Lynch's arms and gave him a hug. "Just what I wanted."

"It had better be," he said dryly. "I went to a good deal of trouble to arrange your escape. I've spent less time and effort extracting a Saudi prince."

"Escape?" Kendra repeated. "What the hell?"

"That's what I said." Jessie got out of the car and came toward them. "But the more Dee talked about it, the more it appealed to me." She nodded at the cargo plane. "That's why that cargo plane landed at a military base earlier today and picked up Dee's orchestra and crew and flew them here." She exchanged looks with Dee. "I didn't really think she could pull it off in four days. But she managed to do it."

"Well, it was actually five days," Dee said. "It took longer than I thought it would for Lynch to get all those pesky documents I needed for me and the guys."

"Yeah, visas and passports can be so pesky," Lynch said.

"I didn't say I wasn't grateful," Dee said. "I just said I didn't count on it. I have a lot to learn."

He was suddenly smiling. "Maybe. But you learn very fast."

"Escape," Kendra repeated to get them back on track. "What's happening, Jessie?"

She shrugged. "Dee decided that the media wasn't going to leave her alone as long as she was easily accessible. This story was like a horror movie with so many elements of scandal, it would tend to feed on itself."

"She's right there," Kendra said grimly. "They've been rabid about trying to locate her since you whisked her away. The reporters have even followed me out to the school looking for her and trying to interview me."

"Told you, Jessie," Dee murmured. "I have to shut it down."

"I never argued with you about that," Jessie said. "But as usual you decided to do your own thing and involved Lynch in creating the scenario. I told you he'd end up by taking over the operation."

"But you also told me that he was probably the only one who could do it." She beamed at Lynch again. "Did I tell you how amazing you are? Or how grateful I am?"

"You mentioned it once or twice." He grinned. "But you could prove it by turning around and getting on that plane. Setting this up on short notice required pulling strings and bribery. I didn't do anything really illegal, but I came close a couple times. It could be awkward for me." He made a shooing motion. "Have a nice flight, Dee."

"She's not going anywhere until I find out the details of just why you're so 'amazing,'" Kendra said flatly. "I've been getting double talk from all of you since the moment you came through the gates." She turned back to Jessie. "You left a message asking me to come here to meet you today. Now talk to me."

"Sorry." Jessie made a face. "Life has been a little hectic lately, and today was no different. My part in this fiasco was to get Dee here without being tailed, and I was a little tense."

Kendra shook her head. "Not you."

"It happens now and then." She shrugged. "Well, as I started to tell you, Dee decided the only way she could get the media to leave her alone and have a chance at the kind of life she wanted was to opt out of the entertainment scene for a little while."

"What?"

"Not entirely," Dee interceded quickly. "But it made sense to me. I have to give everyone a chance to forget the 'big' story and remember who I am." She paused. "And who I want to be."

Kendra frowned. "But I've watched you perform. You love it. Nothing could be more clear."

"I do like it," Dee said quietly. "It's great fun. But what I love is the music. It's always been the music. And lately it's sometimes been hard to put my own music on hold and go out and perform." She smiled. "I've composed three platinum hits in the past two years, and it felt awesome. But I think I can do better...if I have the time. If I can let the music come to me."

"And it will," Jessie said gruffly. "This week she played her latest composition, 'Sun Song,' for me, Kendra. It wasn't half bad..." She added slyly, "For a bloody superstar." Her gaze shifted to the cargo plane. "Anyway, she's heading out of the country for the next year or so. She'll principally be composing but every few months she'll give an impromptu concert at one of the cities near where she's located at the time. Just to give herself a little fun and keep from getting too serious."

"And boring," Dee said. "Heaven forbid I ever become boring."

"I don't believe you'll ever have to worry about that," Kendra said. "Where are you going to start out?"

"A small village about eighty miles from Tallinn, Estonia."

"What? Estonia? Talk about off the beaten track." Her gaze shifted to Lynch. "Why?"

"The media will locate her almost immediately. It's a very small world these days. But where she's going isn't like Paris or Rome. Estonia can be very pleasant, but reporters won't find this village nearly as comfortable, and there are places that are starkly primitive. I've made sure that Dee will be able to disappear in either direction whenever she wants to." His blue eyes were twinkling as he glanced at Dee. "After a while the reporters might even find her boring."

Dee sighed. "I suppose I could put up with it for a little while."

"I'm not sure I like any of this." The horror of losing Dee was still too fresh for Kendra. "Will she be safe?"

"I've made arrangements," he said quietly. "And Dee assures me that she can take care of herself from now on."

"Tell that to Jessie." Kendra turned to Jessie. "You're going along with this?"

"Dee tells me I have no choice. She's her own woman and makes her own decisions." She smiled at Dee. "And most of the decisions she's made for this trip are sound. It's not only the orchestra and crew that are on that cargo plane. She's bringing Colin Parks and his entire security team with her. That's very smart, because Parks will work twice as hard keeping her safe just to save his own career from tanking."

"And it wasn't his fault Noah managed to grab me," Dee said soberly. "Noah was a monster who fooled all of us. Maybe me most of all. He thought he owned the world and couldn't bear that anyone believed anything else." Then she was smiling again. "So stop worrying, Kendra. Now that I know there are monsters out there, I won't invite them into my world. But I won't close myself off, either. It's a wonderful world and I won't be cheated of one minute of it."

"Get on that plane," Lynch said again. "*Now.*"

"Nag. Nag. Nag." She turned and gave him another hug, whispering, "Thank you again."

She whirled and hugged Kendra. "It's going to be fine. Lynch will tell you. And my first concert when I come back home will be for the kids at your school. I promise. I'll see you soon."

Then she tore herself away and was running toward the plane. "Come on, Jessie. You heard him."

"You're going with her?" Kendra's brows rose in surprise. "So much for her being her own woman."

"She will be. I didn't break it to her until we were on our way here that I wasn't leaving her totally on her own," Jessie said. "I'm just going to make sure that she's settled in and doesn't have any surprises to start this bid for independence." She smiled ruefully. "And maybe I'm more dependent on her than she is on me right now. Friendship never stays the same, does it? Ours never has, Kendra." She turned and handed Lynch the keys to the car. "You'll find everything you need in the trunk. Dee wouldn't let me do anything for her, so I concentrated on the instructions you gave me." She gave Kendra a hug and then started running after Dee. "Lynch, I'll tell you how good your arrangements for Dee turned out when I get back in a week or so. They'd better be very good."

"They are."

"What confidence." She laughed as she climbed the steps. "I'm warning you I'll have a checklist." She disappeared into the plane.

"And she will," Kendra murmured. "She's looking on this as sort of a last hurrah in her relationship with Dee. She'll make sure that it's done right."

"I know that, Kendra," Lynch said gently. "Why do you think I let Dee draw me into this? I have to face too many final hurrahs in my life. When I can turn one of them into a new beginning, that's all to the good."

A new beginning...

He meant it. She could see that whatever waited for Dee in this time ahead, the preparations for it would have been done with Lynch's usual panache, efficiency... and care. She had to clear her throat to ease the sudden tightness. "Yes, that's all to the good."

Only minutes later the plane was barreling down the runway, then taking to the air.

She took a deep breath and swallowed. "Gone." She smiled a little unsteadily. "But you might have given me a heads-up what was happening before you sent me that text. I might have been able to help."

"You told me you were going to be busy." His eyes were on the cargo plane just disappearing from view. "And I didn't really want your help. I thought it would be easier for both of us if I just took you by surprise."

She stiffened with sudden wariness. "Surprise?"

"See?" His eyes were twinkling. "I was right. Just the thought of anything unexpected puts you on guard."

"Unexpected?" she repeated. "Like the surprise when you just showed up at the FBI that morning when I thought you were in Tibet?"

"Sort of. But much more pleasant. You were completely stressed out then and had every right to be upset." He smiled. "But that worked out, didn't it? If you let it, this will be even better."

"What are you talking about?" Her gaze flew to Jessie's car. "What was Jessie talking about when she said she'd been working on your instructions for the last week?"

"In spite of what she said, she knew I was working my ass off to make things right for Dee. She thought I deserved a reward." He was striding to the trunk of the car and then unlocking it. "But only if you permitted it. She made certain that you'd be fully on board."

"To do what?"

He lifted the lid of the trunk to reveal two suitcases and a briefcase. "Take a small vacation. She and Olivia got together and decided that these last days had been hell for you, too, and you needed to relax a bit. This is Olivia's contribution."

"Relax?" She gazed at the suitcases. "I can't go on a vacation. I got too far behind while we were searching for Dee. I have to work."

"No, you don't." He handed her the briefcase. "Olivia talked to your associates and arranged for them to fill in for you when you were gone. Check the paperwork. There's supposed to be a note in there from Olivia, too."

She stared down at the briefcase, stunned. "I feel . . . hijacked."

"You are. But only by people who care about you. Nothing wrong with that." He nodded across the field at a sleek white Learjet. "I borrowed that jet from my friend Chad Brooks. You remember him? It should be gassed up and ready."

"And where are we supposed to be going?"

"Well, not Tibet. I thought we'd try Tahiti. Much more desirable climate. Have you ever been there?"

"No."

"Then come with me." His voice was low and infinitely persuasive. "It's time for that truce, Kendra. We have to reach out and take it or it might slip away. Though I promise I won't let that happen. Just take my hand and trust me."

Lord, how she wanted to do it. "A few weeks together might not change anything."

"Or it might." He said again, "Trust me."

She couldn't look away from him. "I don't even know if Olivia sent my passport."

"Olivia is very smart." He was opening the briefcase

and searching through it. He pulled out a document wallet. "Eureka." He brought out two other envelopes and handed them to her. "And these must be the notes she sent you."

The first note was very brief and typically Olivia.

Kendra,

Don't be an idiot. One way or another, you need this.
  Go with him.

Olivia

She opened the second envelope.

And she started to laugh.

Lynch gazed at her quizzically. "What is it?"

She held out the sheet of paper.

"Harley."

The only thing on the paper was a huge paw print.

"I guess that's supposed to signify approval?" She couldn't stop smiling. "Since he always agrees with everything Olivia tells him."

"That's not enough. This time it has to have *your* complete approval."

"How honorable." She was only half mocking. Lynch was one of the most complicated people she had ever known, but he had never been anything but honest in their relationship. This was no exception, so why was she hesitating?

She reached over and grabbed her purse from the front seat

of her car. "But how could I resist such a tender request from both you and Harley?" She headed across the tarmac toward the waiting Learjet. "It would be impossible. Besides, I'm fascinated to see how you intend to construct this truce. Grab my suitcases and let's get going."

# ABOUT THE AUTHORS

**IRIS JOHANSEN** is the #1 *New York Times* bestselling author of more than 30 consecutive bestsellers. Her series featuring forensic sculptor Eve Duncan has sold over 20 million copies and counting, and was the subject of the acclaimed Lifetime movie *The Killing Game*. Johansen lives near Atlanta, Georgia.

**ROY JOHANSEN** is an Edgar Award–winning author and the son of Iris Johansen. He has written many well-received mysteries, including *Deadly Visions*, *Beyond Belief*, and *The Answer Man*.

Iris Johansen and Roy Johansen have together written *Night Watch*, *The Naked Eye*, *Sight Unseen*, *Close Your Eyes*, *Shadow Zone*, *Storm Cycle*, and *Silent Thunder*.